WINTER WIND

WINTER WIND

J.R. Rain

Other Books by J.R. Rain

American Vampire
Vampire Moon
Moon Dance

SAMANTHA MOON CASE FILES
Moon Bayou

JIM KNIGHTHORSE
Night Run
Clean Slate
Hail Mary
The Mummy Case
Dark Horse

THE WITCHES SERIES
The Witch and the Huntsman
The Witch and the Englishman
The Witch and the Gentleman

OPEN HEART SERIES
The Dead Detective

NICK CAINE SERIES
Pyramid of the Gods
Treasure of the Deep
Temple of the Jaguar

THE SPINOZA TRILOGY
The Vampire in the Iron Mask
The Vampire Who Played Dead
The Vampire With the Dragon Tattoo

Winter Wind
Published by J.R. Rain
Copyright © 2015 by J.R. Rain
All rights reserved.

ISBN: 1511815906
ISBN-13: 9781511815901

DEDICATION

To Aiden James, my good friend.

1

The day is warm.

No surprise there. It's early fall in Southern California, which means it might as well be summer. I can't remember the last time rain had fallen. Maybe four months ago. Maybe six. Hell, maybe nine.

I stand on the steps in front of my apartment building and lift my face to the sun, as I do every morning, as I do throughout the day. As I do every chance I get. Surely a strange addiction. The sun does not feel pleasant. It is searing and blistering and if I stand there too long, I will surely burn. But I don't turn away. No, not yet.

It's there somewhere, I think. It has to be. I can feel it. So hot. So alive. The sun isn't quite directly above. But it's before me, clearly above the apartment buildings that I know are across the street. There are some trees there, too. Old sycamores. I can see them in my mind's eye, trunks twisting and flowering into massive mushroom clouds of green leaves, heavy with the dust and grime of downtown Los Angeles.

But I can't see them. And I can't see the sun. Not even a hint of it. Nothing. There is only blackness. Complete and total blackness.

There shouldn't be blackness, of course. There should have been the burning orb of the sun, hanging there in the sky. I should have been able to see it and a smattering of clouds that I suspect are up there, too. I should have seen birds flying and cars whipping past. I should have seen the gentle slope of the street that led up to my apartment in one direction, and down into Echo Park in the other.

But I don't. Because I can't.

Finally, I turn away, pulling down my baseball cap and, sighing, lightly snap on Betsie's harness. We continue away from the stairs, walking carefully along a path that I know circumnavigates the busy apartment complex parking lot. Betsie knows the path. She seems to always know the path, wherever we go. She seems to read my mind, too, which is spooky and exciting and sad.

Betsie keeps to a slow gait, never pulling and always alert to my slightest commands. I love that dog more than life itself, and that is not hyperbole.

As we walk, I use my other hand to reach out with my walking stick, swinging it back and forth like a metronome. It grazes the flower planter on my right and a pole to my left. At least, I think it is a pole. It could have been anything, quite frankly. Still, I remember a pole being here, right here, in the parking lot, back when I could see.

There is no wind. The day is searing. Sweat begins to form on my brow, along the bridge of my Dodger ball cap, and between my shoulder blades. I am hyperaware of my skin—and of anything that touches my skin, including the heat of the sun, a soft breeze and my own sweat.

My probing walking stick hits something solid and I find myself now standing in some shadows. I know this because the temperature has dropped, perhaps five degrees. Betsie stops, letting me know I have reached a roadblock. In this case, I know it's the wrought iron fence that keeps us all so safe in our apartments. I reach out with my hand, letting my walking stick dangle from a loop on my wrist, and find the doorknob and turn it.

Betsie, without any urging from me, is through first. She pauses just beyond, while I step through and shut the door silently behind me. It is a routine we have done thousands of times.

Once I'm through, Betsie is moving again, down the hill, in the same direction we always go. No mind-reading here. We do this every day. Not quite like clockwork, as we go at different times. But usually, it's in the morning. In another time, another life, I would have often turned right, and gone up the hill, to the park trails that wander throughout Elysian Park, trails that few Los Angelenos even know about, trails that overlook the brightly lit downtown skyscrapers and wander behind big, beautiful old homes. Hidden homes.

Someday, I think. *Someday, I will walk those trails again.*

With Betsie, of course.

Always with Betsie.

The sidewalk is wide enough, but if I come across anyone coming up, or moving down quickly past me, I will never know. I can neither see them, nor hear or smell them. For all I know, Betsie and I are alone on the cement path; but that can't be, not truly. Surely we pass people. But I never know it.

We continue down steadily, carefully. My probing stick alerts me to irregularities in the sidewalk, of which there are many: steep angles where driveways cut through, pushed-up sections from tree roots, buckled sections where earthquakes have hit hardest. There's always the oddity, too: A toy left on the sidewalk, or a bike, or a skateboard. Any of

3

which would have me hitting the ground, fast and hard. Again. Each fall is a painful lesson learned.

Now, I move slowly, carefully, *seeing* the path with my lightweight aluminum four-foot walking stick. A tool that is truly an extension of me. My eyes, my ears, my hands, my everything.

I walk in silence. But that's not quite true, is it? There is a faint ringing just inside my ear. A ringing that is always there, and may always be there, according to the doctors. The sound isn't very loud and often I forget it's there… but it's enough.

Enough to drive me mad.

In the months following the accident, as my body healed and morphed into something new, something forever challenging, something forever damaged and broken and suffering, I kept waiting for the ringing to go away. As the weeks turned into months, I was faced with another challenge, perhaps the greatest of them all:

To keep my sanity.

The ringing. Just inside my destroyed ears. A soft hum. Never varying, never rising or falling.

And never going away.

Ever.

I had to find a way to get used to this, to accept this. And it wasn't easy. Sometimes, it's still not easy.

So, no, I'm not walking in complete silence. There is the ringing. Right there, just inside my ears. I'm not entirely sure the ringing was a result of the blast that nearly killed me, the blast that I often wish *had* killed me. These days, I wish this less and less. Early on, not so much. Early on, I placed a handgun near my bed, inside the bed table drawer in fact—never very far out of reach—a handgun with one single bullet meant for me.

It's still there by my bed, although I open the drawer less and less these days.

But it's there.

Just in case.

In case of what, I don't know.

No, I thought, as Betsie and I continue down the broken sidewalk, over misaligned cement slabs but mostly over a straight and narrow path. No. I know what it is for.

It's there in case I grow so mad that I never return to myself, am never the same again. I only hope I'm not so mad that I will forget the gun is there.

I don't know how many steps I take to Chango Coffee at the bottom of the hill. I don't even know how long it takes me to get there. I suspect no more than fifteen minutes. Probably ten or less if I was sighted. Now, as I sense that I'm getting closer, I involuntarily tense up. My already careful steps shorten. The intersection is not chaotically busy. Here, Echo Park Avenue is only one lane in each direction. But the coffee shop lies within a three-way stop. Cars are in a hurry here. They often whip through the intersection. Often recklessly. At least, that's my memory of it.

I continue slowing my pace, and Betsie slows with me. Never pulling, always alert and aware of my needs. She is a saint. My angel. My gift from God.

Of course, a true gift from God would have been to return my sight to me. Or my hearing. Or my speech. Or my sense of smell. Or to return my dead partner to me.

Betsie pauses, and I pause, too.

This is the tricky part. There is no crosswalk here. Nothing to suggest that the intersection gives a damn for pedestrians, let alone blind and deaf pedestrians.

Betsie cost nearly $30,000, a big chunk of my life savings. She has been worth every penny. Her training involved only crossing when there is a gap in traffic. How they trained her, I don't know. She is so smart, so special, and so I wait for my little girl to see me through, to cross when it's safe, to use her best judgment.

I sense no one, hear no one, am aware of no one. But I know that can't be true. This is a fairly busy intersection, the halfway point to the apartments and homes on the hills, and the businesses down below. There are rows of shops here, too. Busy place.

I stand on the corner of Morton and Echo Park, or what I assume is the corner, my guide dog's harness in one hand, and my aluminum walking stick in the other. Rarely, if ever, does anyone help me across, and they don't do so now. I might as well be alone in this world. Or, at least, alone at this one intersection.

Now, Betsie is moving and I am moving, too. Trusting her. I have, after all, no other choice.

No, I do have a choice. I could sit at home and do nothing. Except, of course, I do enough of that already. Not to mention, I love Chango's coffee.

When I'm about halfway across the intersection, in the crosshairs of where the three streets intersect, I know I am fully exposed. So is Betsie. She would never leave my side. Should a car not see us, should a driver be texting now, we would be hit and there would be no way to avoid it.

But today, the drivers are alert and soon, my walking stick touches the far curb. I measure its height quickly with the tip of the stick, and step up into the cool shade under the awning at Chango.

Betsie leads me inside, where, luckily, the staff knows me well.

2

I sit outside with Betsie, holding the hot to-go coffee cup with both hands. Betsie is leaning on my ankle, panting in the heat, her heaving body pulsating against my own. Her weight is comforting. Her touch gives me peace of mind and a small amount of happiness.

There is still no wind. I miss the wind. I hunger for the wind. And for the rain. I realize all over again that I am, perhaps, living in the wrong part of the country.

But I can't move. Not from here. I know this area. A snapshot of it is forever imprinted in my mind. Forever and ever. I live in that snapshot. How could I live where I don't know what the view is like from my balcony, or from my front door, or up and down my street? I couldn't, and I am afraid such a change would be the end of me. The end of my sanity, too.

I suspect that eyes are on me, but I do not know. I suspect young ones want to pet Betsie, but her vest clearly says: "Working dog. Please do not touch." At least, that's what I'm told it says.

Betsie does not need to be petted or touched and fawned over or played with. She is a working dog. She is always alert, ever watchful, her head constantly swiveling. I can feel it, even know it, that she is watching, watching.

She knows what her job is and she does it well for me.

At least, that's what I believe, and I am sure I am not far from the mark.

When the coffee begins to cool enough for me to sip, I do so. Perhaps one of the few luxuries that remain is my ability to swallow food and drink, although both must be done very carefully. If either goes down the wrong pipe, I am in trouble. It's very difficult to cough up through a tracheal tube, which I'm breathing out of now.

And so, I sip slowly, carefully, ingesting just a small dose of the coffee.

Yes, one of my few luxuries is taste. I do have it, albeit in limited form. After all, part of my tongue had been destroyed, too.

The coffee is only really a hint of coffee. I will take a hint. In a life where so much was taken from me, anything at all is a blessing. Early on, I couldn't recognize my blessings. Early on, I was all too aware of what had been taken from me, stolen from me. It has taken me years to appreciate what I still have. And what I have is a hint of taste buds...taste buds that still worked. God bless them.

I taste the crap out of this coffee now, savoring it, swallowing it oh-so-carefully.

My scarred and destroyed throat is of little use. But it still remembers how to swallow. Thank God I can feed myself.

Another gift, I think.

I am about halfway through my coffee when Betsie sits up. She moves away from the shade and the pressure on the harness suggests she is standing alert. Then again, what do I know? One thing is certain: there is someone next to me. I can feel them now, sense them in my own way. Betsie does not growl. Betsie is not aggressive. That had been trained out of her as a puppy. But she is alert and letting the stranger know that I am well protected.

Turns out, it isn't a stranger after all.

3

We are in my apartment.

I am sitting in the corner of my couch, my hands in my lap, my knees together. A docile pose. An unassuming pose. I do not know why I sit like this these days. Perhaps I am afraid to spread out. To expand. To touch something unfamiliar. To get hurt. To be embarrassed. So now, I sit in an upright fetal position, so to speak. Touching no one. Touching nothing. As alert as I can be, which isn't saying much.

With me are two people. My ex-boss at the LAPD, Captain Paul Harris of Robbery-Homicide, and a sign language translator named, I think, Rachel. The translator is sitting next to me. My ex-boss, the gruff-but-fair Captain Harris is sitting opposite me. I know this because I can feel only one person on the couch. And if I am alert enough—and I often am—I can even feel the floorboards beneath me give way ever so slightly, signaling that my plus-sized ex-boss is sitting in the recliner.

If they are speaking, I wouldn't know it. Sometimes, I can detect speech by the way the cushion around me might bounce as the speaker gesticulates with hands and arms. There's no gesticulating going on now, probably because we were only now getting settled. I felt Betsie at my feet, where she would be, I knew, for the rest of her life, God bless her canine soul.

I raised my hands and signed: "To what do I owe the pleasure, Captain?"

Small movements next to me. The translator was relaying my signs into speech. A pause. Now, small movements. If I have to guess, the translator is nodding, and if I have to guess further, I suspect that Captain Harris is getting straight to the point, as he is wont to do.

I wait, hands folded once again in my lap. Betsie is asleep on my left foot. Her breath is hot on my bare ankle. I am in shorts.

And now, something happens that doesn't make sense to most people at first. The translator takes my right hand carefully. I know what's coming next, and so I open my palm. Below, Betsie looks up, undoubtedly assessing the situation, determines that all is well, and rests her chin once again on the top of my shoe.

I wait with my hand open, aware of the woman sitting close to me, aware that this is the first time in many months that a woman has sat so close to me. I am also aware of a hint of perfume. Just a hint, as my sense of smell is mostly gone, too. But sometimes, the right combination of scents makes its way through my damaged olfactory, and hers does now.

Roses. And jasmine. Something woodsy, too. The smell of rain, somehow.

I know I am smiling, and I can only wonder what the other two are thinking of me, seeing me smiling there, with my shades on and part of my face destroyed. Not all of it, granted—and, I'm told, I had lucked out. The scarring isn't hideous. I have been told that, in the right light, I still even look somewhat handsome. I'll gladly take the 'somewhat handsome' part. Then again, I would take many things at this point.

So, I am smiling as she places her hand in my hand, and what happens next has become second nature to me, although it has taken many, many tries to get it right.

Rachel—I think her name is Rachel, I am too embarrassed to ask her again—uses American Sign Language now. Pinkie up, she presses her hand into my palm and I immediately recognize the letter "I."

She pauses, tapping my palm once to indicate a space.

A closed fist with the thumb in is pressed into my palm—then a closed fist with the thumb out.

A—M—

Another tap. More letters pressed into my palm.

S—O—R—R—Y—

Another tap, more letters.

T—O—

Tap.

S—E—E—

Tap.

Y—O—U—

Tap.

L—I—K—E—

Tap.

T—H—I—S—

And two taps to end the dialogue.

All in all, the process takes just a few seconds. I can feel the signed letters being pressed into my palm. It is a cumbersome way to communicate, true, but it is effective for someone like me who can't see or hear.

The captain's words sink in. I haven't seen him in many years. Perhaps even five. I haven't seen many of my old friends from the station, no pun intended. Few could communicate with me, and sitting with me in awkward silence is, well, awkward. Most of my friends are gone. My parents are passed, and I only have one brother, who visits me weekly. He'd long ago mastered sign language, and we have a good time together. Or as good as we can.

I use both hands to sign back: "What do you mean?" But then, I smile, or think I smile. Half of my face is mostly paralyzed, although I am told my smile is still kinda adorable, with a few new dimples thrown in for good measure. Who told me these things? Who'd blow smoke up a blind and deaf man's ass? My ex-girlfriend, of course. My ex-girlfriend who'd cared for me for many months after the explosion. My ex-girlfriend who is now long, long gone, although I think about her often. And dream about her even more. In fact, I've been meaning to look her up again, crazy as that might sound.

Very, very crazy. After all, my ex had made it known that she wanted nothing to do with me after my rehab.

No, I think. *Those words are too strong. She was just exhausted, overwhelmed. Maybe we can get coffee someday soon.*

The idea of coffee with my ex sends a thrill through me. I have not seen her in, what, four years? Maybe she's still single? Maybe she misses me, too? Maybe she's waiting for me to reach out to her?

Maybe.

I suspect I know the answer to most of these questions. Still, the thought of being with her again, touching her, sends a thrill through me.

And the woman sitting next to me, with her small hand once again pressed into my hand, is, I suspect, the source of this thrill.

The explosion mercifully spared the rest of my body. My hands are intact, as are my legs. The blasts had been centered around my facial area. In particular, around my neck region. My voice box had been destroyed. My wind-pipe had been destroyed, too. The close proximity of the explosion had permanently damaged the inner and outer hair cells of my ears, those all-important sensory receptors that pick up sound. And there is no healing or replacing such receptors.

Shrapnel had destroyed my eyes. So much so, both eyes had been enucleated, or removed, leaving me with empty sockets. Early on I had tried orbital implants—glass eyes—but grew tired of them. Additionally, my scar tissue was such that the implants irritated me more than helped. These days, I prefer to hide behind my wraparound sun-glasses...and keep my eyelids closed.

Remarkably, my esophagus had stayed intact, which allows me to still eat and drink with my mouth. However, my larynx—the organ responsible for speech—had been completely destroyed. The damage was so severe that traditional voice aids do not work. Even handheld devices, electric larynxes as they are called, were ren-dered ineffective due to severe scarring at my throat and my inability to hear the sounds. Such devices sent vibrat-ing sound waves into the mouth and throat area, which, in turn, could be shaped into words with tongue, jaws, lips and teeth just as one would have done with sound from the larynx. It is an ingenious device that has been around longer than I would have guessed. With my hear-ing loss, I was never fully able to use the electronic lar-ynx. After all, one needs to hear the sounds coming out to learn how to manipulate them, adjust them, correct them. For now, speech is a lost cause for me, although I tried many times to use the device, and each time, I was told I was unintelligible. I haven't tried again, and doubt I ever will.

For now, I get by using American Sign Language, reading braille, using writing pads, blocks of plastic letters and a new phone app that converts text messages and emails into, of all things, vibrating Morse code, spelling out my texts one letter at a time, much as Rachel the translator was now spelling out words, one letter at a time.

Communication on my end is a little easier and faster, as I can use both hands to sign full words, and so I rapidly ask the captain to what did I owe the pleasure of his company?

There is a pause, and I feel her nodding her head, undoubtedly listening to the captain's response.

Then I feel gentle hands take my own hand again. I open my fingers and she rests her palm flat against mine—and I feel another thrill that made me think of my ex-girlfriend again, and it also makes me wonder for the first time, just what Rachel looks like. That is, until I realize I would never know what she looks like, and I let the thought go.

Still, her touch is gentle and slightly...seductive, but that could just have been my imagination. Truth is, words like 'seductive' had long since departed my vocabulary. 'Getting through the day' are common words. 'Not killing myself' is another common phrase that runs through my mind.

Still, her touch is...pleasant, and it sends shivers through me. The first shivers, I'm certain, in nearly five years.

And now, she is spelling out the words, which she does a little faster this time around, as our connection is already growing. At least, I'd like to think so. She presses each sign firmly into my palm, then quickly forms the next, pausing and tapping between words, until the sentence is spelled out, a minute or so later.

"I need your help, Lee."

I absorb this, and then sign: "You need a driver?"

I feel the couch shake slightly, and I think Rachel might have been laughing. A moment later, the captain's return message arrives: "It's good to see that you haven't lost your sense of humor, Lee."

"My sense of humor is one of the few senses I have left," I sign back.

There is another pause—and what was meant to be another small joke suddenly turns into not such a small joke. Maybe it sounded more like a cry for help, or pity, neither of which I had intended.

Now, I feel the floorboards beneath me move and Betsie jerk her head off my foot. Someone is coming over, and that someone is the captain. He reaches around and wraps a meaty arm around my shoulder and presses his head against mine and holds me closer than anyone has held me in a long, long time.

When he is done hugging me, I can feel his tears rolling down my neck. Either that, or my trachea valve needs another cleaning.

Now, he sits next to me, his legs pressing against mine. He has Betsie's full attention, and for now, she continues sitting up, undoubtedly staring at him, undoubtedly assessing him.

I sense he is talking, and now, Rachel lifts my hand and once again, presses hers into mine.

"I'm so fucking sorry this happened to you. You didn't deserve this, Lee. No one deserves this."

Except, of course, I did deserve this. I deserved this and so much more. I don't respond and we all sit in silence again on my couch. Betsie lowers her head once again to my shoe.

After a short reprieve, the captain speaks again; as he does so, he rests his hand on my shoulder, and this, along with the hug, is the most the captain has ever touched me. My old boss has gotten sentimental over the years. Rachel promptly translates his voiced words into my open palm.

"I hate to do this to you, Lee, but we could use your help on a case. Many cases, actually. One, in particular. A case we call the Big Case, with a capital B and C."

"What do you mean?"

"People are disappearing, Lee," comes his response a few minutes later. "Many people, in fact. Ten, as far as we are aware."

"Any bodies?" I ask, signing.

"None yet."

"Tell me more," I say, and the captain does. This is a lengthy process, one that challenges the translator and, I suspect, the captain's patience. But when he is done, I have the full picture.

And what a crazy picture it is.

4

P eople are disappearing.

It began six months ago. At first, the disappearance of a middle-aged man hadn't gotten much attention. That is, until another middle-aged man disappeared. The media found this suspicious, even for a city as big as Los Angeles. And then, a month later, a woman in her early thirties disappeared. Followed by a mother of three. Exactly a month later. One disappearance a month, roughly. Ten total.

I had missed this story. I read a general braille newspaper that shows up in my mail once a month. The disappearances hadn't made the braille news yet. And if they had, I might have skipped it anyway. I'd spent my career in robbery-homicide, and most of that was in homicide. After the explosion, I needed time to heal physically and emotionally.

Now, there isn't much more to heal other than my mind.

At any rate, I make it a point to skip the lurid headlines, even in the braille newspaper. I tend to focus on politics and sports, and, yes, I've even been known to read an article or two about the Kardashians, although I hated myself afterward.

Anything to keep my mind away from crime and criminals, from death and mayhem, from the very thing, in fact, that had taken so much from me. And from one other, too, of course.

My partner.

But that was, as they say, another story.

Anyway, the disappearances had stopped after ten, all while the police searched wildly for the cause; sure it was one man, and sure they would start coming across bodies sooner or later. So far, no bodies. The last disappearance was two months ago.

I ask all the usual questions, questions I know the captain and his squad have asked themselves a hundred times, but sometimes, it's nice hearing the answers again, even when you think you have all the answers. Sometimes, something stands out, even something you've looked at a hundred times before, in a hundred different ways.

Our dialogue is fast-paced. At least, as fast-paced as we can go under the circumstances. It is stilted and without much, if any, inflection or humor. In this situation, we don't need inflection and humor. Besides, these days, my humor is often lost on most people.

I begin with: "Is there security footage anywhere?"

"Yes, but not much. Two of the missing lived in apartments. We have them exiting the apartments."

"What are they wearing?"

"Jeans, light jacket. One has a backpack."

"Any footage of them at airports, bus stations, train stations? Uber accounts? Lyft accounts? Bank ATMs?"

"Nothing."

This throws me off for a minute. Usually, someone, somewhere, will show up in such an establishment.

"Is there any evidence of foul play?"

"None yet."

"Any witnesses?"

"None have been found or have come forward."

"What time of day do the disappearances occur?"

"Always at night."

"Where do the disappearances occur?"

"Over greater Los Angeles, although generally in West Hollywood, Los Feliz, and one from Echo Park."

"Has anyone asked for a ransom?"

"No."

"Have any of the victims' credit cards been used?

"No."

"Money taken out of banks?"

"Nothing excessive, and nothing at the time of the disappearances or just after."

"Socio-economic profile of the victims?"

"Mostly middle class."

"Do the victims have criminal records?"

I think here he is going through his notes or his files. The captain probably came prepared. A moment later, I feel Rachel pressing letters into my hand. "Two or three, but nothing alarming, and nothing that connects them."

"What patterns have you established?"

The captain pauses here. While the captain thinks this over, I notice that the translator and I are still touching hands. Not quite holding, but her fingertips are nestled between my own fingers as she waits to translate. Her touch is…intoxicating, although I try not to think about it too much. The captain's appearance has done something to me. Jostled something awake inside me. Something that had lain dormant. My investigator's mind.

And so, even as the woman lightly touches my hand, and even while I feel a rare thrill course through, I feel an even greater thrill take hold of me: that of being wanted, needed.

That of being *useful.*

No, I haven't asked anything that the captain and his own investigators haven't already asked, but I am excited to feel myself perk up, pick up, slip right into the game. Yes, it's all coming back to me, which is good and bad. Good, because I'm beginning to feel like my old self. Bad, because I could never feel like my old self. Not the way I was.

"All victims headed out on foot, we know that."

"Any phone calls prior to disappearances? Text messages?"

"Nothing out of the ordinary. Nothing telling. No pattern. But get this: all of the vics left their phones behind. And their wallets, I.D.s, credit cards and money."

"Walking blind," I sign.

I chewed on this, literally, biting down on my scarred lower lip. Not so scarred that I am told it looks deformed. Just puffy from the stitches that had put it back together. Flying shrapnel is hell on a human body.

"You say you have two on the apartment security feeds. Any indication where the vics were heading?"

"Both turned north."

"That's not much to go on," I sign.

"Did the vics live alone?"

"Only three lived alone."

"Did they tell anyone where they were heading?"

"No. Only that they were going for a walk."

"All vics said the same thing?"

"It appears, yes."

"So, all the vics told those closest to them that they were going for a walk?"

"A handful did. Some didn't say anything. Some lived alone, or were alone that that day."

"So, those who did tell someone where they were going, said they were going for a walk?"

"Yes."

I nod when the single word is spelled out. I had broken out into a small sweat. Generally, when a fellow investigator and I hash out motives and leads and evidence, I would pace. Pacing is not an option. Not when I need my open hand for communication.

I sign: "They were told to say that."

"We think so, yes."

"And they were told to meet someone."

"We think so, too."

I sign: "Somewhere out of sight, away from security cameras."

We sit quietly. I wonder what Rachel thinks about all of this. I wonder what she looks like, too, especially the longer we touch hands. Her proximity is exciting. And so is the prospect of working on a case again, albeit in a peripheral fashion. A lot of heady stuff is going on for me today.

Finally, I sign: "I wish I could check out the video feeds."

"Trust me, Lee. We have pored over them. Many of us have. We had the best eyes looking for anything and everything."

"You didn't have my eyes," I said.

There is a long pause, and the captain's heavy hand falls on my shoulder. I feel him speaking, and a moment later, Rachel signs into my open hand. "No, we don't, and I wish like hell we did."

"So do I," I sign.

I feel him nodding as he stands. Rachel signs: "I'm leaving you with the reports. They're in braille. If you have any further thoughts or ideas, get back to me, will you?"

And just like that, they both stand. I shake Rachel's hand, which seems a little formal after spending the past forty-five minutes holding it. The captain gives me another pat on the back, and just like that, I am alone again.

Well, not entirely. I feel Betsie pressing against my leg. I think she has to pee.

5

After Betsie had done her duty and been fed, I sit in my living room with the police report.

I can do things like feed my dog and take her out to pee. My life is a challenge, but not that challenging. If anything, my life is about patterns and routines. For instance, I know where everything is in my apartment. Literally. I have memorized what's in what drawer, from the kitchen to the bathroom to the bedroom. Nothing is out of place, ever. If anything, being blind, deaf and, for all practical purposes, a nonverbal communicator, has made me the world's neatest of neat freaks.

If I need something outside of my home, something that is beyond the small shopping center at the bottom of my hill, I will do so with my brother, who visits every Sunday.

My life is often boring, and for that, I have no excuse. Then again, there is only so much I can read in braille. I may not get to watch—or even hear—*Seinfeld* anymore, but I can read the scripts in braille and imagine the characters acting out the scenes. I often laugh while reading such scripts.

These days, I do not know what my laugh sounds like. The months following my accident, I used to be self-conscious about my laugh. Maybe I still am a little.

Anyway, I have my whole house memorized. I know where the corners are. I know exactly where the hallway begins. I know how many steps from my doorway to the corner of my bed. I can navigate my apartment without the aid of my dog, which she appreciates, too, I think. At home, she acts as a dog should. Her favorite game is catch. Often, I feel her natty tennis ball pressed up against my thigh or my hand.

I often wonder what Betsie looked like, too. She's a golden retriever. I know that much.

I was told she had brown eyes, but, more than anything, I want to see *into* those eyes. I know they have to be intelligent eyes. They have to be. There is an old soul in this dog.

Now, I read through the police report, taking my time, reading through the lines, so to speak, trying to paint a picture with words—and in my case, with embossed braille. I see—or feel—immediately that this case is unusual, in that many reports have been combined to form one big case. Or, the Big Case, as it is sometimes referred to in the report. The Big Case consists of many missing person reports amalgamated into one, bigger case, especially as the investigators recognized the common thread that linked them.

No witnesses. No goodbye notes. No money being pulled from the bank. Cars left behind. Bikes left behind. Scooters left behind. Money, wallets and IDs and credit cards, all left behind. It was as if everyone got up…and walked into the ocean, never to be seen or heard from again. And that is another common thread: no word from the missing, as if they had truly disappeared.

But not quite. In five instances, it was reported that the missing had taken a backpack. In one of the surveillance videos, one of the missing was seen wearing a backpack. In all instances, the missing had donned walking shoes and many of those left behind reported that light jackets and jeans were missing.

What the hell? I think, as I begin again at the front of the thick report.

This time, I focus on the witness testimony, although I use that term loosely. None of the witnesses—or those who lived with the missing—were aware of any suspicious activity leading up to the disappearance. Additionally, none of the witnesses were aware if their friends or loved ones had met anyone suspicious recently. None reported that their friend or loved one had changed their habits recently. One middle-aged man, Boomer Thompson, who had disappeared many months ago, had canceled dinner with his son to go for a walk. Two other witnesses—both wives of the missing—reported that their husbands were simply determined to go for a walk. Determined to get fresh air and get some exercise in. In fact, they both used those exact words.

They were told what to say, I think now, sitting back and stretching my hands, the equivalent of rubbing my eyes. Reading braille takes careful attention, a true synergy between mind and body, fingertips and imagination. I picture each word as my fingers move over them. I picture a lot these days, as I will for the rest of my life.

Of the ten missing, eight are men. Most are middle-aged, except for one old man in his early seventies, the first of the missing, in fact. Or, rather, the first of the missing that was linked to the Big Case.

I feel tired, and absently reach for my watch. When one lives in the dark 24/7, one's circadian rhythm is thrown off. Which is why I must often check the time. It helps to frame the day. I flip open the watch's protective cover and lightly touch the Braille numbers and raised watch hands. 2:35 in the afternoon. I would have guessed later. Evening, perhaps.

Still, a nap will do me good. A nap will do the case good, too. A fresh mind sees things differently. I know this from back in the day, back when I worked homicide.

I lie back on the couch and prop my feet up. There's no closing of the eyes for me.

The darkness is already there. It's *always* there.

Always.

I dream of a beautiful, raven-haired woman who is holding my hand and watching me closely. She is so, so beautiful. Short hair. High cheekbones. Round, brown eyes. Or are they blue? Or violet? Doesn't matter. What matters is how she is looking at me. With so much love in those eyes.

When I wake, I automatically check the time…an hour has passed. As I sit forward, I push up my sunglasses and wipe around my empty eye sockets. Mercifully, my eyelids were repairable. I can still open and close them. I mostly keep them closed—and wear non-breakable, wraparound shades. Goggles, almost. I sleep with them on, often forgetting they're there. They form and hug my face, and keep people from seeing the horror underneath.

This isn't the first time I've awakened from a sleep or nap with tears filling the inside of my shades. I pull them off my face and clean them with a finger, then head to the bathroom.

I feel Betsie plodding behind me. I always imagine her as less formal here in the apartment. Maybe even a little goofy. But outside, I imagine her a proud sentry standing guard.

I have a trach-cleaning kit ready to go, a kit that I prepare each morning, knowing that it's stocked and ready to go when the time comes to clean my tracheal tube, which must be done two or three times a day. It's hell, but it's my life.

At the sink, I first remove the latex, foam-padded tracheal tie, which keeps the tube in place around my neck. I next gently remove the tube from my throat. As I do so, I feel mucus come up after it. Once the mucus has been cleaned, I swab the hole in my throat with an alcohol-based pad, and dip the new tube in a saline solution. Once dry, I re-insert the outer tube into my throat, then snap the inner tube in place.

Then I take a deep breath, and relive the blast again.

Again and again.

6

When all you have is your imagination, sometimes, you cannot turn off the movie in your head. Sometimes, it plays over and over and over.

I worked in the LAPD robbery-homicide division. I mostly worked homicides. I was good at my job. I had a knack for asking the right questions, seeing people for who they were, catching them in their lies, and probing relentlessly until I found a nugget of truth. I was tenacious, I was told. I was quick on my feet, I was told. I was an asshole, too, I was told. Doesn't matter. The truth was what I sought. The truth was what I found. Doggedly. Persistently.

The truth. Always the truth.

I'd been partners with Mitch for a few years. We were a good team. Classic good cop, bad cop. I mostly played the good cop. When I played the bad cop...I played it too well.

I was better at keeping a level head. I was better at watching the perps closely. I was better at watching body language, hearing inflection, watching eyes shift, fingers jerk, breaths shudder.

It was a copycat killing. We knew that much. Some punk shot up a comic convention in Los Angeles. Nearly a dozen were dead. The shooter gave himself up and survived. Those in the department were in shock, traumatized, let alone those who survived the ordeal. All hands were on deck.

We were all working the scene, some of us working overtime, running on adrenaline. Running on anger and confusion and shock.

Police are people, too. We are not robots. Despite what people think, we have not seen it all. Certainly, I'd never seen anything like this.

On this day, I was not thinking straight. We knew who the killer was. We knew what he had done. We were all pissed, horrified, sickened. I'd seen the bodies on the smooth cement floors. I'd seen the shots to the head, the back, to the young and old. I'd seen it all...and I wasn't thinking.

I should have been thinking.

Because what I did next changed my life forever—and ended the life of my partner. My best friend.

It was an apartment off Los Feliz Boulevard.

My partner and I were the first to arrive. Two veterans. Trusted homicide cops. Unlike the Aurora, Colorado, shootings, we had not been tipped off that the place had been booby-trapped, wired with more than fifty explosives.

My instincts were off. I knew it. I was angry. I wasn't seeing straight, thinking straight.

The apartment was on the busiest street on Earth. Maybe that's an exaggeration. Still, if Los Feliz wasn't at least the busiest street in Los Angeles, I would eat my left shoe.

I was seeing red. And not just from the blood of all the victims. I was taking the assault personally. This was my city, goddammit. *How dare you fucking come here and do this to our people?* The people I fought to protect.

No, I wasn't thinking straight at all.

But Mitch was.

I was the first up the flight of stairs. The first down the narrow outer hallway that led to the front door. There was a curtained window next to the door, next to us. The place looked empty. Police instincts. Turned out, it was the last thing I would ever be right about. The place was empty, yes, but not entirely.

———

I'm holding a department-issued Smith & Wesson, my preferred gun. Behind me, Mitch is gripping his Glock 36. We both move along the narrow upper floor hallway carefully. A metal railing is to our right.

I can hear the ever-present traffic outside the apartment complex. If I have to guess, there are probably a dozen or so units here. The place appears run down. But I know better. This is the foothills leading up to the million-dollar celebrity homes above. These apartments might look dingy from the outside, but I suspect they are big and roomy inside. Not like the one-bedroom apartment I live in. But I'm thinking only about bagging evidence. I'm thinking only about the bodies I have just seen. The young girl. The teenage boy. The mother covering her son. All shot.

No, not all. Twelve dead, and twenty-seven more wounded. So much blood...

I pick up speed as I move along the exterior hallway. My own apartment has inner hallways. Not this place. This place looks like a beat-up old hotel. But I know better. I have seen enough places in this town to know that some-times, appearances can be deceiving. These are nicer apartments, camouflaged in grime. Perhaps it's done on purpose, but I doubt it. Neglect, surely. No one giving enough of a damn.

These thoughts are all instant and unfiltered. Mostly, I am moving steadily toward Apartment 2F, my weapon in both hands, my partner directly behind me.

The shooter, once the damage was done, had set down his weapon and waited for the police to arrive. From what we knew, the whole thing had taken less than ten min-utes. We have no idea how many rounds had been fired or how many had been shot. Not yet, anyway, although we can guess.

Below us, a patrol officer appears. A beat cop. Mitch and I are dressed in our finest plainclothes uniform: cheap slacks and a cheaper, long-sleeved, white shirt. It's a good look, actually. Most perps find the look intimidating. Like Mormon missionaries, minus the bikes and Bible thump-ing. And there's no saving your ass from us. At least, not if you were one of the bad guys.

We duck under the wide window fronting the exte-rior hallway, a window shielded by dirty, broken blinds. We don't want someone from the inside taking pot shots at our passing shadows, but, as I said, the place appears empty.

Truth be known, on that day, I felt compelled to move down that corridor. I felt drawn to that door. Yes, the anger propelled me forward, but something else was going on here, something I hadn't ever been able to put my finger on. Not then, not now. But somehow, some way, I felt that I had to get into that apartment. I had to take action. I had to do what I did next.

Which was to reach for the doorknob.

I didn't bother knocking and waiting. There were a dozen people laying dead in their own blood and many more writhing in pain, whose lives would be forever altered by this scumbag. I wasn't giving anyone inside a courtesy knock. Fuck that. Fuck him and fuck anyone inside.

"Lee, wait!"

Those were, of course, Mitch's last words.

Except, I don't wait. I turn the doorknob and am surprised to discover that the door was unlocked. I push it all the way open...

And that's the last thing I remember.

7

Until I wake up in the hospital a day later.

But I wake up into a world of silence and darkness. I wake up a monster. I wake up friendless, as well. My partner, Mitch, who I was closer to than any of my partners, hadn't been so lucky. The entire Apartment 2F had been lined with explosives. Not all of them had gone off. Just the ones closest to the door and the window, which Mitch had been standing next to when he reached out to me, reached out to stop me from opening the door.

He's dead now, having taken the brunt of the explosion. A random bomb had exploded in the kitchen, too, set off for reasons I never understood. It had blown a hole in the wall and seriously wounded a neighbor, although she had survived, too.

One death, two injuries. All because I wasn't thinking. All because I had forgotten my training and abandoned my instincts.

I sigh, still standing there in the bathroom, expelling air through my freshly-replaced tracheal tube.

It's times like this, I want to drink.

But I don't, can't. At least not alone. I can't risk passing out. I can't risk vomiting. I can't risk getting drunk and doing something stupid, like wandering outside without my walking stick, or without Betsie, or even leaning too far over my upstairs railing. Drinking now is never a good idea, although I have had a beer or two with my brother, with his ever-watchful eye on me.

I continue to hold the bathroom counter, aware I'm standing in front of a mirror I had looked into a thousand times before. Did I have more wrinkles now? More gray hair? My brother tells me I look the same, but is he being truthful? I can feel the wrinkles around the corners of my eyes, but are they noticeable to others? I could only imagine that I have not aged well, not with the stress I'd endured, the pain I've felt, the guilt that wracks me daily.

Then again, half my face is pocked by scars. I touch them often. In fact, I usually wake up in the morning touching my scars, which means I touch them while I sleep, too. I think, in a way, I am fascinated by them. Plus, they feel so…foreign. As if I am touching someone else's face. And so I awaken each morning, my fingertips running over my temples and eye sockets and cheekbones, reading, if you will, the story of my accident.

The days following the blast were too hellish to remember in any detail. The fear. The horror. The sick realization. The begging for help. The begging for death. The pain. The treatments. The surgeries. The heartbreak. The loss. The nightmares.

The darkness.

The silence.

Too much to relive, and most of these were memories I would rather soon forget.

I lower my head, still holding the sink. My life has come into some balance now. Some semblance of normalcy. I have my routines. I have my patterns. I know my way around. I do not get lost, and, just last month, my brother presented me a prototype smartphone. It has a braille plastic cover that I can use to find the apps I needed. Also,

I can both send and receive texts and emails—all spelled out in vibrating Morse code.

Now, throughout the day, my hip will sometimes vibrate, indicating a text message. To date, only my brother has text messaged me, although the captain gave me his personal number, and so did the translator, in case I needed her services again.

I push away from the counter and wonder again what Rachel the translator looks like, until I realize I don't care what she looks like. I also realize that I miss her touch and wonder if I will ever see her—or feel her—again.

I take out my cell phone, and find the braille messaging icon, and proceed to text-message the captain.

I do, after all, have some follow-up questions regarding the case. At least, that's what I tell myself.

8

Detective Hammer is an old friend.

He is also a lead detective at the LAPD Missing Persons Unit, which is why the captain sent him over. If memory serves me, the man was damned good at what he did. Additionally, if memory serves me, he often worked with a private dick by the name of Spinoza. A small guy, quiet, who had a helluva past himself. Hammer and Spinoza made an unlikely team, and often worked together on missing person cases. Whether or not they still did, I don't know. And how I remember the little detective's name, I'm not entirely sure, either. I guess you can't forget a name like Spinoza.

Hammer picks Betsie and I up outside the apartment. As I step into what I assume is an unmarked car, I am greeted immediately with the faintest hint of jasmine. My sense of smell is working at nearly a hundred percent capacity. If I had to guess, I would say maybe at eighty percent. For me, this is damn good news.

Before I sit in the back seat, I sign, "Hi, Rachel."

For a reply, I feel a light touch on the back of my hand. I next sign, "Howdy, Detective."

I can almost imagine the stoic Hammer saying, "Enough with the chit-chat."

Maybe he had. The car is moving away from the apartment, and down Morton Avenue, a street I walk every day.

Next to me, I can feel Betsie panting. Her breath smells ripe. I love her ripe breath, which can often penetrate my damaged olfactory system. As we drive, I imagine the homes whipping past us. The dangling telephone wires. The graffiti. The old bungalows. The schools. The chain-link fences. The out-of-the-way shops, of which Chango is a part.

We stop and I am certain we are on Alvarado, although Hammer might have turned down Scott Road. Betsie puts a paw on my lap. I love her stinky paws, too; that is, when I can smell them.

We make the turn and shortly, I feel us coming to a stop. I know the donut shop is the detective's favorite hangout. I know he also takes a lot of heat for that. Or, at least, he did. Okay, he took it from me. When we come to a full stop, I feel another light touch on my hand. Rachel is indicating it's time to get out. At least, that's what I think she is indicating. Either way, I am about to find out.

I open the door, step out, and Betsie follows behind. When we are situated and I have a firm hold of the harness, I feel a small hand reach inside my arm and lead me forward. I go without hesitation, and so does Betsie. As I pass the detective, who is holding the door to the donut shop open, I catch a faint hint of aftershave. Long ago, doctors told me my olfactory had been mostly destroyed. I shouldn't be able to smell. But I do sometimes. Each smell is a miracle. At least, that's what I tell myself.

Once we are seated in the warm shop, I can't help but smile at the assorted smells that come next. Yes, eighty percent, maybe even ninety percent. A hint of choco-late and cinnamon and cake. The smell of old grease. Something that could have been marijuana, too. Hard to say. I also smell dirt and grime and sweat, and suspect there's a homeless man seated nearby. Also, Betsie's attention is elsewhere. On the homeless man, probably. She doesn't like homeless men or women. They, more than any others, are most likely to confront me, and Betsie somehow knows this. Motionless, she watches whoever is sitting next to us...the entire time we sit there. Never taking her eyes off him or her, even to scrounge for donut crumbs that are undoubtedly falling around her.

Rachel takes my wrists carefully and her touch is even sweeter than I remember. She places the back of my hand on top of the table, and then slips her own small hand into my own. Goosebumps ripple through me. No, tear through me. Rage through me.

"Hi, Lee," she signs, one letter after another. "Remember me?"

"How could I forget?" I sign back, using both hands. I return my hand to the table, palm up, ready for her answer. I know I am grinning like a schoolboy.

"Detective Hammer wants to know if you want anything to eat or drink?"

I sign back that I will take a donut and a milk. I tell him to choose the donut, since he is the expert.

"He says comments like that are what get people plain donuts," responded Rachel, her fingers gentle but firm in my palm.

"Tell him to bite me," I sign back.

"He says it's good to have you back, Lee."

I grin. For some reason, I sense Rachel grinning, too, although that had to be my imagination. Then again, isn't almost everything these days in my imagination?

While we wait, presumably as the good detective stands in line for our donuts, Rachel has the good decency to release my hand.

I hate good decency.

My thoughts wander. I'd realized long ago that seeing actually helped focus my thoughts—and also helped distract my thoughts. Now, I had little distraction from the world inside my head. And, boy, oh boy, did my mind wander. Sometimes, too far and wide and for far too long. Sometimes, it is all I can do to rein in my imagination, to wrestle them down, so to speak. Especially when I am alone, when my thoughts are scattered and chaotic, I think I am losing my mind. In the past, all I had to do was open my eyes, blink and rub my eyeballs and focus on something else. Now, well, now I had nothing to distract my inner world. I live, I've come to accept, in one long, rotten dream.

I feel something thud on the plastic table, followed by the greasy aroma of donuts. A soft hand slides between my forefinger and thumb and guides me to a carton of milk, already opened for me. Who had opened it, I don't know, but I have my suspicions. The donut is next to it. A long john, with frosting. My guess: chocolate. I will know soon enough.

Now, as I drink in silence, I feel all eyes on me. The esophagus is functional for me, and so is the masticating process. Yay.

The donut tastes heavenly. It has been awhile since I treated myself to something like a donut. For me, sweets have always been a reward. I guess I haven't had much of a reason to reward myself these days. But I know that's not true. Hell, just making my way safely down to the coffee shop each morning is something to celebrate. Or keeping my sanity. Hell, I should be having donuts each and every morning. Maybe I will.

Shortly, when all of us have had our sugar fixes, Rachel takes my hand again. I hope mine is grease free.

She begins spelling the words out quickly. My injuries have forced me to develop new neural pathways in my mind that allow me to see the letters as they appear in my hand. As if I were watching words appear on a computer monitor. "Another missing person report came in last night."

"Who's working the case?" I ask, using both of my free hands.

"Detective Hammer."

I nod, sign: "Where did the victim live?"

"Beverly Hills."

"How old?"

"Fifty-eight, married."

"Let me guess," I sign, "he told his wife he was going for a walk."

"I see the captain caught you up to speed."

"Any witnesses?" I ask.

"Only the wife. No one's seen him since."

"Any video feeds of him?"

"We're checking on it now, but he lived in an old house. No home surveillance."

"Was he wearing a backpack?"

"Yes."

"Wife know which direction he took?"

"She does not."

I think about this, and ask: "Anything turn up on his cell phone or email or web browser?"

"We're checking that now, but so far, nothing."

"Same M.O.," I sign.

"Yes," comes Hammer's response, as relayed through Rachel's fingers pressed into my palm.

I sign: "Someone's helping the vics disappear."

"That's the way we see it."

"But why?"

"For money, be my guess."

There is silence and I feel myself buzzing. I love this feeling. The buzzing crackles between my shoulders and down both arms and seems to settle somewhere in my solar plexus.

"We've gone through emails and texts—sometimes many months back—but always a lot of nothing. So, what do you think is going on, Lee?"

I think about this, about it long and hard. But before I can answer or think about an answer, another message gets pressed into my hand. It's from Rachel: "He's telling me he trusts your opinion. That you were one of the best. That you are greatly missed."

I smile, and sign back to her, "Detective Hammer must be drunk again."

Rachel: "On donuts. He just ate four of them. Gross."

I smile again, and address Hammer's question: "For now, Detective, I don't know. But it's not good."

"You think he's killing them?" he asks.

"Or maybe he's helping them disappear, for reasons we don't know about."

Rachel, who just signed the question into my palm, continues holding my hand lightly. As she does so, there is the slightest—slightest—movement of her pinkie against mine. Rubbing, maybe. One can hope.

We sit quietly around the bench. Some of us more quietly than others. I don't sense words being exchanged from the other two. Finally, Rachel reaches for my hand, lifts it and presses her fingers into my palm, spelling out the words: "He hates seeing you like this, he says."

I smile back and say, "I hate seeing me like this, too."

"He's smiling, Lee. You made him laugh."

"He's simple like that," I say to her in our private, side conversation. And to Detective Hammer, I sign, "Can you swing by when you find something?"

"He says he will," comes Rachel's reply, and she follows it with another squeeze. A full hand squeeze, this time. It is, I'm certain, the sweetest squeeze I've ever felt. I turn to her…and smile.

At least, I hope I smiled.

9

I am sitting on my balcony. It is midday.

I know this because I can feel the sun on my lifted face. Sometimes, I open my eyelids behind my sunglasses, and when I do…they blink intermittently. All on their own, with no help from me. Sure, I could stop them from blinking, but I don't. I smile, often sadly. Sometimes, I weep at this. Such a wonderful useful tool to keep our eyes watered and healthy and clear, now lost on me. But I smile because the movement reminds me of better times. And reminds me that I am still human. That maybe I am not so different, after all. That is, of course, until I take off my sunglasses, and someone catches a glimpse into the black depths. I am sure they would scream, or gasp, or gag a little.

I drink from my water bottle, wishing it was more than water, but not daring to drink alone. Not ever. Yes, I might hate myself for killing my friend and destroying my body, but I don't hate myself so much that I want to drown in my own vomit.

Some think I don't have goals. My brother doesn't. My brother often encourages me to try new things, to do new things. I respect his opinion. His is often the only opinion I get. My therapist, back in the day, suggested that I try new things, too, to continue to push myself.

I reminded them that not falling down the stairs is often goal number one for me. I remind them that not getting hit crossing the street is a terrific goal, too. I remind them that walking down to Chango in complete silence and darkness is a Herculean task that isn't for the faint of heart.

My brother doesn't want to hear it and he worries about me. He worries that some street punks will take me down, rob me blind. I remind him that I don't carry cash and that I'm already blind. I do not know if he laughs at my simple joke or not. I doubt it. These days, my brother seems much too serious. And it's true, I don't carry cash. It is, after all, hard to count dollar bills, although I do have a wad of cash in my bedroom, each corner earmarked to let me know which bill is what. Still, a credit card works wonders for me. With that said, I don't often buy random things alone. When I shop, it's usually with my brother.

Yes, there is a special place in heaven—and in my heart—for my brother. He does so much for me, so much. Each Sunday, he brings me groceries. Each Sunday, he goes through the mail with me. He pays my bills online for me. He tells me how much money I have remaining. I often tell him to transfer five bucks to himself for his trouble. He usually doesn't laugh at the joke. Or at any of my jokes.

Much too serious, I think now.

He doesn't have to help me. I have a handful of friends in the apartment building who would probably go shopping with me. And I could even hire someone to help me, too. I have suggested this, but he waves it off. At least, I think he waves it off. At any rate, he isn't too keen on the idea of someone else helping me. I told him just last week that I appreciated his help and that I was sorry that I was a burden on him. He signed to me that I wasn't a burden and what were brothers for? I suggested noogies. I'm pretty sure he laughed at that one.

Anyway, as of today, in a few minutes, in fact, I am expecting a personal trainer at my apartment. I know this because my brother just text messaged me a reminder. A simple text, to the point, spelled out via Morse code and my vibrating phone. Welcome to my life.

Truth is, I don't want a personal trainer to come to my apartment. I have no idea if my apartment is even clean enough to host a guest. I shouldn't worry what my apartment looks like, but I do. I also worry about what I look like to others. I shouldn't worry about that, but I do. I dread the moment I open the door and the trainer sees what he's dealing with and we stand there in awkward silence, because all I know these days is awkward silence.

I angle my face toward the sun some more. Behind my shades, my eyelids blink sporadically. The blinking makes me sad and makes me smile, too.

Next to me is a big glass of ice water. Under me, in the shade of the patio chair, is Betsie. She's out cold. I love her more than words can express. With her, I am never alone, and I do not know what I will do when she finally passes. Maybe, mercifully, I will pass with her.

A shitty thought that upsets me more than I want it to. I let it run its course, before making an effort to change my focus onto something else.

The case is perplexing, haunting, troubling, scary and fascinating. It is the kind of case that would keep me up at night, back in the day. The kind of case I would take personally. Now, it's not keeping me up at night. There's little I can do about it, other than ponder it, consider it, turn it inside out and upside down. I know, instinctively, for me to take the case further, I need more evidence. Detective Hammer is my eyes and ears and mouth. I hope he brings back some good evidence to work with, to mull over, to analyze. We'll see.

And as I carefully set my glass of ice water down on the bamboo patio table, the little buzzer clipped to my belt does just that. Buzzes. Betsie jerks awake, instantly alert.

Someone's at my door.

My trainer.

Oh, joy.

10

His name is Jacky and he's a boxing trainer from Orange County. A long drive, surely, for what would have to be deemed a lost cause: teaching boxing to the blind.

Like I said, my brother worries about me, and he's done a lot for me. Certainly more than anyone. If he wants me to take lessons, and Jacky is willing to drive all the way out here, then the least I can do is humor them both. Besides, my brother seems to be in a bad place right now, growing angrier with me, more impatient, and I want to make him happy.

Truth is, I wasn't too worried about being mugged. I had Betsie, and I rarely, if ever, went out after dark. My street is relatively safe and most people know me and keep an eye on me, or so I've been told. I've also been told that most neighbors make it a point to keep their sidewalks clear for me. When I heard this from a man at Chango, a man who used my spelling blocks to speak to me, I got choked up. I didn't think anyone cared or noticed me. It's easy to think that. Truth is, I really don't know how many people watch me go by their homes, or how many keep an eye on me as I cross the streets. Perhaps more people aid me than I know. It is a pleasant thought.

As a lark, whenever I approach my front door, I pretend to look through the peephole, which I do now. Nope, still can't see a thing. I open, having a pretty good idea who's there, since I've been expecting him. When strangers come to the door, I generally wait for Betsie's reaction. Almost always, her tail begins wagging, letting me know the coast is clear.

Her tail wags now. In fact, whoever is in front of me is reaching down to give her wide head a good scratching. I know this because I can feel her pushing up against a hand; that, and her tail flicks me repeatedly.

I smile and nod and hold out my hand. It is greeted by a firm, albeit slightly quivery handshake. And judging by the roughness of it and the callouses, I would guess it belongs to a very old man. And judging by the angle of the handshake, a smallish older man, to boot.

Great, I think, *my brother sends me an old, short trainer.*

Then again, who am I to judge?

Not to mention, my brother swore Jacky is a miracle worker. My brother, who lives in Orange County, apparently witnessed a woman destroy a professional boxer. A woman Jacky trained. Not to mention, my brother has watched a young man spar with grown men, a young man who frequently has to be pulled off the cowering men after just a few rounds.

Trained by Jacky.

Good enough for me, I think, as I step aside to let the man in. After all, wouldn't hurt to take a few lessons. In the least, I can get some exercise in. And if Jacky was a miracle worker, maybe he really could teach a blind man to box.

As he steps inside, I remove the small notepad and pen from my front hip pocket. I flip it open and feel for a blank page. Once found, I write: "Hi, my name's Lee."

It does him no good to write back. I might be aces at reading braille, sign language pressed into my palm, and interpreting Morse code through my cell, but, to date, I haven't mastered feeling pen impressions on paper. For starters, some of the impressions could have been from a few pages back. Mostly, the impressions aren't deep enough, and my hands aren't quite sensitive enough, either.

Which is why I carry a bag of plastic letters in my fanny pack. I also have another bag at home, which I keep on a bar table near the door. Spread over the table are hundreds of small, plastic letters. No doubt the whole setup looks like it belongs in a preschool or kindergarten. I next write on my pad of paper and hold it up for him to read: "Use the letters, if you don't mind."

I do not know if Jacky understands what I want from him, but after a few moments, I feel a light touch on my arm and he guides my hand down to the table and to a row of letters he has spelled out. Good, we're on the same page, so to speak. I reach for the letters, picking each up in turn, and soon a sentence forms in my mind.

"My name is Jacky. Your brother sent me."

I write on my pad of paper: "Oh, good. You are here for my massage?"

A few minutes later, he guides my hand to the first letter on the table. It spells out: "Another comedian. Are you ready to box?"

I write: "Boy, am I. How are we going to do this?"

A few moments later, he guides my hand again to the first letter of the sentence. "I have no clue. We will figure this out together."

I nod and like his can-do attitude. He places a hand on my chest and seems to indicate he wants me to stand still. I do as indicated. Next, I feel the floor beneath me shake a little. The old man, I suspect, is clearing some room in my living room.

He next takes my elbow and guides me to the center of the living room, where, I note, he moved away the coffee table. To where, I don't know. I don't like my furniture moved, admittedly. I need it exactly where it is, exactly where I remember. But I let it slide. He's here to help, I remind myself. He doesn't know he upset my world. Maybe, with luck, he'll return the furniture to exactly where it was. But I doubt it. I will have to memorize a slightly new path.

Here, I release Betsie's harness and snap my fingers and point to the direction of the couch. I feel a slight vibration up through the wooden floor. It feels exactly like a big dog trotting away and leaping up onto a couch. Then again, maybe she's drinking out of the toilet, and I have it all wrong.

Jacky next takes my elbow and turns my torso this way and that; soon he has me positioned in a fighter's stance. I'd taken my fair share of self-defense classes at the academy and a handful of mandatory follow-up classes to know what he's doing…and what to do with my body. I help him out by raising my hands and balling my fists, one in front of the other. Back in the day, I used to be able to hold my own.

So, I stand there with my hips turned sideways, one leg in front of the other, my right arm cocked back, my left hand up for jabs and defense. It's a good stance, and had I been able to see, I could probably fight my way out of just about anything. As it stands—or as I stand—I'm still a sitting duck.

Jacky fine-tunes my hands, then reaches down and positions my feet. I think it's cute that he thinks he can help me. Whoever heard of teaching a blind man to box? No, I never had either, but my brother had been adamant and so far, Jacky is taking his job seriously.

When he's done positioning my feet, he next takes my left arm and extends it out, mimicking a punch. He does it twice more, then pats my shoulder. He wants me to do the same.

And so I do, throwing a punch blindly at about a quarter speed, hoping like hell the little man isn't directly in front of me. He's not. He's standing next to my side. He pats my shoulder again, and so I throw another punch, then another and another, until he reaches out and takes hold of my bicep, stopping me.

He shows me some other punches, jabs and upper cuts and hooks. He has me practice each a number of times before moving on to the next. I am getting winded, but, dammit, I'm having a great time, too. This is already more exercise than I have done in some time.

We take a short break. By break, I just stand there, breathing hard. I have no clue what he's doing. Maybe texting, but probably petting Betsie.

A few minutes later, he positions me again, but this time, he takes my fists and directs them into his. Except, I notice, he's wearing punching mitts. I nod. I get it, I think. He backs away and I aim a straight punch where I think his mitted hands are, and miss completely.

I stumble, nearly fall. A strong hand keeps me up. I feel more foolish than I have in a long time.

But the old man will have none of it. My wrists are seized quickly, so fast that Betsie is startled and I feel her land heavily on the wooden floor. I also sense she is barking up a storm. He releases my wrists—smart man—I kneel down and she comes to me. Yes, she's barking still, panting, getting all worked up. She doesn't like the seizing part. She'd already probably been on edge watching me air box, wondering what the hell was happening. The seizing of my wrists had pushed her over her doggie edge.

I calm her, clucking with my tongue as I sometimes do with her, patting her head. I lead her back to the couch and have her jump up. I motion with my finger for her to stay...then think better of it.

I lead her, instead, into my bedroom and pat her on the head again and silently tell her she's doing a good job, mouthing the words, then shut the door. My loyal dog just won't understand the various humiliating exercises that I suspect I will be enduring.

I come back automatically, having memorized my apartment's layout even before I went blind. Soon, I am back in the middle of the living room and I feel Jacky take my wrists again and lift them. He once again positions my body in a classic fighter's pose. Then directs my wrists to his punching mitts. Then releases my hands again.

This time, I strike immediately, seeing his mitted hands in my mind's eye. I miss completely. I wonder if he's moving his hands, but I doubt it. It's me, not him. My eye-hand coordination is nonexistent. Yes, I can memorize where some things are, over time. I can remember where I set my coffee on a table, or where my fork is on my plate. But this is a new movement. A movement I have not done in quite a long time, if ever. My self-defense classes did not consist of punching mitts. Especially mitts being held up by a man who was, for all intents and purposes, probably a little shaky himself.

Punching anything—let alone hovering mitts—isn't a part of my reality. These days, moving carefully from one room to the next, feeling my way with my walking stick and guide...yes, these are my new reality.

I swing again and again, and miss each time. In frustration, I nearly drop my hands again. But I don't. In my mind's eye, I can almost see the little man willing my hand's up. I take in a lot of air through my tracheal tube, air that's filtered and humidified to prevent irritation of my airway.

Jacky again takes hold of my wrists, steadies them, directs them into his mitted hands, and he keeps doing this, over and over, until I establish a clear pattern, muscle memory. He does this patiently. I think. Calmly. I think.

Finally, he releases my wrists and I don't wait around. I snap off an immediate straight right, and connect with the edge of the mitt. I stumble forward a little, but I am elated. It is a good thing Betsie is in the other room. She might have hurled herself at the little boxer at this point. It is only the edge of the mitt, but I feel ecstatic. I hit something, dammit. From out of the darkness, I've made a connection, and it feels wonderful.

I gather myself and see again in my mind's eye where his hands should be and fire off another punch, this one harder and more confident. If I miss, I am going to lose my balance again. But I don't miss. Quite the opposite, in fact, I hit the mitt squarely in the middle. And I hit it hard.

My next punch connects, too. My third misses entirely. I stumble and regroup and take some more air, and as I did so, the little trainer grabs my wrists and lifts them again. I know that boxers need to keep their fists up, to protect their faces, and to launch their own counterattacks. Jacky isn't letting me forget it, or letting me slide.

I gather myself and deliver another ten punches, seven of which hit their target flush. I am excited. There's a bounce to my step. Even when I miss, I am able to mostly keep my balance.

We next work on delivering jabs, which are quick, short blows launched with the leading hand. In my case, my left hand, my weaker hand. The right hand is reserved for delivering the knockout blows, so to speak.

Jabs do a lot of damage. They keep your opponent off-balance, and, if delivered correctly, they can even break noses. I wasn't looking to break anyone's nose. I wasn't entirely sure why I was learning boxing to begin with.

But, by the time Jacky and I are done with our first session, I can feel myself smiling bigger than I have done in a long time.

At my table with the plastic letters, Jacky spells out: "Good work. But keep your hands up."

On my notepad, as I wipe sweat from the tip of my nose with my sleeve, I write: "Can I ask how old you are?"

He spells out: "No. Next week, we practice with gloves."

"Oh, goody," I write.

He spells out: "Boxers don't say goody."

"I'm not a boxer."

"You are now," he spells.

And with that, he pats me on the shoulder and I feel the front door opening and closing, the vibrations of which travel up through the wooden floor and into my whole being.

11

Betsie is curled up at the end of my bed.

It is near midnight, according to my super cool braille watch with its protective cover and sturdy hands. Midnight doesn't look much different than midday. Early on, I had trouble regulating my sleep patterns. When it's dark 24/7, the body is fooled and sleep cycles got to hell. It's called non-24-hour sleep-wake syndrome, and in those early days, I slept often. I dozed off throughout the day. And when I awoke, I had no clue how long I had slept or what time of day it was and how to control my sleeping.

Thanks to some handy prescription drugs, I had gotten control over the non-24 hour syndrome. And once my sleep pattern was re-established, I got off the drugs. Still, sometimes I find myself slipping back into it, losing track of the day, nodding off randomly. But nothing that's beyond my control. In fact, one technique I use is to monitor the time constantly.

Now, it is near midnight and I can't sleep. But my lack of sleep isn't because of a disrupted pattern. No, I am thinking of the missing people and I am thinking of my ex-girlfriend and I am thinking of Rachel and her small, soft hands. I am thinking of the way her fingers curled around mine—or inside of mine. The way they sometimes nestle in there, as she waits to translate the detective's words. I am thinking that I don't have much to offer a woman, if anything. I am thinking that I miss having someone in my life, someone who loves me, cares for me, and someone I can love in return. It's been a long time.

Too long.

Now, as I lay on my bed, on my back, looking up at nothing but seeing so much in my mind's eye, I ask myself if this is something I want. Do I even want a relationship? Wouldn't I be the world's biggest burden?

I'd been alone for so long. My few friends are mostly gone. Only my brother visits weekly. An elderly woman, who lives down the hallway, visits sometimes, too. We sit at my kitchen table and she spells out a few questions with the plastic letters, and I answer them on my notepad. She never bothered to learn sign language, and I don't blame her. The plastic letters are sufficient. She sometimes brings me cookies and often, she will give me a big hug before she leaves. And not just any hug. She holds me tight and sometimes rests her head on my chest and once, I think she was crying. She feels sorry for me, alone and blind and deaf and nonverbal, as far as she knows. Alone, she thinks, and forgotten.

Long ago, back when I was in college, I flew out to visit some friends on the East Coast. While on the plane, I was having a hard time hearing what the flight attendant was saying to me. She was either a low talker or I just wasn't paying enough attention. Embarrassed, I later told the passenger next to me, "I think I'm hard of hearing." Except he heard me say, "I'm hard of hearing."

For the rest of the flight, he took control of the situation and made sure I was taken care of by the crew and explained things to me carefully. I was oddly…touched. I also didn't want to tell him I could hear just fine. The situation had blown up out of my control and I didn't want him to feel embarrassed or used or stupid or taken advantage of. Hell, it was easy enough to pretend I was hard of hearing, and his concern for me was heartwarming. How he had immediately taken on his role as benefactor. He took it seriously and with great pride. I also sensed his protectiveness over me. I also got a taste of what life might be like for the disabled.

Now, I live like this daily, although there's one difference. My disability is threefold. A hundredfold, truth be known. Also, I could not sense or see the satisfaction that some might be receiving in helping me. Or see their pity.

Now, I often receive help from strangers, strangers I can never voice a thank you to, although I have silently mouthed such words many hundreds of times. I have also received many hundred, if not thousands, of gentle pats on my shoulders and back. Many people will also gently take my elbow and guide me up stairs. I have had others who have hugged me for no known reason. Not full body hugs, but a show of support, of love toward their fellow man, of understanding and compassion. These are all faceless strangers, for whom all I can do is smile, mouth a thank you, and hug them back. I hope it's enough. I hope all those many strangers—and all the many people who have helped me—know and understand just how much I appreciate their love and attention and kindness and gentleness. Sometimes, I don't feel I deserve their help. But their help, their touches and their hidden smiles, have all helped me get through the day, to get through this life of mine.

Now, I think I am ready for more, maybe. And I can't stop thinking of my ex-girlfriend...and I keep thinking about her as I finally slip into sleep.

12

I awake as I often do:
Dreaming of my mother, who had passed nine years
ago. I also awaken to my alarm vibrating under my pillow.
I'd learned to place my cell phone under my pillow while
it charges at night. One of the techniques to battle non-
24 syndrome is to awaken with a set schedule, which I do
every morning at 7:30 a.m.

I turn over, yawn. Outside, the world is awakening, people are getting ready for work, cars are moving
through the Los Angeles roadways. The sun is shining.
The smog is thick. The women are beautiful. The men
are dressed to the nines.

In my bedroom, all is black. So black that sometimes
I feel like I have fallen into a deep well that I can never,
ever climb out of. To this day, I pray that I will awaken
from this nightmare. So far, no luck, although I'm still
holding out that this is the mother of all dreams.

Speaking of which, my mother.

I sit up and scratch Betsie behind her ears and see
my mother in my dream again. She is holding my hand,
sitting right here next to me on the edge of the bed, as
she always does in my dreams. Yes, I dream of her often.
In my dreams, she appears youngish, certainly younger
than she had been when she died of congestive heart
failure. If I had to guess, she is in her early forties and

looking healthy and strong. But we never speak in my dreams. I wonder if it's because I can't speak in real life. I don't know, but I can always see her and feel her, and she always holds my hand in both of hers. She's smiling at me, and never once does she look upon me with sadness. Only with love. The love I feel from her is real, and I miss her when I awaken, as I do now. Mostly, I miss seeing her.

I am not weeping on this morning. Still, it is a challenge for me to awaken from such beauty and love, only to find myself in complete darkness again. My dreams, I think, are my saving grace. In my dreams, I am whole. Sometimes not. Sometimes I am broken in my dreams. But mostly not. Mostly I am alive and well and experiencing the world with all my senses.

On this morning, I awaken with, I suspect, a rare smile, and an even rarer excitement.

Stupid, I think, as I find my way to the bathroom automatically, the path permanently seared into my memory, each step, each turn. I do, however, take care to line myself up in front of the toilet, to guarantee accuracy of stream. My brother tells me I must surely miss as often as I hit. Oh, well. I do my best.

The coffee is waiting for me in the kitchen—the coffeemaker having been pre-programmed by my brother. I need only to scoop coffee in the dispenser each night, which I always do before I go to bed. My plastic mugs—everything in my house is plastic—are always near the sink, and I grab one now, rinse it, then fill it with coffee, which I drink black. Milk tends to produce extra mucus for me, which can be a problem, since I have to extract it out of the trachea hole in my throat.

I take my coffee and work my way through the living room, to my patio, careful of the recently moved coffee table. My poor toes have taken much abuse in these past five years.

I sit on my balcony, in the cool morning air, drinking and turning my face to the sun. Betsie uses a pee pad on the balcony, which I replace every few days. Sometimes, I walk her down to go pee in the morning. On this morning, though, I want to sit and think and feel and wonder and ask and pray. For the first time in a long time, I feel hope and promise and it is a good, good feeling.

Before I get up and get dressed, I send Detective Hammer a text message, using my braille phone. I hope I get the message right. If not, he'll puzzle it together. He's clever like that. I text: "What's the latest?"

A minute later, my phone buzzes, spelling out the words in Morse code, which I string together automatically. "Going through some video feeds. I might have something for you later today. Stay tuned."

I write back: "Staying tuned is what I do best."

Believe it or not, the Detective sends back a winky face, which touches me for some reason.

When my coffee is done, I scratch Betsie behind her ears and note a faint whiff of fresh feces. She had done her business. I give her a good-girl pat. I keep her bowl of high-quality, dry food filled throughout the day. She is free to eat whenever she wants.

Back in my room, I feel my way through my closet, finding jeans and a bowling shirt that, I hoped, looks good on me. Most of my shirts are either white or black, anyway. Once dressed and brushed and groomed, I strap Betsie into her harness and we take the elevator downstairs.

When the elevator touches down and I feel the whoosh of the doors opening, I step out into the small foyer and press the upper right app button on my phone.

The Uber taxi service app.

13

Uber is a beautiful thing, especially for someone in my condition.

Granted, I doubt there are too many people with my condition, but that is beside the point. With a tap of an app, I can summon a taxi anywhere, at any time. Uber isn't a licensed taxi service. Instead, they employ drivers who use their own cars and GPS tracking. Via the app, it's billed directly to my credit card. Months ago, my brother had set me up with them, coaching me how to use the app and summon a ride. He also set up my user profile to mention that I'm disabled and have a service dog. I'm sure some drivers pass on me—drivers, apparently, can pick or decline services—while others might be sympathetic to my plight. Although what I deal with on a daily basis seems a bit more than a plight. Maybe a plight with a capital "P."

Anyway, ten minutes later, I feel Betsie react to someone coming up to me. I suspect it is the Uber driver and I wave, while also giving Betsie the command to heel. Betsie, as always, immediately obeys.

Have I mentioned that I love that dog?

Next, I feel a hesitant hand guide me forward and shortly inside the backseat of a smallish car. I'm not a smallish man, but I make do. Betsie hops over my lap and sits on the seat next to me. How she manages to miss my crotch is always a miracle.

When I'm fairly certain the driver is seated, I show him my notepad with the address already scribbled on it. Also included are my notes to please drop me off in front of the main entrance. He pats the back of my hand. He understands, and so, I sit back, and a moment later I feel the forward motion of the vehicle.

And we're off.

The drive shouldn't have taken more than fifteen minutes, and I don't think it does. Whether or not the driver drove in circles around the city block to jack the price up, I would never know, but I think I would have caught on, eventually.

Since my accident, I have to rely on others for help. I have to trust others implicitly. I have to believe there was good in people and that most have my best interests at heart.

This was hard for me to do at first. Almost impossible, in fact. I had seen the darker side of human nature. I watched how petty jealousy turned into violence. I watched how greed turned some men into animals. I watched it all, worked with it all, fought it all, chased it all, hunted it all. I arrested it and removed it from society. Day in, day out. For fourteen years. I looked killers in the eye. I questioned them, challenged them, hated them, pitied them. Sometimes, I was duped by them, too. Sometimes, I even believed their lies. All par for the course. Usually, I got my man or woman. Usually.

And now...

Well, now, I am expected to forget what I know is stalking the city streets on any given night...and to trust my fellow man. Now, I am supposed to let down my guard and just hope for the best. Now, I just sit here in the back seat and hope that my Uber driver is a good man. If not, then bad things are going to happen, and will probably happen to me. Of course, not if Betsie has any say in the matter. And she does. A big say. A big 'woof' maybe.

I have to believe that this man will take me where I'd hired him to. I have no way of knowing where I'm going, unless I had the route memorized, and I don't. I have to believe that he isn't going to, say, drive me to a back alley, where I could be robbed and shot and left for dead.

I have to believe this; I have little choice otherwise.

I enjoy the vibration of the car. I enjoy anything tactile, tangible, physical. I enjoy heat and cold, even extremes; indeed, I enjoy sweating and shivering equally. I enjoy, mostly, how such sensations take me out of my head and bring me back into my body. Now, I enjoy the vibration that seems to come from everywhere; up through the floorboards, up through the seat, the small flow of air from the air conditioner. I revel in it all and sit back in my seat and pat my dog and run my fingertips through her longish, soft fur.

I could, of course, rely completely on my brother, but that's not fair to him, or healthy for me. Not to mention, I sense we are reaching his breaking point, of what he's willing and able to do. I don't want to break my brother. I want only to spend time with him. I want only to be a brother to him. Not a project. Not a burden. Not a hassle.

I stay up on sports, because I know he loves his Dodgers and Lakers. Me, not so much. But I want to be able to discuss the latest trades, the latest standings, the latest news. Of course, my news via the braille newspaper is generally a week behind, but I make do.

It has been many years since I've driven to my ex-girlfriend's apartment. I don't have the route memorized, turn by turn, but I have a fair idea where we are, and when I feel the car come to a stop, the timing seems about right to me.

A moment later, the driver's door opens with a whoosh of warm air, followed by my own door a few seconds later. Now, a slightly more confident grip takes hold of me just inside my elbow. I am led outside, along with my dog. Once I am standing on the curb, I feel a pat on my back, and I nod and smile and hold out my hand. A dry but firm hand shakes it. I will never know my driver's name or his race or age or anything. I know only his heart. He is friendly and attentive and I like his hand. It is firm and confident and rough and friendly. I feel his heart in his hand and I wish I could see him...

Maybe I am happy I can't. I've never felt someone's heart in their hand before my injuries. Now, I see people in different ways, and sometimes, it's not so bad.

Before he leaves, he gently turns my shoulders and takes my wrist in his. He raises my hand and uses it to point in the direction of the building. I smile and nod and the next thing I know, he has wrapped his arms around me and pulls me into him and hugs me very tight. He releases me and holds me at arm's length and I can only wonder what he is thinking or saying, or what other people are thinking or saying.

When he leaves, I take in a lot of air through my tracheal tube, hold it, then start toward my ex-girlfriend's apartment.

14

ers is a secured apartment building.

One needs a key to get in, or one needs to be buzzed in. Now, as I stand before the glass doors—doors that I see again in my mind's eye—with the heat of the morning sun on my neck, my right hand firmly holds Betsie's harness, my left grips the walking stick, and I realize the foolishness of my decision.

After all, I have no way of buzzing her or contacting her or figuring out how to use the newfangled intercom system. And, since this is L.A., the apartment isn't manned by a doorman. Or even security.

I dated Gwen for two years. We loved each other, yes, but our connection was never so strong that we discussed a future together. Nor was it so tenuous that we broke it off. I think we were both waiting for a reason to either move forward together or break up. The explosion seemed to have made the decision for us.

But maybe she's reconsidered? Maybe she misses me, too? Maybe she doesn't know how to reach out to me?

Maybe, I think, as I scan the area in my mind's eye, trying hard to remember the details. There's a cement planter out front that doubles as a long bench. I'm sure of it.

The sun grows hotter on my neck. Now, I feel people from the sidewalk staring at me, probably wondering if they should help. I could let them help me. I could ask someone, via my notepad, to buzz Gwyneth Morgan for me. But so far, no one's approached me, nor do I seek anyone out. Yet.

So, I turn and, using my walking stick, feel my way over to the planter and have a seat but the cement is hot and I worry about my dog's paws. Would they blister in the sun? Probably, but I don't recall much in the way of shade around here.

I do the next best thing. I use myself as shade and position Betsie in front of me, hoping that much of my shadow falls over her. She won't complain either way. She will sit there and pant and wait until the cows came home, through burning paws and thirst and heat, until I get up and leave.

Herbal, pungent and flowery plants surround me, all mixing into what I imagine is a heady concoction. For me, the scents barely make it through my damaged olfactory. Still, I can detect them occasionally. And *occasionally* is good enough.

Beggars can't be choosers.

Yes, my sense of smell comes and goes, triggered by God knows what. But I'm always appreciative when it hits me, and it hits me now, and I revel in what I am sure is pungent acacia and sweeter deer grass. Years ago, I took an environmental biology class and learned the names of most drought-resistant plants in California. By proxy, I got to know their scents, too.

I revel in them now. Sharp at times. Flowery at others. All permeated with the earthy, mushroomy smell of moist soil. This is Beverly Hills, after all. To hell with the drought in California. The street plants need to be watered. Either way, I love it all, revel in it all. Crave it all. Hunger for it all. I wish more scents would hit me. I wish I could smell the exhaust from nearby Doheny Street. I really did. No matter how foul or offensive. I wish I could smell the cigar of a man smoking nearby. I wish I could smell sweat and perfume and cologne and gasoline and oil and halitosis. I wish it would all come to me often, in wave after sweet wave. Or pungent wave. Or foul-smelling wave. Hell, I'm not picky.

I do not check my time. I don't need to. There's no reason to. I know it's midday, and I have nowhere else to go. I am where I need to be. In front of my ex-girlfriend's apartment…waiting.

For what, exactly, I don't know. For her to recognize me, perhaps. For her to invite me in. For her to tell me that she has missed me this whole time and has wondered about me but wasn't sure if seeing me was a good idea. That she wants to know all about me and my life. I could, of course, fill her in easy enough. The last five years have passed without much incident, unless you counted the many times I'd fallen, or gotten lost, or learned a new way to communicate, or received a false hope that doctors might be able to help me speak again.

And she would hold my hand and show me that she had mastered sign language in the time we've been apart, with the small hope that she might see me again, and now, here I am and all is right in the world.

I am saddened by how unlikely these scenarios seem, even in my own fantasy.

It has been four years and six months since we last dated. And just over four years when I last heard from her, back when she had told me she was now dating an attorney. She told me this, of course, through the use of the plastic letters on my kitchen table, back when she had been returning some of my stuff. She had never bothered to learn sign language.

I let that thought go and lift my face to the sun, feel the wind in my hair, catch the faint smells, feel the heat of the cement planter. Sometimes, when I'm indoors, I feel…nonexistent. So much so, that I will sometimes snap my fingers and wave Betsie over just to feel her hot breath and wet tongue on my skin. Just to reinforce that, yes, I am alive. I am not dead, not a ghost, not a memory, not a stray thought.

Outdoors is different. Outdoors, I can feel the wind and the sun, the cold and sometimes, even the rain. Outdoors, I can pick up stray scents and sometimes even get jostled by a pedestrian, or someone trying to squeeze into the table behind me at Chango. Outdoors, I feel part of humanity, connected to this earth.

Now, as I sit here in the sun, I almost forget why I am there. Indeed, I am reveling in the heat and the scents and the wind and the weight of my dog pressed against my calf when I notice something else. Betsie's tail is wagging, slapping against my shoe. The wagging is followed by another sensation. The smallest, smallest touch on my left forearm. Someone is here.

Betsie's tail continues to swish over my shoes. She's panting now. Excited, relaxed, playful. Whoever's next to me has her attention. My guess, it's a woman. Betsie always seems to prefer women. Maybe she gets that from her dad.

The small touch on my forearm comes again. Very small, very light, the fingertip slightly cold, despite the warm day. It hits me. A child. A girl, probably. Maybe even a little girl.

I am instantly alert. Why is a girl approaching me on street? Is she alone? Where's her mother? The touch comes again, followed by more tail wagging from Betsie. If I have to guess, and I kind of have to these days, I would say Betsie is getting some serious scratches behind her ears.

After waiting for the touch of a mother or father or even a nanny—this is Beverly Hills, after all—I realize it's just me and the girl. I reach into my shirt pocket—all my shirts have pockets—and take out the small notepad with the attached pen. On the cover of the notepad, I've written the words: "I'm sorry, but I'm blind, deaf and mute."

I always wonder if my handwriting is holding up these days, although I haven't had any complaints yet. Then again, there might be a special place in hell for whoever criticizes a blind man's handwriting. "Mute" isn't the most acceptable term, but it gets my point across nicely.

I have no idea how old the little girl is, or if it is even a little girl. Betsie's reaction has a lot to do with it. She doesn't react this way to just anyone. A man would have had her on guard and pressing against me. Either a little boy or girl, but I'm leaning toward girl, mostly based on the tiny and cold fingertip. And Betsie's wagging tail.

I also don't know if the little girl can read, but I take my chances. I hold up the cover of the notebook for her to see and point to it, and then give her the thumbs-up sign. Then I flip through the notepad, searching for the dog-eared page that would indicate my next blank page— after all, writing on already used-up page wouldn't do at all. When I find the blank page, I flip the notebook open and write:

"Where's your mommy? And remember, I can't hear you."

I hold up the page and wait a heartbeat or two, then feel gentle hands tug on my pen and notepad. Whoever's there wants to write me a message in return. I smile and shake my head and write:

"I can't see your writing either."

That should be enough for the curious little girl to get going. But she's playing with Betsie, because I can feel Betsie just itching to jump. Except Betsie never jumps. Never does anything she's not supposed to do, which makes me sad sometimes. Dogs and little girls should play together. Betsie knows she's a working dog, and takes her job very seriously.

Betsie is still reacting positively to whoever is there, panting against my inner leg. The girl hasn't left, and a moment later, a small hand picks up my left hand. She opens my hand, and to my surprise, I feel the smallest fingernail—a ragged fingernail that has been chewed and not clipped—write into my palm one big letter at a time, slowly.

"H-I."

I nod and smile and mouth the word "Hi." I then flip back to the page where I had written: "Where's your mother?" And hold it up to her to read.

She takes my hand again, a little bolder this time. "She is fighting with Tom. He's her boyfriend."

"Fighting where?" I write on my pad.

"In the kitchen." Except she doesn't spell kitchen right. *Kittchin*.

I write: "You shouldn't be out here alone."

She writes the next words slowly, and I can imagine her little tongue sticking out as she focuses on each and every letter in my palm. "Yes, Mommy will be mad." Mad is spelled *madd*.

I keep all my old notebooks in a big dresser drawer in my bedroom. Not the drawer with the gun next to my bed. No, the drawer beneath my socks, socks that are all white and the same size. Makes my life easier. Anyway, the drawer with my notebooks is about half full. Notebook after notebook of my scribbled conversations to strangers. My one-sided conversations. I do not know why I hold on to them. No, that's not true. I think a part of me wants to leave behind a legacy of who I am and what has happened to me and who I met along the way. To whom I would leave this legacy, I don't know.

I wonder if Gwen is still single. I wonder if she still lives here. God, I hope she still lives here. There is something about being here that felt right. I was excited, nervous, hopeful. It was midday. Gwen worked from home, where she ran a small interior design business. Mostly, she popped over to residences and charged a consulting fee. Sometimes, she got bigger jobs, too. Mostly not. Which was why she lived in a smallish apartment in Beverly Hills, rather than a biggish apartment, or even a home. She had been content to take the small jobs. I always suspected she didn't like to work very much, even though she ran her own business.

I shouldn't be here, I know. My confidence is shaky at best. I want to get up and head home. But I power through my insecurities. It had cost me good money to be delivered here, and I was going to see it through, as best as I could. Besides, wasn't there a little girl even now petting Betsie, a little girl who might have even wandered off?

I flip to a clean page, and write:

"You need to go inside now. You should not be out here alone."

I hold it out to her to read. The light tickles on my forearm are from her as she leans forward and reads my writing. Writing that I hope is intelligible.

So insecure, I think.

Now, she takes my hand again, and a single, small finger spells out big letters in my palm. "Not alone. I am with your doggie."

"How old are you?" I write, balancing the notepad on my knee this time.

A single, looping number drawn on my palm. She is eight. But she isn't done writing. The words continue to form. Sometimes she stops them and literally makes an erasing motion on my palm. A lot of cuteness. So much so, that I am aware all over again that I want kids of my own. I would sigh, if I could.

She finally spells out: "You had an accident?"

I nod, and mouth the word, "Yes."

"I am sorry," she writes.

"I am, too," I write on my notepad.

More writing in my palm, more erasing, and finally, she forms the sentence: "Do you pray for God to help you?"

I turn my face to her, and briefly wonder what she would think if she saw my empty eye sockets. I would scare her and give her nightmares, no doubt. Finally, I shake my head no.

Her writing is bolder now. "You should pray. God will help you."

I give her a half-smile, and think about what I want to say, and finally write: "Maybe I will."

I sit motionless, while she continues holding my hand. After a minute or two, she opens my hand and spells out: "I will pray with you."

I am about to shake my head, when she reaches forward and shushes my silent lips with her little finger. I smile and would have laughed if I could have. Hard to laugh through a tracheal tube. Poor excuse, I know. I could make the motion of laughter, and sometimes, I have. But no real sound comes out of me, from what I'm told.

"Please." She writes in my hand.

I nod. Okay.

She squeezes my hand, excited. Then spells: "Repeat after me, okay?"

I smile and nod again. There won't be much repeating on my end, but I can always mouth the words.

"Dear God," she begins, spelling slowly into my palm.

"Dear God," I mouth.

"Please help this man see again."

I begin to mouth the words, when I feel the tears come to me. I fight them back a little and repeat her words, mouthing them. "Please help me see again."

Now, she holds my hand, squeezes it, pets my dog, and then, the little girl is gone, running off, I hope, back to her apartment. Maybe her mother has stopped arguing with her boyfriend.

I stay put, wondering how long I will need to wait. I can't give up.

Two hours later, Betsie stands, turns and growls low and deep. I can feel her growl vibrate through my shoes, which she's presently standing on. I reach out and pat her head. But not so much that I discourage her from doing her job. I need her to growl for me. I need her to warn me—to protect me—from whoever and whatever is coming. Then again, we are in Beverly Hills, so maybe it's a wild Kardashian trailed by paparazzi.

And so, I continue to pat Betsie's neck, gauging the severity of the situation. Someone is approaching us, that much I know. Betsie is reacting to each step. But she is not lunging and not barking, just growling low in her throat, I think. Whoever is coming toward me is a man.

Or...

Is it possible?

Betsie never did like Gwen. And the feeling was mutual. I remember my brother, at the time, saying to me through sign language into my palm, that it took a special kind of bitch to not get along with a seeing eye dog.

Betsie does eventually calm, although I can feel her chest vibrating ever-so-slightly. A low, subsonic growl, perhaps. Whoever is approaching is not a threat—Betsie would have gone ape-shit. No, Betsie simply doesn't like whoever's approaching.

I take a chance, flip to a clean page, and write "Gwen?" nice and big. I hold up the page to whoever's approaching.

Back in the day—during those six months Gwen and I had been together after my accident—she hadn't bothered to learn much sign language, if any. Instead, we developed our own language. For instance, she would often tap on my shoulder twice for yes and squeeze it for no.

As I sit there, and as the growls in Betsie's chest cavity deepen, someone taps my shoulder twice.

It's Gwen.

15

Her apartment is so familiar.

I am sitting in the living room. I turn my head, getting my bearings. The kitchen is there, in front of me. The bedrooms to my right, down the hallway. The balcony in front of me, through the living room, where we had sipped many glasses of wine together, watching the glittering city far below.

Once, while drinking with Gwen before the accident, or, B.A., as I think of it now, I remembered listening to the woman next door on the phone. From what I gathered, she worked for a psychic hotline. I remembered the details the woman gave over the phone, and I often wondered how accurate she was...and if I should ever schedule an appointment with her. Then again, that was five years ago. What were the chances she was still around too?

I decide to lead off with that question, and open to a fresh page in my notebook. While I do so, I feel the cool air from the AC unit on my forehead. It feels good. I had burned while I waited outside. Sometimes, I like the feeling of being burned. Not a serious burn. Something minor, enough to get my attention, and to keep my focus on something other than, say, the tracheal tube. Or the ringing in my ears.

A cool glass of water gets pressed into my hand and I nod my thanks. I note there's no ice. Ice would have been nice. Before I drink, I reach into the backpack that's sitting at my feet and remove a small plastic bowl—an old Reddi Wip container—and fill it with a few fingers of water from the glass. When I feel Betsie lapping away, I drink from my own glass.

I can almost feel Gwen's disapproval. Probably water splashes out into her carpet. I next remove my packet of plastic letters and set them on the coffee table in front of me. I remove them carefully, so that they don't clatter across her table. For some reason, I am feeling tight and nervous. Gwen always has that effect on me.

I ask myself again why I am here and don't have a ready answer but push forward anyway. Gwen, I know, is my best chance—perhaps my only chance—at finding love. Sad as that might seem.

"Hi," I mouth to her, feeling myself flush slightly, although that could just be the sunburn setting in.

Whether or not she says hi in return, I'll never know. A small touch on the back of my hand. Gwen's indication of hi. Betsie doesn't like Gwen touching the back of my hand and growls low and deep. I can feel the thrums of the growl as Betsie presses against me. I pat my dog with one hand and rest the fingertips of the other on the glass coffee table. Now, I can feel micro-vibrations rise up through it; Gwen is arranging the plastic letters.

When finished, she taps the table; I reach out and she guides me, somewhat roughly, to the first plastic letter of the first word. I feel each in turn, rapidly, piecing together the sentence in my mind, one letter at a time:

"Forgot all sign language, sorry. What are you doing here?"

Yes, my plastic letters even come with plastic question marks and exclamation points. So far, I don't think anyone's ever used the exclamation points.

I consider what to write, and finally decide on:

"I've missed you."

I don't sense any movement on her part. No gentle pat on my shoulder. No loving hug. No peck on the cheek. No reaction at all. She's not spelling out how much she's missed me, too, or how much she regrets ending things the way she had—via a text my brother had to read for me nearly a week later.

And so, after a few seconds of uncomfortable silence—and for me, that's saying something—I quickly scribble on my notepad: "And I just wanted to see how you are doing."

Now, she's spelling out words again. I sense the glass table shuddering more than before. I imagine her spelling the words emphatically. Betsie is on high alert. Sitting straight. Ears erect. Muscles tense. I do my best to calm her down, patting her and holding her with my left hand. Her harness is looped over my left wrist.

A sharp tap on my shoulder. She is done spelling. This time, she doesn't guide my hand to the first letter. Instead, I go to the same general place on the table where she'd begun the last dialogue. "I am fine. How are you?"

And that's it. No playful banter. Nothing inviting, encouraging or sweet. Then again, maybe I was reading too much into plastic letters. At least, she asked how I was doing.

A part of me knows this is a bad idea. But I deny that part of me. Dammit, I'm in Gwen's apartment, a place I hadn't stepped foot in since, well, since before my accident. I'm here now. And, good or bad, I am going to see it through.

I balance my notepad on my knee and write:

"Still waiting on my driver's license."

An old joke between us. At least, that's what I tell myself. Truth is, Gwen never laughed very much at my jokes, even when I was trying to make the best of a bad situation.

Anyway, I get no response at this attempt either. No pat on the back. No gentle hug. I wonder if the pen has gone dry, although I don't think it has. It had flowed smoothly enough over the page. With that said, I can feel palpable tension in the air. Betsie feels it, too. I've never seen my dog react this way, not for such a prolonged period. That is, not since the last time she was around Gwen.

"Remember our old joke?" I write on the pad.

No response. I assume she nods. Or maybe she's just staring blankly at the freak show seated in her living room, breathing through a tube in his mouth, his plastic letters spilled across her nice coffee table, his dog growling at her, his face flushed and slightly burned, his need for acceptance and love so overwhelming that he endures this embarrassment.

I write: "We've had some good times. I miss that. I miss you." I hesitate before I write the next sentence, then shrug, and dash off the next line: "You still dating the attorney?"

But I don't show her the page. Not yet.

Instead, I almost close the notebook and shove it back in my shirt pocket. I ask myself again why I'm here, and suddenly, I don't have a clear reason. To reconnect with the last woman I had loved. The last woman who had loved me. The only woman, I think, who could possibly love me now.

Finally, I nod and hold the page up for her to read.

There is a short hesitation, and then I can feel her manipulating the plastic letters on the table. A moment later, a slightly smaller, less aggressive tap on my forearm. I pick the first letter up, then the next, my thumb pads and finger pads stroking each rounded or angular edge carefully, forming the words in my mind as I do so. When I get to the last letter, I nod and do my best to smile.

Her words are to the point. Everyone I communicate with these days gets straight to the point. There's little banter anymore. Another thing taken from me. I sigh at that. Apparently, spelling out a flippant, cute, offhand comment was taboo when dealing with the blind, deaf and silent.

"The attorney is gone but I am engaged to someone else."

I'm still nodding as she reaches over and spells something else out. She guides my hand to the first letter.

"I am sorry."

I nod some more and smile and feel more sad than I should. I should have known she would have moved on. I should have known she would want nothing to do with me. I should have known there wasn't a chance in hell that she would still be interested, or missing me, or even caring whether I was alive or dead, since I hadn't heard from her in four-and-a-half years.

I think she senses my pain and confusion and self-hate, and I am a little surprised when I feel her hand on my forearm. It's warm and gentle, and then, she pats me. And then, I feel her lean forward on the couch and feel the coffee table shift slightly with her efforts of spelling more words.

Whatever she is spelling takes some time, and while I wait, I pat Betsie's head lightly. Gwen's apartment is cool. The couch feels new. There is a slight scent of...there it is…a man's deodorant. I am sure of it. No doubt wafting down the hallway. But I could be wrong. I am surprised I can smell it, but today is a good day for my olfactory. Anyway, she is not lying. There is a man in her life. Maybe smelling the deodorant is a gift to me, helping me understand that she really has moved on.

She touches my hand again, and guides my fingers to the first letter. The sadness is still in me. Not shock, just deep sadness. But her kindness is helping me some. I pick up each letter slowly. My concentration is all over the map. Mostly, I hate myself for coming here and subjecting myself to more pain. Of course, she has moved on. Of course, she has gone through a few men, too.

I absorbed each new letter, dropping them into place in my thoughts. Each new letter forms words, and the words begin taking on meaning and depth and profundity, and, as they do, my groping fingers move slower and slower. It takes a while to feel my way through these longer sentences. Finally, I pick up the last letter and sat there motionless, holding it.

"I was not strong enough for you, Lee. I know this is hard for you to read. I see you are hurt. And I see you still have feelings for me. I miss you, too. And I often wonder how you are doing, but I am afraid to ask. It was a shitty way to break up with you. I am sorry. More sorry than you can ever know."

I set the last letter down and take out my notebook—which I always, automatically, return to the pocket at my chest, and flip to a new page:

"A lot of plastic letters. I have a hand cramp now."

Now, I do feel her laughing, the couch cushions bobbing up and down a bit.

She leans forward again, spelling out something new, then guides my hand to the first plastic letter. Her fingers, I note, are shaking a little…and feel ice cold. Her single sentence says, "Maybe we can be friends?"

I turn the final letter over in my hand—the question mark—and set it down. I pull out my notepad, then write:

"I'd like that but…"

I pause and hold up the notepad so that she can read what I wrote, then point to Betsie who's leaning against my legs and who hasn't, I am certain, taken her eyes off Gwen. I think about how she broke up with me. I think about how she has never bothered to follow up with me, inquire about me, help me, or care about me. And so, with a heavy heart but also a small smile that may or may not have found my lips, I resume writing. And hold up the pad again:

"I don't think Betsie likes you."

16

I don't usually drink, but tonight, I make an exception. I also almost never get drunk, but tonight...well, we'll see.

It is late evening and I'm sitting on my balcony with my legs up on a plastic footrest and Betsie lying somewhere beneath my outstretched legs. I'd had a heckuva productive day. I'd taken a ride to Beverly Hills and effectively put an end to any crazy notion that Gwen and I would ever be together again. Maybe I should have been relieved. She had been a handful back when we were dating. The more I think back on our time together, the more stressed I remembered feeling. Stress I didn't need. My job was stressful enough.

I drink from a highball glass, filled with Jameson, neat. I sip slowly, carefully, enjoying the warmth of it down my damaged throat. I can almost follow its heated path through my organs, along my bloodstream. I am quickly becoming buzzed.

My last one, I think. *Maybe.*

The buzz is a welcome relief. I am enjoying letting my mind go a little. Enjoying the freedom, the expansion, the release from my broken body.

I imagine my thoughts spreading out a little further, filling the entire balcony, from corner to corner... and leaking out over the ledge and spilling down to my neighbor below. The feeling is...liberating, and

I go with it for a few minutes. I imagine, briefly, that I am the building itself, that my mind fills the apartment building and rooms and hallways and stairwells and elevators. I imagine what it would feel like to have people move through me, flick on my light switches, slam my doors.

Weird, I know...but I go with it.

My mind reaches out further, out beyond the apartment, beyond the parking lot and out over the trees. I feel myself seeing everything, smelling everything, alive and everywhere and free.

Free from my broken body.

And soon I sleep.

———

A buzzing in my pocket.

I awaken colder than I had been in a long time. I reach for my cell phone and turn off the alarm, something I do every morning at this time. Usually, though, I wake up in bed.

Shivering and wondering if I have gotten myself sick, I push out of the plastic deck chair and somehow, simultaneously, scratch Betsie between her ears. I can feel her panting. It's always a good morning for Betsie.

I did not get drunk last night. Three shots max, enough to get me buzzed and spend the night out on the balcony. Then again, this is Southern California. Fall nights are not very different than summer nights. And, hell, even some winter nights.

Now, I'm in the kitchen making coffee with the Keurig, since last night was spent drinking—and not remembering to prepare my coffee maker. My brother had shown me in detail how to work the Keurig, guiding my hands over the various buttons and lids and features. I thought I was getting the hang of it quickly enough; that is, until my brother walked out in frustration to control himself, only to return and guide me, somewhat roughly, through the final stages of coffee making.

Now, I hold the coffee mug's handle while the coffee dribbles in. I can feel the heat rising from the mug, over my knuckles, up to my face. When finished dribbling, I mix in the vanilla coffee creamer. Before I sit with my coffee, I reach into a Tupperware container on the kitchen counter and toss a chicken treat to the only girl in my life who matters, to the girl I know is waiting patiently at my feet. I suspect Betsie snatches the treat out of the air. One bite, maybe two max, and I suspect the treat is already long gone.

I move over to the small bar table by the door, the table littered with plastic letters. I push some aside and set the coffee mug down. I reach down to scratch Betsie's long flank, and feel her tense. She snaps her head around. She barks once, I'm certain, judging by the bolt of energy that surges through her. As she barks, I feel my phone vibrate at my hip. Someone has pressed my doorbell, which is synced with my phone. Another fancy gadget my brother had gotten for me.

Where would I be without him? I don't want to know. I also don't want to think about it.

I do my usual joke of pretending to look at the peephole. Then I open the door, holding Betsie's harness tightly. She might be perfectly trained, yes, but she's still a dog protecting her master. I like that about her.

As always when guests come unexpectedly, there is a moment or two of awkwardness, perhaps awkward silence, although I'll never know for sure. I help the situation by smiling encouragingly and holding out my hand.

I wonder who will take it.

17

Almost immediately, a soft, small hand takes my own, and I know by the touch, the pressure of the fingertips, the way the thumb moves over the back of my thumb, who it is.

Slender fingers form words quickly in my palm. "Guess who?"

I smile and nod and move away from the door. I feel her step past me, and then feel another person step past me too, a person whose pat is firm and rough and manly. I can smell the faintest of whiff of aftershave or men's deodorant. Either way, I know it's Detective Hammer.

In the relative safety of my apartment, I don't need Betsie's services and I always imagine she acts more like a normal dog in here than out there, where she is a working dog. Even now, I imagine her tail is wagging as she gives Hammer and Rachel a good sniff or lick or shoulder bump. Or, if they're lucky, she's even stuck her nose in their crotches. Either way, I imagine her tongue hanging out, maybe even spilling a drop or two of drool, and, of course, looking cute as hell. All in my imagination, of course. I have never seen my dog...and never will, and that's a damn shame.

Once we are inside, I ask if they would like some coffee. Via Rachel's fast and expert signing, the response comes back yes, but that she will make it for us. I insist on making it and she lets me, which I am grateful for. The Keurig is fast and soon I am signing if they want milk and sugar or some of my vanilla creamer. Both want the creamer, and I take it from the fridge and let them add their own, which they do. We are all in my little kitchen, which, for some reason, doesn't feel crowded but cozy. A cool blast of air suggests that Rachel has put the creamer away, and now, she is touching my elbow, subtly directing me to follow them and sit with them, which I do, through the kitchen and living room and over to my couch.

Rachel eases down next to me and I catch a faint hint of perfume and shampoo and coffee and vanilla and dog breath. I think the five greatest scents ever. My sense of smell is working overtime these past few days. I couldn't be happier. Well, maybe I could. Just a little.

I note that our knees and thighs touch and that sends a thrill through me that all but obliterates any lingering sadness from the day before. I remind myself that Rachel is just about as likely to fall for me as Gwen had been. Still, I like touching her leg. I feel my heartbeat picking up a little. Yes, a roller-coaster of emotions for me. I'd gone months—years—of giving little thought to women. And now, I'm swinging wildly from one day to the next. I'm not sure how I feel about that. And then Rachel shifts a little next to me, sliding her thigh along mine, and a new thrill rushes through me all over again.

Actually, I think, *I feel pretty darn good about it.*

After pleasantries are signed, Detective Hammer gets to the point, which I suspect he had probably wanted to do from the moment he first stepped inside my apartment.

Soon, Rachel is relaying his message into my palm: "A body has been found."

I sign back to her, which she relays to the detective. "One of the missing?"

Soon, we are in the flow again, each message only taking seconds, rather than minutes to relay.

"Yes. He was found floating in Long Beach Harbor, tangled in some lines."

"Cause of death?"

"Single shot just behind the ear."

"Execution style," I sign. "Suspects?"

"None yet."

"Who found him?"

"Yacht owner."

"When did he first go missing?" I ask.

"He was one of the originals. Maybe a year ago."

"How was he I.D.'d?"

"Dental records. He was in rough shape, had been floating for a few days. Crabs and other nasties had at him."

I make a face for Rachel's benefit. Truth is, I have seen such floaters before. Many of them. The horrors of my job still had little effect on me. Back in the day, I could look at the most disturbing crime scenes, the most mutilated of corpses and not get a reaction, even as my partners would turn away, or turn green...or get sick altogether. As for Rachel, I don't know her story, and I hope she is okay relaying these messages, graphic as they are.

As if reading my mind, she squeezes my hand a little and signs just for my benefit. "I'm okay."

I nod. Hammer has resumed talking. Although he is sitting across from me, I can feel Rachel nodding along while he speaks. She stops nodding and now signs into my palm.

"He disappeared a year ago. Like I said, one of the first to go missing. In fact, he's officially the third to go missing. No one heard a peep from him. He leaves behind a wife, a kid, a decent job at Boeing in Long Beach."

"Near where he was found floating?" I ask through Rachel.

"Right," comes the response a few seconds later. "Nothing from this guy in a year...and then he shows up out of the blue, floating in the harbor, shot behind the ear. But there's more."

I nod and wait, keenly aware of Rachel's hand lingering in my own. But I'm not thinking too much about her hand. No, my mind is racing, putting together the pieces of the puzzle. Like old times. Detective work is problem-solving...and often problem-solving is working backward. In our case, we work backward, starting with the crime. And with my job—or my old job—the crime always involves a corpse.

Finally, I sign, using both hands: "What's the victim's name?"

"Jesse DeFranco."

"Any chance Jesse is *un*connected from your case?"

"Anything is possible. You know that, Lee. Except Jesse's case reads like all the others. Except, of course, he's the first to show up dead."

"Perhaps the first of many."

"Jesus, I do not want to think about that, Lee. It's bad enough that they are missing. Worse, if they start showing up dead, too. And a year later, to boot."

"Did you just say 'to boot'?" I sign to Rachel, who translates for me.

"I did," comes Hammer's response. "And don't fuck with me, Lee."

After a moment, I sign: "Why a year later, you think?"

"My guess, he attempted to disappear. And didn't do a very good job of it."

"Or had second thoughts," I interject.

"So, he comes back a year later, maybe thinking everything's okay, or to let his family know he's okay."

"And someone pops him," I sign when Rachel is done relaying Hammer's scenario.

"But who?" asks Hammer. "And why?"

"Maybe whoever helped him disappear."

We are silent. At least, I think we're silent. Finally, after maybe a half minute or so, I feel Rachel nodding, encouraging Hammer. Soon, she is signing into my open hand, pressing her small fingers into mine and, well, sending shiver after shiver through me.

"Can we agree that the missing eleven people had help?"

I nod. "Agreed."

"No skimming cash out of their bank account. No removing themselves from social media. No awkward final conversations with friends and family. They're just..." Rachel pauses slightly, then adds, "gone."

"Did any of them have any reason to be gone? Any gang relations? Any pending IRS tax fraud investigations? Any domestic violence?"

"Typical problems. Nothing too outrageous. One guy, Danny something or other, owed money to a bookie. Another guy was facing jail time. Many were in debt, but typical stuff."

"What's typical for one person might be unbearable for another," I sign.

"Enough for them to want to disappear?"

"Maybe," I sign. "Let's talk about this last disappearance, James Kirkpatrick."

"Fire away."

"Where did he live?"

"House on Vermont in Los Feliz."

"The very first victim lived in Los Feliz," I add.

"Right. One of the few links we have."

I nod. "We have evidence, via apartment surveillance footage, of two victims turning north."

"Initially turning north," counters Hammer, via Rachel's impulses in my hand. "What if they turned down another street?"

"Maybe," I sign. "But Los Feliz is north."

"But so is Alaska. What's your point?"

"What's north of Los Feliz?"

"Nice homes, hills, Griffith Park."

I nod, thinking. "I would suggest searching surveillance footage up and down Los Feliz. Lots of apartments there. Lots of footage."

"Because Los Feliz Boulevard is north of him?"

"Right."

"And for some reason, all vics are gravitating north, into the hills of Griffith Park?"

"Maybe they're zombies," I sign. "But humor me."

"Fine. Anything else?"

"Yes," I sign, thinking. "See if the park has security footage, too."

"Will do."

I nod and sign privately to Rachel: "Would you mind hanging back for a few minutes?"

She pats my hand, yes.

Detective Hammer stands and drops a heavy hand to my shoulder and squeezes. I sense that he wants to give me a hug, but doesn't. His loss. Since losing many of my physical senses, I've become a helluva hugger.

Rachel sees him to the door. I'm damn good at tracking footstep vibrations within my own apartment. I also sense a slight decompression of air around me as the front door opens and closes. More vibrations up through the floor, more footsteps, and now a small hand on my shoulder, a hand that slides down and slips into my own hand, before signing:

"Would you like some wine?"

"I don't have any," I sign back.

I sense her laughter. "Luckily, I just happened to bring some."

18

I sit and wait.

Rachel is in the kitchen, working. I know this because Betsie is watching her every movement, should a scrap of food accidentally fall. Betsie's head moves a little more and I feel the floorboards shift. Betsie's tail thumps once, twice, over my loafers, and I hold out my hand. And just like that, the cool stem of a wine glass appears. Magic.

Rachel sits next to me. I catch more of her perfume and ask myself if this is really happening.

It is, I think. *At least, I think it is.*

If I'm dreaming, I don't want to awaken. Intimate or not, friend or not, I can't remember the last time I'd been alone with a woman in my apartment. Actually, I do remember. It had been Gwen. Yes, definitely. It had been the day before she sent my brother a text message—my brother who had been my cell phone liaison for me. A text message letting him know that she was sorry, that she just couldn't do this anymore.

Now, I find myself drinking wine with a woman I have never seen and will never see, whose voice I would never hear, whose ears would never hear mine. A woman I knew only by touch. A woman whose touch I was already beginning to love.

I next feel something clink against my own glass, and I smile, raise my own glass, and sip from it. Champagne and orange juice. As I swallow, I feel almost human. I feel almost loveable. I feel almost worthy. Amazingly, I also feel flirty.

I set the glass down on the coffee table before us. I slide my right ring finger over my left knuckle and make a drinking motion: "Early for drinking?"

She takes my hand in hers. And presses her fingers in mine: "They're mimosas. They're permitted."

I grin, release her hand and sign: "The alcoholic's answer to drinking in the morning?" I open my hand on my lap for her reply.

"Exactly."

It's a choreographed dance we do. I release her hand so that I can use mine to sign, then she takes my one hand and signs into my palm. We exchange information like this quickly, now almost effortlessly. It is already second nature to me…and yet…

And yet each time she takes my hand, a thrill courses me. *Uh oh.*

I am not sure what to ask now, although a million questions race through my mind. Not counting my failed attempt to talk to Gwen yesterday, I am long out of practice of flirting and making small talk.

"Are you trying to get me drunk?"

"And take advantage of you?" she asks, pressing her small fingers into my palm.

Now, when I go to release her hand, her fingers hold mine a little longer. Finally, she does release them, and I sign, "Something like that."

My heart is thumping—somewhere up against my artificial tracheal tube. I'm finding breathing difficult, but not in an alarming way.

Calm down, cowboy.

I reach for where I'd left my glass, find it smoothly enough, and take a long pull on it.

This isn't happening.

But this *is* happening. I feel her repositioning herself on the couch. I think she is now sitting cross-legged, facing me. She takes my free hand and wants me to sit the same way. I nod and do so, and fold my long legs under me and face her. To be safe, I reach over and set my mimosa down.

Once done, I sign the only thing I can think of:

"What do you look like?" Immediately, I feel my face burn hot, and I hurriedly sign: "Not that it matters or anything. I mean, I'm just curious. Never mind. Forget I asked!"

I can feel the couch bounce a little with her giggles, and I imagine she's holding her hands over her mouth and looking at me in such a way as to suggest that I'm either adorable or she is regretting staying behind.

When the couch is done bouncing with what I hope is adoring laughter, there is a short period of…nothing. And now I am certain she is regretting being here and she is going to tell me that she has somewhere better to be.

I breathe in deeply, the air rattling in the tracheal tube. A tube that needs to be cleaned soon. My life. Whether she leaves or not, the short time I've spent with her has already lifted my spirits—especially after yesterday—and I'm about to thank her for her help, when she takes my hands in hers. Both hands. This is new. Generally, she signs into my right or left hand, whichever is closest to her.

Now, both hands move over my own so slowly that I nearly whimper at her warmth, her caring, her sensuality—all of which, I know, might just be in my head. None of which might be actually happening. For all I know, she is trying to keep me from tipping sideways. I suspect all the hair on my body is standing on end, and, yeah, I'm definitely having a hard time breathing.

Breathe, I tell myself. *Relax. Clean it later.*

Her touch calms me, excites me, liberates me. And now, she is guiding my hands toward her, up toward her face, and I feel myself shaking and wanting to laugh and not knowing what to do with myself, exactly.

Too much, I think. *Too much excitement for one day.*

The prospect of touching Rachel now is so overwhelming that I pull my hands back and find myself rocking on the couch. I turn away and do my best to wipe the tears that come from empty eye sockets, careful to not push away the sunglasses too far, careful not to reveal the monster beneath.

Once again, she seems to read my mind—or understand my fears and deeper issues—and I next feel something I hadn't felt since my accident: someone touching my face, which she does now, slowly, tentatively, carefully, even while I try to turn away from her. Her fingertips move over my cheeks, over my cheekbones, and slip under my sunglasses. I turn away a little when they do, terrified by what she will find. She pauses, still holding my face, and I realize she's not going anywhere. Not yet, at least.

I relax a little and breathe and now she cups the left side of my face—the most damaged side of my face, with her palm. I feel her thumb brush away what I know is an errant tear. I try to sign, but she shushes me by holding my hands down. I don't need to explain myself, her gesture suggests. She understands. I nod once and crack a half-smile and I wonder if she is smiling back.

She next takes hold of my hands in both of hers and I wonder all over again what is happening. Whatever it is, I am eternally grateful to the woman in front of me. Just these few minutes of physical contact will last a lifetime, something I will treasure forever.

But she is not done with me. No, not by a long shot.

She guides my hand up to her face...

19

Her skin is so soft.

So soft and delicate and perfect and fragile and strong and smooth. I feel that I am touching the face of an angel. Of something brought down from heaven, just for me to experience in these few short moments.

I am unsure of how much to touch—that I have violated her face too much, too long—when I feel something so heartbreakingly beautiful that I nearly lose it right there. I feel her smile. I feel her cheeks rise and the corners of her eyes crinkle.

It is the first smile I have felt in years. No, that's not right. It is the first smile that I have felt *ever*.

And as I hold her left cheek in my hand, I feel the warm drops. They work their way down over my thumb and onto my wrist, down my arm, down, down. Wetness, warmth, tear drops. Lubricating my skin against hers. I do not think it's my place to brush them away, and so I let her tears flow, and I give her a small smile, and I know my hand is shaking. I do not know why it is shaking. Perhaps the effort of holding her carefully. I imagine her face as a fragile flower, afraid of damaging it in my big clumsy hand. Except I know that is not true. My hands, if anything, have become less clumsy. They are my feelers. My antenna, my connection to this world. I see with them, laugh with them, explore with them, and

I explore her face now, even as her warm tears continue to flow.

My fingertips move through her hair—gossamer, silky, ethereal—so soft as to almost not be there. I am again reminded of an angel. I move my hand over her ear, covering it completely, cupping it, lightly stroking it with thumb and forefinger, committing it to memory. She's not wearing earrings, although I can feel the tiny holes in her lobes. Two holes, in fact. Rebel. I am fascinated by these tiny holes and explore them longer, front and back. And she lets me. And she gives me the time I need. I don't know how much time I need, but I sense we are in no rush, and for that I am thankful.

I move my hand away and sign: "What color is your hair?"

"Light brown," she replies into my hand, and I smile and add the splash of color to the portrait of my mind.

Still, she holds my left hand in hers, fingers interlaced in mine, and so I reach for her face again with my right. She dips her cheek into my hands. It's okay, she seems to say. She wants me to do this, and so I do, exploring her, exploring the unknown. The known unknown, perhaps. Never before have I touched a woman more intimately. Never have I, say, explored her eyebrows. But I do so now. I move my fingertips over one now, with the grain, so to speak. Her brow is not plucked; it feels full and proud. I move my hand carefully over her eye, and feel it moving just under her lid, shifting and moving and following my fingertips. Jesus, I had forgotten how strange and beautiful an eyeball could feel, orbiting and rotating in its socket, such a gift from God. And such a nightmare to lose them. I leave her eye and brush down her slender nose that has the slightest of bumps in it. Maybe she is ashamed of the bump. Maybe she is proud of it. I love it more than anything I've touched on her so far. The bump fills in her face for me, giving it personality and depth and distinction. God, I loved that little bump.

My fingers fan out over her nostrils and trace them, but that seems too intimate, too exposing, and so I move on to the space above her upper lip, my finger finding the divot that probably has a name. I explore the divot and find it sexy, exciting, a hidden quiet spot that is uniquely hers, but now mine, too. I feel some small fuzz there, too, so soft as to almost be my imagination.

Now, I am moving down, down to her lips, and I can feel the excitement building in me.

Her upper lip. It's even softer than I am expecting, yet I can feel a clear edge to it, where it meets the skin above her lip. Her mouth is open a little. I can feel her hot breath on my palm. I can also feel the last, waxy remnants of a lip balm. I trace her upper lip carefully, soaking it in, feeling her teeth just behind it. Feeling the occasional wetness, the delicate skin.

My hand is drawn, inexorably, down.

Down, down…

Her lower lip is everything I'd hoped it would be and more. Then again, any lower lip would have done. But this…wow…this is fascinating.

It is exactly twice as big as the upper. Thicker, wetter, somehow softer. I stroke it with my thumb and forefinger, pinching it slightly, pulling it out slightly. Her lower lip, if anything, seems separate from her body, a full, pliant, pillowy strip of flesh that seems made to be loved, to be kissed, to be played with, to be explored. I can feel her hot breath blasting over my knuckles, down from her nose and sometimes through her mouth. But not just breathing, panting. Her lower lip is wetter, more inviting, and my thumb now glides over her lubricated skin, and now something is happening to me, a reaction I am not entirely prepared for, a reaction that I am certain I need to stop, to somehow control.

I have no business doing any of this. Except this wasn't just my business, was it? It was her business, too, and she was here and pushing her face into my hands and breathing hard and I could feel her heart beating through her damn lips, although I know that is impossible, or is it?

I am breathing harder, too. I know I should move my hand away from her lips, except I don't want to move my hand, and I don't think she wants me to, either, but what do I know? My instincts are so far off that for all I know she's screaming for help.

Except I'm pretty sure she's not screaming. No, she's moving into my hands, undulating a little, writhing a little, and now, she does something I am certain I imagined. Yes, surely this is my imagination.

This can't be real...

Except she does it again and again, and I am left reeling, beyond thinking and feeling.

She's kissing my thumb and finger, pressing her lips against them, even sucking on them a little. Had I ears to hear, I am certain I would be hearing small smacking sounds. Now, I imagine the sounds. I hear them as if they are happening, small, sweet, hungry smacking sounds, of lips coming together and then opening again, of saliva sealing and unsealing.

And now, I am doing something I didn't think I would ever do again—especially after yesterday.

I move forward toward her. Toward her face, even as hers moves towards mine. I guide her lips to me, and briefly imagine a space shuttle precariously docking with the International Space Station, and when the connection is made, when my lips melt into hers, I sink into heaven.

So deep I never want to return.

20

It is the next day.

I am sitting with Betsie in the sunlight, in Griffith Park, not too far from where Jesse DeFranco was last seen, one of the original disappearances in the Big Case, and the only one, so far, to turn up dead.

Turns out Griffith Park doesn't have surveillance cameras, but the adjoining Greek Theatre does. Griffith Park is huge. There are many entrances and many roads. Perhaps the most popular entrance is the one that leads past the Greek Theatre, and on up to the Griffith Observatory, made popular by a handful of rebels back in the day.

Detective Hammer had scouted the location and found the camera, positioned nicely in front of the theater...and along the major walkway into the park. These days, most video is stored permanently on cloud servers. Easy enough to access. Anyway, he'd gone back to the day Jesse had disappeared, and proceeded to review the digital files, and lo, there was our guy, heading into the park, bearing a backpack and a water bottle and shades and a hat. The clothing matched what his wife reported he had been wearing. It was him.

His disappearance followed the same pattern—only his murder was the aberration. His disappearance and death could have nothing to do with the other ten. Except I think it did.

I scratch Betsie between her ears. She is panting steadily. The day is too hot for late fall, but welcome to Los Angeles. I am wearing a bowling shirt and cargo shorts and sneakers with low socks. I feel my legs heating up, perhaps even burning. In a few minutes, I will do my best to find some shade, but for now, I am enjoying the burn. I know this park well enough, but I do not know it so well that I know where the benches in the shade are.

Were the other ten murdered as well? I suspect not. These were designed disappearances. All pre-planned, all staged to look like true disappearances. According to Hammer, none of the bank accounts were drawn from again. No credits cards were used. No phone calls were made from known phones. No tell-tale signs of cash were withdrawn over time.

Maybe they were all killed. Maybe they were all dumped into the ocean, and only Jesse washed ashore.

Maybe, but I doubted it.

I lift my face to the heat of the sun and think of Rachel and our kiss…and smile bigger than anyone who is blind, deaf and nonverbal should smile. She left quickly after the kiss, but not before we made loose plans to see each other again, for dinner. Date and time to be determined.

I smile at that and turn my thoughts back to the case. People disappear for any number of reasons. From the law, from gangs, from life, from bad marriages, from boring marriages, from alimony, from abusive husbands. In some cases, there are programs in place to help some people disappear, especially women in bad relationships. Very, very bad relationships. So bad I have seen case workers plan a woman's escape as carefully as anything in the special ops. Many of these women are controlled and abused by very powerful men, men who are often beyond the law. There are people out there who will help liberate such women. The women go on to start new lives with new identities, far away from those who wish to control them and abuse them.

Yes, there are many, many reasons to seek escape. Some run from responsibility. Some run for their lives. Some run from the law. Some do it well, and truly disappear. Some not so well. Some are found by the very people they hope to disappear from. In most cases, the police are involved. Some people can slip away quietly, to never be seen or heard from again. Most are single, without family and friends. True drifters. Indeed, some might have changed their identities countless times.

And then there are those who help them disappear. Those who will provide false identities, forged paperwork. Many of the documents are crap, but sometimes a forger proves to be particularly good. New identities are purchased. And people disappear to lead new lives. Or so they hope.

Many go as far as to change their appearances, too. Some will gain weight or lose weight, change hair color and even get plastic surgery. Many leave the country, disappear to tropical islands or to South American jungles. Some disappear into the wilds of Alaska. I hope they find peace. I hope they find safety. I hope they can live out their days with some modicum of joy.

Many, of course, leave behind broken hearts. A mother who will never see her son or daughter again. Brothers and sisters and friends who are left with questions. If done right, the missing will leave no trail, no inkling as to where they might have gone. Most do not do it well. Most screw it up somewhere. It takes a clever, clever person to continuously fool police, investigators, border inspectors, new friends, new spouses, new employers. Somewhere, there's a slip up. And one such slip up is what I suspect happened here.

Jesse DeFranco came back for a reason. And the reason he came back had gotten him killed. I had Detective Hammer looking again into Jesse's personal life. We would see if any contact was made.

The person who helped Jesse disappear—and the other nine—probably wasn't a bad person. They were doing some good in this world. Helping others find new lives. And they were good at what they did. That is, until Jesse showed up dead. Many staged disappearances are obvious. Some are not. Some really do look like a true mystery, with the victim seemingly vanishing forever. Hell, maybe some of them really do vanish. Or have been abducted by aliens or were dragged off into the forests and feasted upon by Bigfoot. Others wind up in shallow graves at the side of a highway, their murders unsolved, their bodies rarely found, their stories forgotten.

Every staged disappearance is different. Investigators know what to look for. There are tells, as we call them. Signs, evidence. Some will take a plane somewhere, or a train or a bus. Others let it slip to friends and family. Many of the dumber ones will leave Internet browser clues, receipts, credit card trails.

Apparently, in this case, all the missing victims have disappeared from this city and this city only. None have left behind telling receipts. No whispers to friends or acquaintances that they will be going. No abandoned cars in parking lots. All seemingly walk into oblivion.

Then Jesse DeFranco shows up a year later, floating in the harbor with a bullet behind his ear, execution style.

So what the hell is going on? I think, and reach down and pat Betsie's head. I've never been able to tell if Betsie enjoys being patted or scratched. I think she puts up with being patted, while secretly hoping for more scratches.

We're not dealing with a serial killer, I think. Someone helped these people disappear, and then someone killed Jesse when he tried to come back. More than likely, those are two separate cases, not one and the same. More than likely Jesse was killed by whoever he was running from… if he was running from someone.

The exterior camera of the Greek Theatre had picked up Jesse walking alone, along a sidewalk in the late evening, wearing a hat and backpack. The entrance into the park goes well past the Greek, and winds through the hills all the way up to the Griffith Observatory. Jesse could have met someone at any point along that winding road. There are many dozens of picnic tables and parking spots. Dozens of turnouts.

Yes, Jesse could have very easily met the person who would ultimately help him disappear here in this park. Not very far from where I'm sitting now. Or, perhaps, in this very spot, too. Perhaps the person had picked him up. Taken him to a safe place. Given him the necessary paperwork and money and credit cards. Perhaps helped him cut his hair, dyed his hair. The preliminaries to disappearing.

Of course, I could have this all wrong. Maybe there really was a serial killer. Maybe someone was luring people up into these hills and killing. Maybe. Then why did Jesse show up a year later, shot and dumped in the harbor?

Not a serial killer.

His murder is, more than likely, related to why he needed to run in the first place.

Then why had he come back?

Did he think the heat had passed? That everything was hunky-dory? Did anyone say hunky-dory any more?

So, then, why am I sitting here, in this park that sits at the foot of the Griffith Observatory, in the hot sun, while my dog no doubt wishes like hell she was anywhere but here? A park that was, by all standards, huge. Hell, it even sported it's own mountain chain, let alone the Los Angeles Zoo, Griffith Observatory and thousands of acres of hills and trails.

Anything could be out here, I think.

Back in the day, I often hung out at the location of a crime. I immersed myself in the scene, especially when I didn't have all the answers yet. I mostly had the answers now, except who had killed Jesse and who was helping people disappear.

Okay, maybe I don't have all the answers now.

How did Jesse and the others meet this contact? A friend of a friend knows someone who knows something about something? Probably. Sooner or later, with enough palms being greased, you make the right—or wrong—connections, and such a deal goes down. I also know there are dark places on the Internet where some people go looking. A man offering new identities could presumably be on such a site. I wasn't too worried about how the missing found their contact. No, I was wondering what happened to them after they met him here in this park.

If the guy is legit, he's offering them the kind of services that will truly help them disappear.

Except...

Ah, yes…except most people want to be paid for such services. And, no doubt, paid a lot.

Except, yes, and here's the crux of the matter—and the reason I'm here now, puzzled. There is no evidence of such services being paid for. No large sums of money going missing from bank accounts.

So, then, how do these eleven missing people—all of whom were from average incomes—pay for help to disappear?

There it is. The reason I am here in the park. This reason, and no other.

They never paid for their contact's services. At least, not in cash.

So, how, then, are they paying him? Or her?

I nod, rub my face, and I'm about to really think this through when Betsie leaps to her feet, ears alert, tail wagging.

Someone's coming.

21

Now Betsie is fighting against the leash, which she never, ever does, and I turn toward whoever is approaching, more curious now than ever—even as I do my best to restrain my clearly excited dog, a dog who had been trained by the best to control her excitement.

All bets are off. All training has been forgotten. My dog is beside herself...with joy.

Now, I can feel the stranger patting my dog, who is now standing on her hind legs, her thick tail smacking and swooshing over my bare calves. I stand at the commotion and try my best to rein her in, but there's just no denying Betsie. As I hold her back, I can feel a stranger heartily patting her sides. Betsie tries to jump up, and it's all I can do to keep her from knocking over whoever's here, whoever is petting her and patting her and getting her so worked up—more worked up than I have ever seen her. I just stand there, holding the leash, cocking my head, utterly stunned and totally helpless.

Finally, the patting stops and Betsie settles down, but barely. I do the only thing I can think of. I remove the notepad from my shirt pocket and hold the cover out to the stranger.

"I'm sorry, but I'm blind, deaf and mute."

There is a pause, and even Betsie seems to finally settle down. A moment later, her furry butt plops down on my shoes. This is followed by a hand on my shoulder, a hand that turns into a gentle pat. It is, in fact, the only polite way to get my attention. After all, I'm not going to see an extended hand for me to shake.

After the gentle pat, I smile and nod and hold out my hand. Anyone my dog likes is all right by me. Besides, I am eager to see who had swung by to say hi, eager to see who had gotten my dog so excited.

A warm, small, and gentle hand takes my own extended hand. There is a strength to the hand. An edge. As if the hand has experienced life to the fullest and has come out the other end a warmer and wiser and gentler person.

I have no idea whose hand I am shaking. Hands, for me, are the only identification I have for most people. I know hands. I remember hands. I remember their size and shape and temperature. This hand is a new hand to me...and yet...

And yet Betsie knows the man well.

The hand grips me in a warm and friendly way, too. And then the man's second hand closes over the back of my own, cocooning mine in both of his...holding me firmly but gently. I sense gentleness in his hands, understanding, and something close to, well, love.

He turns my hand over and signs into my open palm: "Let's sit."

I think my mouth dropped open, but, of course, no words come out. I nod and sit again. He sits, too, and Betsie is between us, hunkered down on my shoes, alert and excited and watching us.

We sit quietly for a few seconds. The stranger has not yet released my hand, and that is okay with me. His touch seems natural, comforting, even a little intoxicating.

What's going on?

The wind is cool and the sun is warm, and I detect a hint of freshly cut grass on the wind. A minute or two passes. I am looking forward, toward what I think is a sharply angled hillside that leads up to the Griffith Observatory. I breathe slowly, evenly, through the tube in my neck. I often wonder if I ever make any sounds as I breathe. Does the hole occasionally whistle? Gurgle? Do I breathe loudly, or softly? I know for me that breathing is sometimes an effort. Sometimes, I fear the hole will fail or collapse or get filled with so much mucus that I can't draw in enough air. Sometimes I panic and scare myself. I remind myself at those times that I am safe and that my tracheal tube has been carefully constructed. I remind myself that there is always an answer. And if I can't find an answer…or if it somehow eludes me…I have a final answer waiting for me next to my bed.

The wind picks up and lifts my hair and moves through my bowling shirt. It is only later, perhaps after a few minutes, that I realize I am still holding the stranger's hand.

Just as this dawns on me, he turns my hand over and spells into it slowly with a firm, steady finger: "Hi, I am Jack."

22

I reach for the notepad in my pocket again, but the same gentle hand stops me. He turns my hand over again, and spells out a single word in my palm: "Sign."

I nod, and sign: "Do I know you?" Jack sounds an awful lot like Jacky, the old Irish boxing trainer. Except, I am certain this *Jack* is not the *Jacky* I had recently met. Very certain, in fact.

I hold out my hand for him to sign into. Instead of signing, he continues spelling out the letters, which, for me, is sometimes just as easy—and more accurate. He taps my palm with the tips of three of his fingers to indicate a space in the words. It is an efficient way of communicating, and he does so easily, fluidly. The words seem flow to me readily, easy to absorb, appearing in my mind's eye like a ticker-tape at the bottom of a CNN broadcast.

"A part of you knows me well."

I use both hands to sign: "I do not know what that means."

"Few do—and those who do, know me well."

I cock my head a little, then sign: "That was a lot of fancy doublespeak."

I sense him laughing, and then feel a hearty pat on my back. "Let's start over. I am Jack. You do not remember me, but that's okay. It is as it should be."

"But you remember me?" I ask, signing, still confused.

"Oh, yes, Lee. I remember you well."

115

"You know my name?"

"Let's say, I have a good a memory."

"Did you just draw a winkie face?" I sign, trying to puzzle out what he'd added at the the end of his last sentence.

"Isn't that what the kids do these days?"

I shrug, sign: "I wouldn't know."

"I suppose you wouldn't, Lee."

"Are you my boxing trainer?"

"No, Lee."

I turn toward him, drop my hands in my lap, gather my thoughts and memory and sign: "I'm sorry, but where do you know me from?"

"You wouldn't believe me if I told you."

"Try me."

"Soon," he spells out into my palm.

"Well, my dog seems to know you."

"She is a good dog. More angel than canine. She is here to serve you and help you; she is proud of her job."

"Um, what?"

"She also loves you unconditionally, Lee. She lives for you and your needs."

"Who are you?" I sign again.

I can feel my heart picking up a little. Each time the man—and for some reason I suspect he is an older man—signs into my hand, I get nearly uncontrollable shivers. And flashes in my mind. Brief flashes. I see my mother before she died, smiling at me from her deathbed. She shouldn't be smiling. Her body is literally dying. Another brief flash of the ocean. I used to run along the Santa Monica beaches on the weekend. I was a true weekend warrior back in the day. But at least I was consistent. Every Saturday and Sunday, I would run for as long as I could, pushing myself each time to go further and further. Another flash, another vision.

This time of a golden retriever with big brown eyes, staring at me from over her furry paws, eyebrows raised, watching my every move. Other than Betsie, I've never owned a golden retriever, and try as I might, I can't remember a friend who owned one either. Certainly I had seen them being walked, or in commercials. But I don't remember having one look at me with such...love.

"What's happening?" I sign. "Who are you?"

The man next to me sits motionless. I reach my hand out for him to sign into, but he doesn't. Not yet. Instead, more visions come to me: of my first girlfriend, of my first kiss, of the sky at night, of the surrounding San Gabriel mountain peaks. Finally, after a steady stream of vision, he takes my hand. But not to sign into it. Instead, he takes it and holds it within both of his, and I am surprised by what I feel next. It is something I am certain I have not felt in many years, even before the explosion. As he holds my hand in both of his, as his two hands completely close over my own, as I feel their warmth and strength, I feel what I am certain is love. Radiating through his hands, through his strong grip that even now is shaking, but not with the effort of gripping my hand, no, but with the outpouring of love, the transmission of love, from him to me.

What's happening?

I don't know, but I don't question, I don't resist. Hell, I couldn't resist him if I tried. The old man has my hand and there isn't a damn thing I can do about it. Or *want* to do about it.

And so I sat there and let this man named Jack hold my hand, and let his love flow through me...

———

Finally, he releases my hand, his fingers uncurling, one at a time.

I am acutely aware—as I sit next to this stranger who may not be stranger—that something has happened to me. I do not know what or how or why. Just *something*. I can feel it stirring within me, like a living thing awakening. It's an energy, and I feel it flowing through me, swirling, moving. I imagine a sea creature moving over rocks and through coral and over shipwrecks, a moray eel looking, looking, looking.

No. Not looking. Growing. Spreading. And...

Healing. And not just healing my broken body, but my broken spirit. I almost sense it mending my cells, my psyche, my heart. Wherever it touches, I imagine new growth, new life.

I'm dreaming. I'm in bed. This isn't really happening.

Whatever *this* is. Just a man. Just an older man showing me some compassion. And holding my hand. And pouring love into me. Unlike anything I'd ever felt in my life.

I can feel myself shaking now. But not out of fear, and not even out of excitement. I'm shaking with whatever is moving through me, whatever has transferred from him to me. Love? Healing? Both?

Using just my left hand—my free hand—I spell out the words: "What is happening?"

He turns my hand over. "Love is happening," comes the carefully written response into my palm, each line, each swirl, each loop, each curve, sending another shudder through me. Another and another and another...

"Am I dreaming?" I spell out.

"No, Lee."

"How do you know my name?" I ask again, now using both hands to sign. "And no doubletalk. Give it to me straight."

He spells: "Once a cop, always a cop."

I nod, and I can feel myself sweating now. I wipe my brow and pull at my collar, getting some air. Just as I'm wiping my palm, he takes my hand again, and spells: "You spoke to a little girl the other day."

I turn to him. If I could have blinked, I would have. Instead, my mouth drops open. I wonder if I've made a sound. I don't know. I am flabbergasted and don't know what to say—or to sign—and so, I sit there unmoving, quiet.

"She asked you to say a prayer with her, do you remember, Lee?"

Now, I do blink. Behind my shades. Worthless blinks, but it's the only response my body has, the only reaction I'm seemingly capable of. Finally, after twenty seconds, I nod.

"She prayed for your sight to return, and you prayed with her, praying as best as you could. 'Dear God, please help me see again.'"

I am breathing as calmly as I can through the tracheal tube. I can feel it sputtering a little. It needs to be cleaned soon. The old man is holding my hand lightly again, and I feel more and more energy coming from him. I can feel it spreading over my shoulders, moving up and down my spine. I've felt such energy before. But this energy feels... foreign. Not my own. Introduced, so to speak.

"How sincere were you, Lee?"

"What do you mean?"

"How sincere was your prayer? Do you believe that you can see again?"

I smile now, certain I am dreaming, but knowing there is a small chance that this could really be happening, and an even bigger chance that someone is playing the world's sickest practical joke on me.

I sign, "I have no eyes, Jack."

He holds my hand with one of his and pats it with his other. A grandfatherly gesture. "Very well. We shall go with Plan B, as they say."

I release his hand, and sign: "What does that mean?"

But he is already standing. I feel him reaching over and patting Betsie's head. Her tail wags so hard that my shins might bruise. He's leaving, I'm sure of it.

"Wait," I sign, holding out my hand into the darkness.

A long moment later, I feel his strong and gentle hands take my wrist, turn it over, and spell out the words: "Help is coming."

I sense him moving away…and he is gone.

23

It is later, and I am just stepping inside my apartment.

Uber is a godsend. Without it, I would still be struggling with the bus schedules and the long walk back to the apartment. With it, I get door-to-door service.

Speaking of godsend, I cannot take my mind off the man I had just met. The man named Jack. The man who knew about the little girl and my prayer. A man who had asked if my prayer was sincere. And when my answer didn't fully satisfy him, I was told, "Very well. We shall go with Plan B, as they say."

No. It's not that my answer didn't satisfy him. My answer showed my own lack of faith.

I carefully hang up my keys on the keyring next to the door. I release Betsie's harness and she trots off—I suspect over to her bowl of water. I bet she drinks loudly, really slopping up the water.

If not for my injuries, I would still be a homicide investigator. I would have seen five years' worth of murders and the worst of humanity. I would have interviewed hundreds of witnesses, seen dozens upon dozens of bodies. I would have done my best to connect the dots to find the killers...or, in the least, to find answers.

I would have looked at the facts, the evidence, interpreted witness statements, decide who is lying to me and who is not. Ultimately, it is the facts that tell the stories, that hold up in court. It is the facts that solve cases, facts that put the bad guys away. I've lived by facts. Emotion has little to no use in my business. Emotions get in the way. Emotions cloud facts.

Emotions get you blown up, I think, and head over to my refrigerator.

Once there, I find the beer easily enough on the second shelf. I'm not so cool that I know where everything is in my refrigerator, but I have a pretty good idea. I twist off the cap and drink the beer down, knowing I need to soon clean my tracheal tube.

The old man—Jack—hadn't asked about my emotions. No. He had asked if I was sincere and if I believed. Believed in what? Miracles?

I shake my head and drink, surprised and amused and alarmed that I had taken the conversation seriously. He was, after all, an old man. Rambling, delusional. Except, of course, he had known about the little girl.

And my prayer.

I drink more of the beer, and am surprised that it is already gone. How the hell that happened, I don't know. I open the fridge and reach for another one.

The answer to the old man's question—and I am certain he was an old man—is that I have very little faith. Very, very little.

If any.

Yes, I had prayed with a little girl. Her request, after all, hadn't been entirely unreasonable. It had been sweet, and I needed more sweetness in my life. And so, I had gone along with her words, repeating them, or mouthing them. And, yeah, maybe for a nanosecond, maybe even less than that, I could feel the hope of her words, and they had gripped me, briefly. But I had let the hope go instantly. Hell, I had forgotten about the prayer altogether.

Until the old man Jack came along.

So, what's going on here? I think into the empty kitchen, lifting the second beer up to my lips.

The answer is: I haven't a clue.

Strange shit. And then I add: *Sorry about the* shit *part.*

I'm about to head over to the couch and finish drinking the beer and pet my dog and, no doubt, dwell on all of this and more, when I feel my cell phone buzz in my pocket. Three straight buzzes. Someone is at my front door.

———

I feel paws pounding over the Pergo flooring.

No doubt, Betsie is barking up a storm. Always good to let people know that the blind man in the apartment has a big, protective dog. Nothing wrong with that. Except, this is Saturday afternoon, and the person at the door would be my brother, Robert.

At the door, I sign: "My brother from the same mother."

An old joke. A stupid joke. My lame attempt to get things off on the right foot, especially with the tension lately. Instead of signing back into my palm, I feel him brush past me.

I shut the door, turn around, sign: "Everything okay, Rob?"

There's no response—not for maybe a half a minute or more.

And then, I feel him take my hand. There's a slight pause before he signs into it: "I'm sorry, Lee."

"Sorry for what?"

"I'm sorry, Lee," he signs again, and it occurs to me that my brother is weeping. I don't know how I know this. Maybe I sense a shuddering in him, a change in the air flow around me, warmer than normal hands. I don't know.

But, yes, I am certain of it.

My brother is weeping.

24

I ask if he wants to sit; he doesn't want to.
I ask if he wants a beer, and he says no, which isn't such a bad thing, since I had just opened the last beer, I think. Still, if he had wanted a beer, I would have given what I had left of it.

And so, we stand there some more, just inside the front door, one of us weeping and the other confused as hell. I can feel Betsie's tail whooshing against my ankles. She always loved my brother and was, undoubtedly, doing her best to patiently wait for the scratches that had yet to come. Okay, maybe there are two of us confused as hell.

After a moment, I sign: "Is everything okay?"

"No," he signs quickly back into my outstretched hand. My brother and I have been signing like this seemingly forever. I know my brother's fingertips better than any brother should ever know. My brother is a sloppy signer, not always finishing his signs, and often seguing too fast into the next letter and leaving me to guess what he is saying. I usually guess correctly. Or maybe he just never bothers to correct me.

I wait. Betsie waits, too. Her tail has stopped swishing. I can almost see her looking at my brother, head cocked to one side, ears perked up. Big, brown, wet eyes looking concerned. The way only a dog can look.

"You sure you don't want to sit?" I ask.

He taps my shoulder twice for no, our own private sign language. Our brotherly sign language. Now, I'm getting concerned. My brother doesn't exactly have a history of having made good choices. To this day, he still asks to borrow money, and so, I give it to him. He never repays. Ever. Despite saying, each and every time, that he will. Then again, what use did I have for money, other than to provide for my basic needs?

It is better to help him, I often think, than to never see him. I'll take what I can get. He is, after all, the only family I have…and the only person who visits me on a regular basis.

And so I stand there and wait, wondering what my brother has gotten himself into. Wondering if I am going to have to pull another favor to bail him out again. The last favor was when he'd been arrested in a prostitution sting. Apparently, my brother frequents the back pages of want ads, the kind of back pages that can get one arrested. I had called in a very big favor…and my brother had been spared, although he'd spent a night in jail, for which I don't think he's forgiven me.

Like they say, you can pick your friends, but you can't pick your family.

Over the last five years, my brother has done much to help me. I would love to say that we've grown closer because of the experience—that my brother is a better man for having helped me, that he's matured and grown and become more responsible, that he embraced the situation and rose to the challenge. I would love to say all that and more, but I can't. My brother is, if anything, growing more bitter with each visit, more resentful. I do what I can to make his life easier. I do all the chores and errands I can safely do, so that when he gets here, there's only the matter of, say, going through my mail with me. Or of going online and paying bills and transferring funds. Or, if he has the time, of going through my emails with me. He usually doesn't have the time. I haven't checked my email accounts in many months.

And so I wait with my dog, who's sitting obediently at my feet, waiting for the attention that my brother never gives her. I hold her harness, although I know she will never run. Holding her harness is, if anything, for my own peace of mind.

What happens next hasn't happened, I think, ever. Definitely not since my accident, and I doubt before, either. My brother hugs me tight, snatching me in both hands and pulling me toward him. He buries his face in my neck and, yes, I can feel his hot tears against my skin. I stand there, stunned, holding Betsie with one hand. Finally, I reach up with my free arm and hug my brother in return. Now, he is weeping into my neck, hard enough that I am certain my neighbors can hear. Or not. Maybe he's crying silently, with lots of wheezing and gasping. But I don't think so. I think my little brother is crying loudly. After all, Betsie is trying to claw her way up to him, reacting to his sobs in ways that she generally reacts to my own.

As I hold my brother in return, as perplexed tears find their way to my own eyes, I am thinking my brother has finally turned the corner. Finally letting go of his anger toward me. Finally embracing our current situation, tough as it might be.

Finally, he pulls away and I feel his tears still on my cheek and I am smiling like a goofy, proud older brother. I leave one hand on his shoulder and pat him and nod, and mouth the words: "Feel better now?"

As I hold his shoulder, I feel him shake his head, and then he takes my hand from his shoulder, holds it before him, then signs into it: "I can't do this anymore, Lee."

"Can't do what?" I sign, completely confused.

He takes my hand again, and I can feel him sobbing some more, perhaps even harder. "This," he signs, "will be my last time."

Something inside me shuts down. Maybe my lungs. Maybe my ability to process thought. Hell, maybe my heart. And so I just stand there, too stunned to move or think or respond or to feel or to hope or to believe.

"I'm leaving, Lee," he continues into my palm. "I'm leaving California. Moving to Florida once I pass a few tests. I met a girl. We're happy. I need a break from this. All of this. It's too crazy for me. Too much. I can't handle it anymore."

I release Betsie's harness and point inside. I feel her trot off into the apartment. She will stay. She always stays.

"I'm sorry, Lee," he signs. "I'm sorry."

I raise my hands. "Will I see you again?"

"I'm sorry, Lee."

He hugs me again, crying and convulsing. I pat his back and mouth the words, "It's okay," even though I know he can't see them, even though I am not sure I even mean them. No, I am certain I don't mean them. I continue patting his shoulder and the back of his head as he sobs into my neck, and with each sob, I know that things won't be okay. With each sob, I know the likelihood of me seeing my brother again drifts further and further away.

He's really leaving me. A part of me doesn't blame him, although a bigger part of me is too wounded for thought or feeling or action.

All I can do is pat his head and tell him it's going to be okay, even though he can't hear me or see my lips moving.

He holds me at arm's length, no doubt staring at me, soaking in his pathetic older brother, and then he leaves.

And just like that, my brother is gone from my life.

25

I sit on the edge of my bed.

My mind is empty. My heart feels empty, which is a new feeling for me. Not even when my brother had read Gwen's breakup text had I experienced such emptiness. I do not know what to think, or do, or who to turn to—or even if I want to turn to anyone. I do not open the drawer with the gun in it, because I will not harm myself because of the whims of my brother.

But the feeling of abandonment and loneliness is not to be denied. I look forward to those few hours with my brother. I know now that he did not feel the same. So much so that he is leaving the state, leaving me forever.

I am loosely holding the bottle of beer—my last beer, the beer I would have given my brother had he wanted it. He didn't want it. In fact, he doesn't want to have anything to do with me again.

And it goes like this for another half hour or so. Me, wallowing in self pity. Me, often looking toward the spot where the dresser would be, where the gun would be. Me, wanting to just hold the gun, to feel its reassuring weight, but afraid to do it. Terrified to take it out of the drawer. I suspect that if I take it out of the drawer, I will use it on myself. I don't want to use it on myself. Not now. Not under these situations. Not ever. But I think I might. I just might. I just might put it in my mouth and pull the trigger. I'm feeling just bad enough to make a super poor decision.

Super, super poor.

Better to leave the gun in the drawer. Better to not feel its comforting weight, its balanced weight, its cold steel and smooth trigger and perfectly formed grip. Too perfect. Too easy to use.

The feeling of reaching for my gun is very, very strong. So strong that I catch myself more than once leaning toward the drawer. I know in that drawer is my death. I know it. But still…

Still, I want to hold that gun. More than anything. I want to heft it in my hand, feel the texture of it, the engineering of it. The ache I feel for that gun is real and it scares the fuck out of me. But I do not turn away. I do not stand and leave. I continue sitting there, facing the gun, staring at it as surely as if I had eyes to see.

I find my fingers have even formed the shape of the gun handle, my index finger hovering over an invisible trigger, my thumb pressing against an invisible hammer. My hand has formed this all on its own.

No, I mouth to no one, now rocking on the edge of my bed. *No.*

I am certain that if I remove the gun from the nightstand it will be the last thing I ever do. I am certain that I will bring it to my mouth and pull the trigger, whether I want to or not. It will just happen. Automatically. As if on its own volition. Compelled by forces beyond my control.

And all because my shithead brother bailed on me.

I might kill myself someday. But not because of him. Not because of this.

I know of another reason why I am not reaching for that drawer. Yes, definitely another reason. I don't want my brother to have my suicide on his conscience, too. My brother is a shithead who makes poor decisions. Something like this, I know, might push him over the edge, too. My brother would be forever lost, I think.

Two brothers gone.

I should not care what happens to him, not after abandoning me, but I do.

Let him go. Better for him to be free and alive, than to feel bound to me and miserable.

All these thoughts and more. My mother wouldn't be happy if I open that drawer. Neither would Betsie. Betsie is my girl. She needs me. And as I finally stand, looking down to where the nightstand would be, I feel Betsie press against my leg, tail wagging.

I reach down and pat her and, as I leave my bedroom, I think of Rachel. She wouldn't be happy if I open that drawer, either.

As I exit my bedroom, I flip off the light because it feels natural to do so—and normal to do so—never mind that there hadn't been a light bulb in my bedroom in five years.

26

We are driving.

I am sitting in the back seat of Hammer's unmarked car. At least, I think it's unmarked. Sitting next to me holding my hand is Rachel George. I only recently learned her last name was George. Then again, I only recently learned that she might not find me too offensive.

We keep our hands low, resting on the seat between us, presumably so Hammer can't see us. But Hammer is a cop. Cops notice things others miss. Anyway, I don't give a crap what Hammer can or can't see, but Rachel seems to care. I discovered the other day that Rachel is a freelance translator, working exclusively with sign language, and the LAPD is her major client. I assumed she felt keeping our relationship on the down low, for now, was beneficial to her business. And since this was the first time in a long, long time that I'd even formed the word 'relationship,' well, I was more than game to follow her lead.

Earlier, I received a text from Hammer, which said he was on his way over with Rachel; they were going to pick me up. A witness had called and Hammer was heading to meet him and he wanted me there. I typed 'OK.' I almost felt normal.

Considering I had planned to sit on my balcony and do nothing—and to definitely not think about the gun in my drawer—this was a pleasant distraction.

Now, as I hold Rachel's hand, the gun is all but forgotten, although my brother is still heavy on my mind. Her hand is small and timid and I begin to wonder if she is thinking the other day was a bad idea. Then again, it was her idea to hold my hand now.

She squeezes my hand as we round a corner, and signs quickly into my palm, "Are you okay?"

"Rough morning," I motion back.

"I'm sorry," she replies. "Want to tell me about it?"

I think about it and almost tell her, "Maybe later," but I can feel her concern for me, the way she now squeezes my hand just a little tighter, the way her thumb works back and forth over my hand. And so, reluctantly, I release her hand and sign: "My brother is moving."

She pats my hand before signing into it: "Is he your only family?"

I nod. "Both my parents have passed."

"No other siblings?"

I shake my head.

"Where is he moving?"

"Florida," I spell out.

There is a long pause, and I think she understands the implication. I think she understands that my brother was, for want of a better word, my caretaker. I think she gets that my brother has abandoned me. I won't say it, of course. I won't badmouth my brother. Not now, not ever. He did his best. He just couldn't do any more. I wish him the best, wherever he is.

Instead of telling me everything is going to be all right, or that my brother is an asshole for leaving, or that

I am screwed, she takes my hand again, this time in both of hers, and lowers it to her lap. She squeezes it gently, warmly, her thumbs stroking my knuckles, and holds me like that for the rest of the drive. Yes, I think, I might have fallen in love with her in that moment.

27

I am led into a cool room.

We are on the ground floor of what feels like a small home. Then again, I could have been led into a cave or into a McDonald's. Still, the air feels stuffy, with a hint of musk and old cigarettes and mildewed carpet and furniture. At the moment, my sniffer seems to be working well enough, and that's all I can ask.

No, I can ask for a lot more…a lot, lot more.

Holding the inside of my elbow, Rachel leads me deeper into the house. I am certain that, to anyone looking at us, the gesture looks innocent enough. But I can feel the way her fingertips sink in a little more than they should, the way her thumb applies enough pressure to let me know she is thinking of me, concerned about me.

All of which is nearly too much for me to contemplate right now. I just lost my brother…and seemed to gain the love of a woman. I inhale deeply through the hole in my neck, find my balance, and allow myself to be led deeper into the home, where I am shown a chair and I sit. Betsie sits nearly on top of my feet. Where I go, she goes. Period.

I feel a chair scraping over the wooden floor next to me, and Rachel sits next to me, takes my hand, signs: "How you doing?"

"Good. We are in a small home?"

"Yes. In Burbank, not far from the Toluca Lake."

I nod and wait. Rachel sets my hand back down on my knee, where it will remain until she's ready to sign into it again. I sense that Hammer is probably telling the witness who I am, asking for permission to have me present, explaining my situation and putting the witness at ease. I try to look as pleasant as possible. I know my face has small puffy scars around my eyes, and bigger scars around my neck. The bowling shirt's collar covers most of those latter scars. The big sunglasses cover, I hope, a lot of the smaller puffy scars. Although once a big man, I must surely look frail and non-intimidating.

I do not know what's happening in the room. I do not know where the witness is sitting or if Hammer is sitting or standing. I suspect standing. These days, I do not often go into people's homes, let alone a stranger's. I try to picture what the home might look like. An old afghan over a couch. A dusty piano in a corner. A cat watching me from a windowsill. I see sunlight coming in through the window and the open front door with its broken screen door, dust motes drifting in and out of the light, glowing like mini-constellations.

Then again, I could have been in a bachelor's home, too, with a Pulp Fiction poster up on the wall, a Foosball table in the corner, and twin recliners with built-in beer can holders. Hard to know without asking. I don't ask. I wait. As I wait, I feel eyes on me.

Definitely a cat.

Now, Rachel takes my hand again—and, as always, a shiver courses through me, so strong that I am certain she feels it, too—and begins to rapidly sign into my palm.

"The man says he's okay with us being here, and with you listening and maybe even asking some questions."

"Who is he?"

"A friend of the victim. Remember Jesse DeFranco?"

I nod. Jesse is the floater. The only missing person to turn up in the past year. I wait and feel more eyes on me. Okay, maybe not cat eyes after all. Maybe there's a child in the room, watching from, say, the hallway. Maybe a child and a cat.

She takes my hand again and signs quickly, doing her best to keep up with the conversation, all while spelling one letter at a time. She uses a form of shorthand, of which I do my best to piece together into something coherent: "Hammer is asking the witness why he called for this meeting. Witness name is Arthur. He's an older guy, gray hair, looks like hell."

I nod as she pauses, but then signs rapidly. She denotes Hammer's and Arthur's turns with only an "H" or an "A" before signing the conversation as fast as she can.

Arthur: "Jesse called me last week, maybe a day or two before he was murdered, before I heard about him on the news."

Hammer: "What did Jesse say?"

Arthur: "Said something bad had happened to him, real bad."

Hammer: "Did he say what?"

Arthur: "Said not over the phone, he wanted to meet me."

Hammer: "Did you meet him?"

Arthur: "No."

Hammer: "Why not?"

Arthur: "Apparently, someone got to him first."

Hammer: "Did you hear from Jesse again?"

Arthur: "No."

Hammer: "Did he say where he'd been this past year?"

Arthur: "He didn't, but he did say he had just escaped."

Hammer: "Escaped from what?"

Arthur: "He didn't say, but he sounded real scared."

Hammer: "Did he say anything else?"

Arthur: "Just that he wanted to meet."

Rachel rests her hand in my own, a surprisingly intimate gesture that I hope no one else sees. That is, until I realize I don't care if anyone else sees. She resumes signing. "Hammer wants to know if you have any questions."

I nod, sign: "What number did he call from?"

There is a pause, and Rachel signs: "He's looking at his phone now, Lee."

"Thank you," I sign, then add: "Sweetie."

She squeezes my forearm in a manner that suggests she might really like me, which is baffling to me, but I go with it. A moment later, she releases my arm and signs into my open hand: "He doesn't know the number. Hammer is writing it down, says he will run it."

I sign: "Did he say where he was calling from?"

Rachel signs his response: "No."

"Did you hear any background noise?"

"No."

"How long have you had your number?"

"Eight years, maybe longer."

"So, it's reasonable the victim could have remembered it?"

"Yes, he knew my number. I know his, too."

"What was the duration of the call?"

"Two minutes and seven seconds."

"Who hung up?"

"He hung up on me, said he would get in touch when he could." There's a pause, and then Rachel continues: "I was stunned. Almost too stunned to speak. I asked him where he'd been, but he only said he would get back to me, but that he was okay."

I signed, "Do you have any reason to believe he disappeared on purpose?"

"I always suspected he did. I mean, he mentioned it once or twice, years ago. I never thought he was serious."

"Disappeared from what?" I ask.

"Life. His marriage. His job. His responsibilities. He always wanted to start over. Thought he would do it right the next time around. Keep in mind, he only mentioned this maybe twice, and that was years ago."

"Did he contact you after his disappearance?"

"Only just a few days ago."

"Prior to his disappearance, did you loan him money?"

"No."

"What's your relationship with him?"

"Friends for a few decades now, maybe longer. I've been sick over his disappearance this past year, always waiting to hear from him, or hear from his ex-wife. Hell, hear anything."

I nod when Rachel is done signing. "That's all the questions I have."

I suspect Hammer is giving the man his card, telling him to call him should he hear anything else or remember anything else. And then, Rachel takes my elbow and guides me to my feet.

And we head out. A ragtag team if ever there was one.

The eyes watch me leave.

28

We are in Hammer's car, sitting in the heat with the windows down, as Rachel informs me the detective is calling the number. She then informs me there is no answer.

Assuming I'm not jumping in the middle of a conversation, I sign: "Let's go over Jesse's personal life."

The car shakes as the detective, I assume, has turned in his seat and is looking back at us, speaking directly to Rachel, who relays his answer into my palm: "By all accounts, he wasn't happy. He and his wife had talked of divorce for years."

"Kids?" I sign.

"Two, in high school."

"Job?"

"Worked as a city bus driver."

"Criminal activity?"

"None that we know of."

"Debts?"

"Typical debts. Maybe higher than most."

"Gambling debts?"

"By all accounts he wasn't a gambler."

"Any reason for him to fake his own death?"

"No obvious reasons, other than he wanted out and seemed too much of a pussy—sorry Rachel—to just leave his wife."

I think about that, and sign: "He was scared on the phone."

"Seems that way."

"So, who scared him?"

"Probably the same asshole who killed him."

Rachel taps the back of my hand, her indicator for me to wait. She rests her hand in my hand. A fat glob of drool lands on my forearm. I reach over and pat Betsie's panting chest. Five minutes later, she comes back on the line, so to speak. "Detective just received a call. Coroner's office. He wants you to know that the victim, Jesse DeFranco, was malnourished, starving perhaps. The man also had rat meat and possum meat in his system. The detective doesn't know what to make of this. Wait, there's more... you're not going to believe this."

I wait, feeling the old excitement of the hunt returning.

"The coroner just called again. The victim had tuberculosis."

"You're right," I sign back, "I don't believe it. How long had he had it?"

"Hold on, I'll ask."

I wait while the various questions and answers are relayed via the detective to the coroner's office, then back to the detective, to Rachel and finally, to me.

"Seems to be a new case. The symptoms haven't shown up yet."

"How long do the symptoms take to show up?" I ask.

I wait twenty seconds for the answer. "Depends. Sometimes a year, sometimes longer."

"So our missing victim disappears for a year and winds up with a new case of tuberculosis and a bullet to his head."

"Yeah," says Rachel, "that's what they're telling me."

I sign: "Please ask Hammer to give me a list of all the victims' medical histories."

I wait while Rachel relays my request. A moment later, Rachel signs into my hand: "He wants to know who died and made you king of the world. But you'll have them in a few days." She pauses, then adds, "I told the detective I would bring them over to you and help you read the report."

I smile and squeeze her hand and turn my head, toward the window, toward the warmth, toward where the light of day would be. Something is gnawing at me.

I sign: "Ask the good detective to check for any incidents in and around Griffith Park in the last year. I'm not talking petty crime. Something unusual, something that stands out."

Her response comes a few minutes later. "He says to quit making him look bad, that he would have thought of that on his own."

"Tell him there's no room for hurt feelings when working a case."

"He says you need to get laid."

"Is he offering?"

"Guys are pigs," she signs into my hand and sits back, but I feel her chuckling to herself.

I smile and turn to the warmth, to the light, and find myself thinking about the case. There is an answer here. I can feel it.

And it's close.

29

I t is afternoon when I get home.

I am eager to get my hands on that list. I should have asked for it earlier. I had assumed the victims weren't victims. That, in fact, they had perpetrated their own disappearance. I am beginning to think differently. How differently, I don't know. What the hell is going on, I don't know that either. There is more here, I am sure of it.

Rat and possum meat? Tuberculosis? What the hell was going on?

I turn this over in my mind, over and over, as I pour myself a bowl of cereal, resting my hand mostly over the lip of the bowl, gauging when to stop the milk. I give it a half inch from the lip, and cap the bottle and replace the box of cereal over the refrigerator, exactly where I always keep it, and the milk on the lower right-hand corner of the refrigerator, exactly where I always keep it. Both cereal and milk had been low. I would have to go shopping again. My brother and I should have gone shopping yesterday. The selfish fucker could have at least gone shopping with me one last time before dropping his bomb.

For the first time, I let myself get mad. Raging mad. I don't break things; I don't throw things. I just stand there and feel the anger wash over me, through me, and it quickly morphs to sadness, as I think about the hard decision my brother made. It couldn't have been easy on him. He had reached his limits. I had broken him.

I breathe through the tracheal tube. Mucus rattles. I'll have to clean it soon. But not right now. No. Right now, I want to eat my cereal and think, which is what I always did when working cases. Food and thinking. Food and thinking.

And so, I sit in my living room and think in complete darkness, carefully eating my bowl of Wheaties and considering the full implications of what I'd learned today.

A man had been on the run, had called his closest friend. A number he had probably known. Presumably, he had borrowed a phone. The victim was scared. The victim had no known reason to be scared, no known reason to be on the run. He was malnourished, with rat and possum meat in his stomach. He had contracted tuberculosis. How?

I shake my head, eat my cereal.

I would like to know where he placed that call from. I nod to myself. Yes, that would be very, very important to know. And so, I set aside my bowl of Wheaties and take out my cell phone, and text the detective, carefully pushing each raised button, silently thanking again the inventor of such a device. I ask my question, then rest the phone on my lap. For me, there is nothing more lost than a misplaced cell phone.

I am three bites into my next round of Wheaties when the cell buzzes in my lap. I don't need to pick it up to piece together the coded message that comes through.

Yes, Hammer had gotten a hold of the owner of the phone number. Apparently, the owner had been approached by a wild man who begged to use his phone. It had happened at the entrance to Griffith Park.

Exactly where I had been yesterday.

I thought about that as I finished my cereal, letting my pooch lick the bowl clean.

I'm cool like that.

30

A busy day.

I'm not used to busy days. I'm used to my morning walks to Chango. I'm used to sitting on my balcony and feeling the sun on my face. I'm used to reading in braille. I'm used to re-reading that week's newspaper. I'm used to cleaning my tracheal tube, of petting Betsie, of the occasional neighbor who stops by just to give me a hug. I'm used to my showers and dinners and walking the interior of my apartment, touching everything, picking up everything—from books I can't read, to picture frames I can't see—and then putting them down again. I'm used to sitting quietly, hours on end. I'm used to dozing off and wondering what time it is, and am often surprised that it is either later at night or early in the morning or sometimes just a few minutes later, too. My days are simple. They have to be. Or, at least, I have convinced myself they have to be.

Now, just as I settle down with the latest James Rollins adventure—well, the latest release from my braille book club—my cell phone vibrates at my hip.

Busy, busy day. At least for me.

At the closed front door, with Betsie by my side, I lower my face to the peephole—grin to myself at my private joke—and open the door, holding my dog firmly by the collar.

Her reaction is what I'm waiting for. Her reaction is what I need to help gauge the intent of the visitor. Will Betsie recognize them? Will she feel threatened? Cautious? Excited?

Betsie doesn't move, not at first. A man, then? But then Betsie warms up quickly, and I feel her tail wag once, twice, slapping against my ankles. A woman, perhaps? Maybe a stranger? I raise my hand and motion 'Hi' and lift out the small notebook from my breast pocket. I show the unknown visitor the pre-written cover: "I'm sorry, but I'm blind, deaf and mute."

There is a slight pause, and I am about to show the stranger the nearby table of plastic letters, when I feel strong arms around my neck and shoulder and I gasp, which doesn't quite have the same meaning when it's through your tracheal tube. Betsie lunges at first, barking, but she settles almost immediately; I settle, too, because the arms are now holding me close, a hot face pressed into my neck, the smell of jasmine and a hint of maple syrup wafting up. The weeping is powerful and long and I hold the stranger in return, as Betsie wedges between us.

I stand there, flummoxed—and wondering if flummoxed is even a real word.

My first thought is that it is Gwen, regretting her decision, but the woman is too small. My next thought is that it might be Rachel, but the woman is too stout. After that, I'm out of suggestions. Not to mention, Betsie's own reaction. Betsie would have been growling had it been Gwen, and far more excited had it been Rachel.

When the woman is done sobbing, as my hand pats her thick hair and thick shoulders, as I mentally check off the list of all the women I know, of all the women who know where I live, of all the women I know who might suddenly appear at my door, weeping, one name finally rises to the surface, and when it does, I gasp for the second time.

When the full realization hits me, when all the pieces become painfully clear, I find myself fighting tears, too—and not succeeding very well. When we are done holding each other tight, I show her the table of plastic letters near the door, and she releases me and I stand there breathing deeply through my tracheal tube, trying not to show that each breath is a struggle, trying to be strong for the woman in front of me.

I sense her working the letters. Finally, when she is done, she touches my hand and guides me to the first letter.

"I miss him so much," it spells.

I remove my notepad again, and flip to the first blank page—as indicated by the dog-eared corner—and use my felt-tip pen to write: "I do, too."

We stand like that for maybe a minute. I might have thought she left, if not for the fact that Betsie is still sitting next to me, tail still wagging intermittently.

A few months after the accident, after I had mostly healed into the monster that I am, I had asked my brother to take me to visit someone. He had, although he had resisted, which is the story of our past five years. Anyway, with my brother waiting outside, I had met with the family I had torn apart. I had written my apology beforehand and presented it to them. I had waited, seemingly forever, until I had felt a hand on my shoulder, then an arm around both shoulders, and, before I had known it, the wife of my now-dead partner hugged me harder than I deserved. That's all, a single hug. I never heard from his two teenage daughters. If they forgave me, I don't know. But her hug had sustained me all these years. It had been enough, even if I never knew the exact meaning behind the hug. But I had felt forgiveness and sympathy, and it was more than I could ask for.

And now, here she is again.

I put pen to paper and write: "Not a day goes by that I don't think of him."

She takes my hand, notepad and all, in both of hers, and holds it warmly. She'd been holding a tissue in one of her hands, damp with tears.

When she releases me a minute or two later, I write: "I am so sorry—"

But she stops my hand, apparently reading my words upside down. I feel her brush past me, leaning over the table, spelling out words for me to read.

"No more apologies, Lee. It was an accident."

I absorb her words and then nod. I wonder what her life has been like these past five years, without her husband. How were the kids coping? Did they forgive me as readily? Mitch had not just been a partner. We had been friends. Gwen and I often did things together with his family. I had known his little girls well. I had felt a part of his family.

Over the years, I had often wondered if I would feel Mitch around me. I never had. No surprise there. People move on when they die, don't they? They don't stick around and torment their disabled ex-partners. Then again, maybe he was presently haunting me and I don't know it. Maybe he swung by every once in a while, hung out in the far corner and watched me sadly before disappearing again. Maybe that's why Betsie would look up every now and then and seemingly bark, although she seems to be doing this less and less these days. Maybe she had gotten used to him.

I keep these thoughts to myself, as I keep most thoughts. I live in a world of eternal, internal dialogue. If I don't like the way my own thoughts flow, or the kind of thoughts I thought, I would have surely gone mad by now. Then again, the jury is still out.

We continue standing there, facing each other, one of us, no doubt, looking at the other, perhaps sympathetically, perhaps pitifully, undoubtedly with a heavy heart, while the other just stands there, sunglasses covering his eyeless eyes, oblivious to everything but his own never-ending thoughts and his own beating heart.

Now I feel Shanna step past me again, working the plastic letters on the table. I wait and breathe and listen to the silence and listen to my heart and feel Betsie wiggle a little against my foot. I hadn't noticed, but one of her big, undoubtedly stinky, paws is plopped right on top of my big toe. I wiggle my toe and she shifts her weight but doesn't move.

Finally, after a few minutes of what I can only imagine is spent in concentrated spelling, Shanna takes my hand and guides me to the first letter, a letter that spells out a long sentence:

"You have suffered enough, Lee. Let Mitch's death go. He is in a better place. Rebuild your life. You have been given a second chance. Do something. Do something great. Don't be afraid to live. Mitch would want that."

And with that, she gives me another hug, not quite as full-bodied as the first, cradles my face with both hands, and leaves.

31

Jacky doesn't come alone.

Apparently, my brother, in his haste to leave me, had forgotten to cancel his deal with the old Irish boxer. Then again, Jacky had taken it upon himself to show up unannounced.

At the door, and trying my best to comprehend the situation, I realize that it's Jacky my boxing trainer, and a friend. I soon find myself, after a slightly awkward exchange using the plastic letters on the table, pumping the hand of a man named John Wang.

It is early. I had been sleeping just moments ago. In fact, I am not one hundred percent certain that I'm not dreaming. One minute, I had been asleep—and the next my hip was buzzing. Betsie is at my feet, tail wagging excitedly. At least she is wide awake.

It takes me a moment to realize that John Wang is still holding my hand. In both of his, no less, reminding me a bit of the old man Jack in Griffith Park, the old man who had seemed to know all my secrets. Or one big one:

My prayer.

Now, while John Wang continues holding my hand in both of his—and while I continue trying to wake up and ascertain what the hell is happening—Jacky is busy working the letters at the table. John Wang continues to shake my hand, although his shake has turned into something much more than a shake. He's outright holding my hand, whoever he is. I smile and try to pull back, but he doesn't release it, not yet. His hands are warm, kind, strong, firm. And, if I had to take a stab at another adjective, I would say…electric. Indeed, his hands seem to be alive with… energy. Something, something I can't quite place my finger on, although my whole damn hand is on it, apparently.

Finally, Jacky takes my elbow, and John Wang releases my hand. A sort of connection is broken, and I am left reeling a little as Jacky guides me over to the table and plastic letters.

Definitely dreaming.

The old boxer leads me to the first plastic letter. I pick up each in turn, spelling out: "John is an old friend of mine. A martial arts expert. A true master's master. He was in town, and I asked him to see you."

I hold up the letter "Y" as my notepad is in my bedroom, next to my dresser.

Jacky gets busy spelling with the letters again. "Never mind that. He will teach you much. I have to leave. You are in good hands, lad."

And, as my mouth drops open, the old Irishman pats me on the shoulder, gives me a half hug, and then is gone, leaving me alone with John Wang.

A master's master.

32

I am not sure how I feel about this, but I also realize I do not have much choice in the matter. Besides, Betsie seems okay with it, although she doesn't seem overly excited. Subdued would be the best way to describe her.

John Wang takes my elbow gently and leads me into my living room. He then bends down and pats Betsie two or three times on the head, and she dashes off somewhere into the apartment. My guess, my bedroom, where I sometimes find her curled up on my bed. In my spot, no less. The hairy booger.

I stand just on the edge of my living room, where I feel the floor shaking and vibrating beneath my feet, as the master's master is moving some furniture around. Maybe I am using the title facetiously. I had never heard of a person referred to as a *master's master*. What was he so damn masterful at? Kicking and punching?

After a short wait, he takes my elbow again and guides me forward, and then down onto a cushion. My couch cushion no less. I step onto it gracelessly—story of my life—and then he guides me into a sitting position, in the center of the cushioned couch square. I note that he takes a seat on the wooden floor in front of me, bypassing the cushion. We have yet to speak directly to each other. Which might be a problem, since I don't have my pen and notepad handy.

I sign: "Do you know sign language?"

I don't get a response, nor do I really expect to. I can feel him breathing not too far away, and I am catching traces of garlic in the air. He is sitting directly in front of me. Our knees, I am certain, are almost touching. I am distinctly aware that things are about to go off script for me, into waters I suspect I am not so familiar with or comfortable with. What the hell has the little Irishman gotten me into?

I lower my hands to my knees and wait, breathing smoothly through the hole in my trachea. I had cleaned and installed a new tube just last night. My airway is open and clear and I can almost take a full breath. I do so now, drawing it in deeply and smoothly and wondering where Betsie was and where my brother was and where Rachel was, and what John Wang wanted with me. I wondered where Rachel lived, too. Did she have roommates? Was she divorced? I knew only that she did not have kids and that she was about eight years younger than I was. I knew little of the woman I had so thoroughly kissed the other night.

Warm hands slip into my own, lifting them, holding them, his thumbs resting on the backs of my hands. My own fingers curl over his a little, and I feel uncomfortable holding a stranger's hands, even though the gesture isn't intimate. He could have been a psychic or a palm reader holding my hands. Or someone in church, back when I used to go to a Pentecostal church in my teens. His gesture has little to do with showmanship either. I have a sense that he is…balancing me somehow. Steadying me. And giving me a little of himself, too, although I am not sure why I feel that way.

He grips my hands a little tighter, raises them off my knees, up before me, supported by him. I feel his unmistakable and undeniable strength. I suspect he could leverage a lot of damage with those hands.

He holds my hands like this for a few minutes. When my hands start to drop, he lifts them firmly, holds them before me, a gesture that seems to tell me to focus and sit still.

I'm still dreaming.

We sit there for Lord knows how long. Twice I might have nodded off. And once or twice, I realized I might have been in a meditative state, too. I know this state, although I don't usually refer to it as *meditative*. I can slip into it often, that place between sleep and wakefulness, that place that is sometimes very, very hard for me to distinguish the real from the unreal.

Two or three times I attempt to withdraw my hands— but there is no escaping that grip, not if I don't want to struggle. He has my hands and, for the time being, he isn't letting go.

As the minutes pass and as more and more warmth and energy and God knows what else flows from the man named John Wang to me, I feel myself slip more and more out of my body, out of this world, or out of my mind. I am not sure which. A sense of dreaming, perhaps. A sense of standing back and watching something happening to me. I seem to be becoming…unmoored from this place and time.

Maybe I've been drugged.

But I doubt it.

I'd recently had a similar experience, hadn't I? Back when I'd felt myself expanding further and further away from the balcony, filling the parking lot, stretching out to the trees and sky beyond…

Now, I felt myself rising only a few feet above my body, as if I were standing directly behind myself.

Yes. I must surely be asleep or drugged.

I also sense that someone is standing before me as well. A man smaller than me, although I don't know how I know this. But I sense him there, standing before me. A small man.

Dreaming.

How else to explain that I feel myself standing outside of my body, and see the shape and outline of a man standing before me, a small man? I don't know how to explain it. I don't know what is happening to me.

But I do know that I somehow feel separate from my body, separate but still connected, a sensation I am not fully prepared for, but one that isn't entirely uncomfortable. In fact, it feels liberating. It feels like freedom.

Freedom from my own mind.

Somehow, I continue to sense the smallish man standing in front of me. Not quite seeing, but perceiving somehow. Surely my imagination. And just as that thought crosses my mind, another thought appears.

And not just a thought.

A single word:

Vibration.

I focus on the word, because it is not a word I normally use, not in this context. And as I focus on the word, I felt its truth. Yes, that's it. I am sensing the vibration of the man before me. How I sense it, I don't know. What, exactly, *vibration* means, in this context, I don't know that either. But this word feels right. I am perceiving his vibration.

And not just *his* vibration. I can see me, too. But my perspective is somehow from above. As if I am standing directly above my sitting body. Above and behind a little. It's as if I have somehow stepped *into* my imagination...

There I am, sitting on the cushioned square, with a small, gray-haired man holding my hands. My imagination, surely. Yes, obviously. But somehow more than my imagination. Much more. All surrounded in a staticy, blue-green light.

What's happening?

And for an answer, I get the surprise of my life when I hear the softest of whispers appear in my thoughts, a whisper with the hint of a Chinese accent. A whisper that appears, seemingly, just inside my ear:

"You are seeing, Lee Jordan."

33

The sound is so starling, so life-changing, that I gasp and try to sit back.

Except the man in front of me doesn't release my hands, doesn't allow me to sit back. Doesn't allow me to move much at all.

So strong.

I feel myself breathing evenly through the tube in my throat, a tube that leads directly into my lungs. The tube uses an artificial filter. It has to. I have no other way to extract pollutants and impurities from the air.

Am I asleep? I hear myself ask, the words forming haphazardly in my thoughts, scattered and almost incoherent, not as cleanly and neatly as the accented words.

Who, exactly, do you expect to answer this question, Lee? Your subconscious mind? If so, the mind can play all sorts of tricks on you. You know this better than most.

Then who's speaking to me? I ask, now using the back of my tongue to sub-vocalize each word carefully.

No need to form the words, Lee, comes the voice again. *We are here together, in this place without words. In this place of vibration. Thoughts are vibration, you know. As is everything that comes to you and from you. As is everything that fills the world and the Universe. I am here to teach you to see the vibration.*

Are you sure I'm not dreaming?

In that moment, the man before me squeezes my physical hands. The gesture is small, but it sends a jolt through me, and briefly rockets me back into my body, I gasp and raise my head and I am back in the living room again, feeling the warmth of his hands, the softness of the cushion, the slight tingling of blood being cut off to my right foot.

I think you know who sent me here, Lee.

Jack, I think, forming the word at the back of my throat, despite being told not to. I wasn't used to speaking with my thoughts. Hell, who would be?

Jack goes by many names, Lee.

I imagine he does.

Good, you are doing good. Let the thoughts flow.

You can really hear my thoughts?

I can, Lee.

All of them?

The ones I choose to focus on. The ones I believe are relevant to our present situation. Those thoughts come to me freely. Those thoughts vibrate similarly. I tune in to that vibration.

Am I dead?

Not yet, Lee. But if you keep talking about that gun in your drawer, then you might be before your time.

I have a time?

We all do, Lee. Many of them. A few of yours have come and gone.

What do you mean?

Windows. Or exit points.

The explosion, I think.

That was one, certainly. Others have been each time you sit next to your dresser, contemplating the gun.

I think about that often.

Too often, Lee. Let it go. The voice in my head continues: *There have been other exit points, but each time, you've refused them and continued on.*

A person can do that?

They can, Lee. And I am not in your head. Not really. In our present state, we are speaking to each other rather naturally.

Through vibration?

Right, Lee.

Is this what it's like to be dead?

Very similar, but not similar. Remember, I am not dead either. I am a man, like you.

I nearly snort. In fact, I think I might have snorted. A vibrational snort, maybe. *You hardly seem like any man I know.*

I feel him smile. Or perhaps I am seeing him smile. He does seem to be taking on my shape in my mind's eye. Hard to know. But I do know he's smiling, somehow.

More words appear in my thoughts: *I am just a man who has some skills.*

What kind of skills? And why are you here?

There is a long pause...and then I feel him squeeze my hands back in the physical world. Finally, the words appear in my mind—or wherever the hell they are appearing: *I am here, Lee, to help you see.*

34

I nearly open my eyes.

But I don't. Not yet. First of all, I really don't believe this is happening. Second, I haven't felt threatened. Third, I'm enjoying this relaxed state of mind I've found myself in. It's peaceful, blissful. I feel free. Free from my mind, where I spend all my days and nights, forever and ever......and ever.

His hands squeeze mine gently.

Shall I continue, Lee?

Please, I think, and as the word comes and goes, I wonder again if I am doing nothing more than having a conversation with myself. Or asleep in bed, spooning with my dog.

If so, appears the lightly accented words, *then it's not so bad a conversation, eh?*

I smile at this and nod and feel myself drifting gently above my sitting body, floating perhaps, yet still moored to my body below. I do not know if I am really floating or imagining I'm floating. If I am in my head, or outside of my body.

Maybe a little of everything, comes John's thoughts.

Fat lot of good that does me.

You're doing great, Lee.

For a newbie?

I sense a smile, then: *Yes, but you have been doing this for longer than you know.*

Doing what?

Vibrating, perceiving, knowing, understand, feeling.

Who are you?

I am a healer.

Jacky said you are a master's master.

A title I did not give myself, but I am honored to receive it.

Why does he call you a master's master?

Because I've been doing this for a while, Lee.

Doing what?

Manipulating the energy around me, focusing it, using it, working with it, guiding it, directing it.

Through martial arts? I ask.

At first. Martial arts is a very physical representative of flowing energy—energy we call chi, although others call it prana or well-being or the Holy Spirit. It is the same stuff, and it can all be directed.

Directed how?

By giving your attention to what you want. Some of us are better than others. Some of us spend a lifetime—many lifetimes—learning how to direct it.

Do you help others?

Yes, Lee.

Are you an angel?

We can all be angels, if we so choose. We can all be devils, too.

You choose to help others?

I do.

Where are we right now?

Here, in your apartment.

I don't feel like I'm in my apartment. I feel...higher somehow.

I have raised your vibration, Lee, so that you can meet me in this place.

What place?

The frequency of healing.

That makes no sense.

Maybe not, but it will.

Fine. So our bodies vibrate...lower?

Correct.

How am I vibrating higher?

I am helping you, Lee. I am guiding you up through the frequencies.

This is all very weird.

I imagine so, come his words.

But also...comfortable too, I add.

You have been here before, Lee. In fact, this is where your higher self resides.

Higher self?

Your soul.

This is a lot to take in.

I imagine it is.

I'm enjoying this communication, I say. *I am enjoying the freedom of it, the speed of it.*

I imagine so, Lee.

Can I talk to others like this?

Of course.

But they will need to meet me up here, in this higher frequency.

Very good.

But not everyone can, I say.

No, but all have the ability.

Fat lot of good that does me.

I sense him smiling. *Now, are you ready?*

I am...I think.

Good. Now open your eyes.

But I don't have eyes.

Here you do, Lee. Just as you have ears and a voice to speak.

I think I understand, but I'm not sure. In this place—this place of vibration and spirit—there are no physical maladies. Or so I think.

I do not know how to open my eyes.

Try, Lee.

I'd been seeing swirling images and shadows during my unlikely conversation with John Wang, but I mostly thought they were my imagination, but now, I am not so sure. I have never imagined such light and shadows before. I live in my imagination. I know it well. The light I am seeing—a swirling, bluish light—is new to me. Just as hearing John Wang's voice just inside my ear is new to me.

I spend the next few moments struggling with self-doubt, questioning my sanity, my wakefulness, my coherence, and, when I finally push past all the questions and concerns and confusion, I decide that this is worth pursuing, this is worth taking seriously. I decide that a lot has gone into this moment in time. Whether real or imaginary, I had nothing to lose in seeing this through. Literally. To see through the darkness. If possible.

I don't understand what's happening.

Do you need to understand, Lee?

It would be nice.

A small chuckle washes over me gently. I don't so much hear it, as feel it. And now a long string of words, softly accented, appear in my thoughts: *Very well. Everything is made of vibration, Lee. Even modern science is finally catching up with this concept.*

Fine, I think. *So the world is made of vibration. That still doesn't help me see the vibration. Unless you forget: I don't have eyes. I have nothing.*

You have more than eyes, Lee. You are much, much more than your physical apparatus. You have spiritual eyes, so to speak. You must learn to open them.

We are silent for a few moments. Hell, maybe longer than a few moments. I feel myself sort of…drifting in the place between places, this world of good vibrations.

How am I hearing? I ask.

You are interpreting the vibrations, Lee. It is easier for you to believe that you can hear in this space, than to believe you can see.

So, that's what it comes down to? I ask. *Belief?*

That has always been it, Lee. Since time immemorial.

But I do not know how to open my eyes, I say again. I'm feeling some anxiety now. Panic.

I feel, way down below in my physical body—a body that I am connected to but somehow drifting above— John Wang release one of my hands. Shockingly, surprisingly, I feel him gently remove my sunglasses. As they slide from my temples and off my face, I hear his words: *Then open your physical eyes, Lee.*

You won't like what you see, I say.

I've seen worse. Now, breathe. Calm down. Good. Breathe. You can do this, Lee. You are hearing me, speaking to me. In fact, your physical lips are moving even now.

Which made sense. This telepathic stuff, or vibrational stuff, was new to me. Hell, it would be new to anyone. I had no doubt that my physical lips were forming the words that I was sending telepathically. Perhaps seeing would be no different. Perhaps opening my physical eyes would prompt my spiritual eyes. Or something like that.

Something like that, Lee. Very good…

Except hearing you and speaking to you could very well be my imagination. Seeing you…seeing you would be something different altogether.

Like you said, Lee…you have nothing to lose.

And everything to gain?

You have no idea, Lee.

I take in some calming breaths, but I might as well be a distant observer. The physical effort of breathing seems to be happening to someone else or, at best, only as a memory. In this place, at this time, I do not feel disabled or injured or weak or lacking, I feel free and unhindered and expansive. I continue to breathe, slowly. He is right, of course. I am speaking to him—or, at least, to someone, even if it is my own subconscious. Still, if I can hear him and speak to him in this world of vibration…then maybe, just maybe, I can see him, too.

Maybe.

*Good, Lee, good…*comes his voice from a distance, drifting to me as if from across a great void, reverberating over me, surrounding me, lifting me, encouraging me.

Who are you? I ask.

Never mind that, Lee…it is time.

Time for what?

To open your eyes.

It had been years since I last opened my eyes willingly. And never in front of anyone. But I do so now, in front of the stranger named John Wang. The stranger who is a master's master.

I open my physical eyes, slowly, lifting the sticky, heavy, useless lids, and in so doing, I open something else.

I open my spiritual eyes.

35

I am dreaming.

I have to be. This can't be real. What I am seeing... can't...be...real.

I am, in fact, not floating above my body. That had been a misperception. A trick of the mind, perhaps. Or an effect of whatever drug I'd been slipped.

The light. That's what I see first. Bluish light. No, blue-green light, filtering in through my lids, blasting all the way to the back of my skull. My instinct is to shy away from the light, but this isn't physical light is it? And I don't have physical eyes.

Go with it, Lee, comes a quiet voice just inside my ears. *And quit thinking so much. You can think yourself out of this place and back into your body. We don't want that. Not now.*

I did just that. I quit analyzing, quit questioning.

I continue staring into the bluish-green light, light which seems to come to me in waves. Pulsating, vibrating waves. If I look deep enough—and I do at first—I can see what I probably shouldn't be seeing: smaller light particles, zigzagging and swirling, forming the bigger waves.

I wasn't drugged. I wasn't asleep. I wasn't imagining this. I wasn't hallucinating. I wasn't high. I wasn't giving in to suggestion. I wasn't dead or crazy. At least, I don't think so.

Maybe this is really happening, I think, as the magnificent waves of blue-green light pulse toward me and through me. Through everything, in fact.

I see more than just the blue-green light. I see everything it illuminated in my apartment, as well—everything it touched and surrounded. Everything, everywhere. Nothing escapes the light. From where it streamed, I don't have a clue. But I am willing to bet it has always been there.

What I am seeing? I ask.

It's called Source Energy, Lee, it flows continuously, abundantly and powerfully. You are tuned into it. But it is more than light, Lee. You perceive it as light. But it is, in actuality, the vibration of creation you are seeing. It is the source of all creation. The source of all love, light, peace—the source of all that which is good.

And none that is bad? I ask.

The light does not determine good or bad, Lee. Bad only occurs when the light is pinched off, closed off, or shut out.

And then it hit me, and it hit me hard.

Is this light…God?

There is a small pause in our dialogue as I watch the glowing particles drift in and out of my existence, flowing, glowing, twisting, vibrating, illuminating, expanding…

Yes, Lee. Or, more accurately, you are seeing God's love, pouring to you and through you. Ever it flows. Continuously, abundantly, lovingly, peacefully, eternally. For all time and forever more, you have God's attention and love and continuous support. It is up to you, and only you, to learn to perceive it.

I'm not, you know, very religious…

Does this look like religion, Lee? Are these pages to a dusty old book flowing to you? Or are you seeing God in real time?

I'm seeing something.

Something is enough, Lee. Let it flow. Let it flow through you. Feel the love. Feel the appreciation that source has for all that you are doing. You are loved, Lee, even if you don't know it or believe it or feel it.

Then what's the point? I ask.

There is no point, Lee. You make of this information as you wish. You do with it as you wish. The Creator—the source of the love you are seeing—has no demands, no desires.

Then why bother? I ask.

That's for you to answer, Lee.

And if my answer is...screw it all?

Then all would be screwed. But still, you will be loved, and still, He will be there, waiting, flowing.

For what purpose? I ask.

To create, Lee. To expand. To stretch further and further. To go places even God hasn't gone before. To create families and stories and inventions and homes and dreams and books and movies. To create that which has not been created before. With each new idea, with each new spark of interest, the Universe expands and grows and that, in a nutshell, is the purpose.

But I haven't expanded in many years, I say. Or think. Or whatever.

Expansion doesn't have to be the next great invention, Lee. It can be a desire to grow in small ways. A decision to be happier. A stirring for a new haircut, taking a cooking class, trying a new recipe, trying out a new route to work. Sometimes, these smaller expansions can be as delicious as the big ones.

Is someone hungry? I ask.

Another chuckle. *The key here, Lee, is that the Creator, the Universe, God, call it what you want, is expanding whether we know it or not.*

I am dwelling on these words, when John Wang continues: *But there is something here that you might be missing,*

Lee, something that is useful for all those who seek and hunger for more.

And what's that?

This powerful force of creation that can be utilized, can be directed, can be used to enhance your own life. This is, after all, the force that creates universes. You are seeing but a small sample of it around you. Learn to use it, to play with it, to love it, and to live within it...and you might be very, very surprised at the results.

I nod, although I do not know if my physical head nods or not. A part of me nods. An idea of me nods. Either way, I find myself scanning the room I've lived in in darkness for half a decade.

This is really happening, I think. *I'm seeing it. I can see the man sitting in front of me. I can see my couches, I can see the coffee table moved over to one side. All of which look exactly as I remember. Except...*

Except...I'm not seeing the exact couch. I'm seeing a ghostly hint of it, an echo of it, the vibration of it.

I can feel my heart thumping in my chest, harder and harder as I look around more and more. This is real. This is happening now.

This is magical.

I see John Wang sitting in front of me, holding my hands, legs crossed, head bowed slightly, eyes closed. The light waves surround him powerfully, and seem to emanate from him as well.

Yes, I think. Magic...

I am taking all of this in and more, when I see movement to my left. I don't so much turn as shift my focus to my left—and there she is, trotting into the living room from the kitchen, water droplets, sparkling like so many diamonds, dripping from her muzzle. A long, wet, glowing tongue unfurls and sweeps along her muzzle. She does this a few more times as she continues to stare at John Wang. And when she's done licking her lips, she turns her gaze fully onto me.

Betsie... my baby girl.

I knew she was a golden retriever, I just wasn't prepared to see how big she was. Hell, I wasn't prepared to see her at all. I never, in a million years, could have predicted last night, when I went to bed, that I would wake up and, in a few short minutes, begin seeing my sweet doggie.

It's her. It's really her.

Unless, of course, I'm dreaming. I have often dreamed of her. In my dreams, she's smaller, more petite. This dog before me is all business. Thick-chested. Long, curling fur. Paws that could take down a small plane.

Her stinky paws.

I am most impressed by her muscle tone, which ripples under her flowing fur.

We should all be so ripped, I think.

She stares at me for a long moment, undulating slightly in the blue-green light. No, I can't see her golden color. I can't see color of any type. But I can see shades and depth and detail. Not striking detail. But enough.

More than enough, I think.

She blinks long and hard, pants a little, and when she does, her dark lips curl into what I will go to my grave thinking is a smile. A beautiful, perfect smile. And then she looks over at the couch. Looks at me again, and then trots through the living room—the vibrations of which reach me now—and hops up on the couch. She turns once, twice, then curls into a tight ball of eighty pounds of pure muscle and love and devotion.

I am left reeling and emotional and fighting tears.

Never, never could I have hoped to see my doggie, and there she is now, on the couch, and bathed in blue-green light. In fact, everything is bathed in blue-green. My hands, the room, the man in front of me, the shimmering particles in the air. It is, I think, the most beautiful color I can imagine.

It is called Winter Wind, says the accented voice, his words reaching me now as if from a great distance.

Winter Wind, I say to myself forming the words in my mind. The words seem fitting. The room is, indeed, the color of a bleak winter landscape. *What would happen if I were to stand?* I ask.

You would lose your focus and everything you see before you would disappear.

So then, I must always be in a state of deep meditation?

For now, Lee, but I will teach you how to work with the Winter Wind, to use it more readily. Now, let's continue…

And continue we do, for another hour or so, but I am often distracted, not always listening, looking at my dog, my apartment, the light coming in through the sliding glass doors, at the picture frames that sit forgotten on book shelves and the entertainment center. There's my old TV, still in its same spot, although long since unplugged. There's a picture of Gwen and me, of my brother, my now-deceased parents. All filtered through the greenish-blue lens of the Winter Wind, not quite turquoise but almost. That the word 'turquoise' would even occur to me again was a miracle.

When the hour is up, I sense a change in the room, a retreating of light, a sort of drawing back…

No, I say, as the light begins to fade. *Please, not yet…*

The energy is always there, Lee. The well-being flows continuously, with or without me.

Trust me, I couldn't see this without you.
You will, Lee, with practice.

And with that, he releases my hands—and the world goes black, as I'm plunged into total silence and blackness. I reach out blindly to the little man in front of me—I know he is little, now that I have seen his staticy image in my thoughts, and hug him tighter than I'd intended, tighter than I'd ever hugged another man. Even my own brother. To John Wang's credit, he hugs me back, patting my shoulder.

Finally, my hands drop onto the Pergo floor, and I feel John Wang rise to his feet. Smoothly, I suspect. A moment later, I feel the floorboards shifting and shortly after that, the subsonic vibration of the front door opening and closing.

Alone and still on my knees, I find myself weeping into my hands. Which is about the time Betsie comes over and curls up on the couch square next to me. Right there in the center of the living room floor. I remember again her longish fur, her thick paws, her thick tail.

I'd seen her. Oh, yes; I'd seen her.

36

It is the next morning and Rachel is with me.

Prior to her visit, I had gotten a text message from Detective Hammer—a message spelled out in Morse code—that he had updated the file with medical histories. Additionally, he'd found something interesting and was adding it to the updated file, a file that Rachel would be bringing over.

I'd spent last night and this morning going through the instructions left to me by John Wang, instructions for me to access the Winter Wind on my own. So far, nothing, and with each try, my hope diminishes, to the point that I'm now questioning the experience altogether.

No, I think again, perhaps for the hundredth time. *It happened.*

I either believe it happened...or else, I'm losing my mind. And I don't want to lose my mind. Not now, not ever. I don't want to have to open that drawer. Yesterday morning had been so beautiful, so earthshaking—that even if I never have another experience like that again, even if I am never able to access the Winter Wind again— that one experience was enough.

At least, that's what I tell myself.

I debated telling Rachel about John Wang and the Winter Wind, and decided I would wait until I had some control over it—or until I gave up on it entirely.

Now, while we take a break and she is in the kitchen making us more coffee on the Keurig, I wish like crazy that I could rise above myself now, up into that blue-green world of shapes and energy and light, and see what she really looks like. How did she look standing at the counter? How did she look when she smiled? How did she look when she concentrated and signed and kissed and held me? How did she look when she kissed me?

Soon, she returns with the coffee and I smile and mouth the words 'thank you,' and when she sets the steaming mug in my hands, I sip it and love it and soon we are going through the reports again.

That she needs to hold my hand to communicate with me is a pleasure and intimacy that few of the sighted will ever experience. As always, her touch is light and firm and sensual. Sometimes, her fingertips tickle me, often they caress me. I know her signs well now. Sometimes, I can predict the word and nod before she is finished. Always, I sit there with a half-smile on my face, even as she lays out the life stories of those who have gone missing.

I had read the initial report in braille. I knew the names. I knew their stories. I hadn't known their medical records. So far, none of the missing had any diseases worth noting. In fact, all of them seemed damned healthy. Almost too healthy.

Soon, we come upon a new name, the latest addition to the file. An addition made by Hammer just the day before.

"His name is Mack Carpenter," she signs into my hand. "Retired. Lived alone. Wasn't reported missing for weeks. There's a notation here from Hammer saying that the victim may or may not be related to this case. Hammer is guessing not, which is why he had been left out of the

Big Case. But you asked him to cull the surrounding area for anything of note, and this is the only thing of note he could find."

"When did he go missing?" I sign.

There's a pause as she reads the new file. "Over a year ago, before any of the others. Hammer's notes indicate that Mack Carpenter's disappearance is being investigated, as of now, as a separate case."

I nod. "What do we know about Mack Carpenter?"

"A retired veterinarian with the Los Angeles Zoo, where he'd worked for over forty years. His home was paid off. His cars were paid off. His wife died a decade earlier from cancer. He lived alone. Nice retirement benefits. No sickness that the daughter knows about. No mention of suicide and no demons in his closet, as far as she's aware. As in, no gambling, drugs or vices that could have gotten him into trouble."

"In short," I sign, "he had no real reason to disappear."

"Hard to know," she answers into my palm.

"What are the circumstances of his disappearance?"

She goes on to read the rest of the report. Mack was much older than the other missing persons, and his disappearance hadn't been discovered for weeks, not until a neighbor had reported not seeing the old man for a while. No body was found. No sign of any foul play. Unlike the others, Mack Carpenter had taken out a large sum of money—most of his retirement, in fact. Additionally, they found a Greyhound bus receipt on his credit card. Apparently, he'd purchased a ticket to Arizona. A search of the local Greyhound surveillance had turned up nothing and the case was eventually pushed aside. No body. A missing old man. The department had bigger fish to fry, especially as others started showing up missing, others that followed a predictable pattern.

She finishes signing and rests her hand in my own, and as I think about the Case, playing the names over and over, the circumstances over and over, sensing Rachel's serenity, feeling her body warmth, something happens, something beautiful and magical and startling—and it only happens for the briefest of seconds.

Blue-green light flashes in my mind, fills my thoughts. For the briefest of moments, I am in the Winter Wind... and I see myself sitting there next to a smallish woman in a long dress, who wears thick glasses and whose hair is bobbed just above her shoulders. And then the vision is gone and I'm plunged back into darkness.

37

I'm at Chango, sitting in the shade, a mug of hot coffee in one hand and Betsie's harness in the other.

The walk down had been gradual and methodical, like always. We'd crossed the three-way intersection without incident. I had ordered and paid with my credit card, scribbling my name where Olga the barista had guided my hand to do so. They all know me here—and we all know the routine. In fact, many of the workers had even learned sign language over the years, often signing greetings into my open palm.

The shade is nice. The sun is nice, too. In about an hour, the sun will angle over the nearby line of trees and shine full force onto this very spot. As I sit and drink and feel Betsie panting against my leg, I sense what I sometimes sense when I come here. I sense someone sitting opposite me. In fact, sometimes even Betsie looks up and looks over. But I don't feel the table shift with the weight of, say, someone's elbows, or the ground vibrate with the scraping of a chair.

No, I only sense a presence. And it's a strong presence. It has weight to it. Heft to it. It has intent and focus. That is, if it existed—which it doesn't, because there's never anyone sitting opposite me.

Just my imagination.

The hair on my neck is standing on end, as if there's an electric charge to the air. As if a goose has walked across my grave.

Someone's here.

And again I reach out across the table, reaching for something or someone that isn't there. Indeed, I only feel the coolness of shade, the cold table, and not much of anything else.

I must look ridiculous, reaching out. I am sure others are looking at the pathetic blind man reaching for something that is not there, confused and lost and miserable.

Chango and I go way back. It is here that my now-deceased partner and I often started our days. It is here we often discussed our cases and developed plans of attack. It is here where we often got word of new homicides. It is here where we had laughed and goofed on each other, and made friends with the locals. It is here where we revisited the horrors of our jobs and found strength in each other, whether spoken or not.

It is here where I feel my friend the most.

If I hadn't known better—if I hadn't just verified that the seat in front of me wasn't taken—I would have guessed that a living, breathing person had just sat across from me.

I drink my coffee carefully, sipping. I breathe easily through the new tracheal tube I had installed this morning. Also this morning I had done the meditative exercises that John Wang had shown me. Unfortunately, the Winter Wind still eluded me when I sought it...and only seemed to come when I least expected it.

I smell exhaust, although I do not hear the cars or motorcycles. I catch a faint whiff of a clove cigarette. Although my sense of smell seems to be working better and better, I hadn't smelled anything this morning—not even my coffee—until the exhaust and the cloves.

Take what you get, I think, and sip and feel Betsie shift at my feet. Betsie is a remarkable creature, as well-trained as a canine can be...but she is still a dog. Passing animals attract her attention. Children do, too. No, she would never leave my side, but her attention will shift with something that catches her eye, even while she waits obediently, protectively, for my next command.

There is a small, gusty, cool wind this morning, just enough to ripple my hair or ruffle my shirt. The sound of the wind is something I miss the most. Hearing it blow over ears and through branches and open car windows... it is nature at its best, alive and moving and seeking.

I can feel it on my skin now, in my hair and inside my bowling shirt. The hair on my forearms shifts, too, and I feel myself smiling—and feel myself slip away, but not really away. No, I am slipping *up*, if possible.

Here, but not really here.

Green-blue light fills my head and, perspective wise, I seem to be standing behind my body, looking down at the table, although I cannot see myself. No, that's not true, I see a shape, a shadow, something...but I feel it's not important to search for myself in this world of light.

Instead, I focus on the hint of a man sitting before me—and not just any man. It is my deceased partner, Mitch Anderson. At least, what looks like him. I see the shape of a man, elbows resting on the table, hands loosely forming the shape of a coffee mug. The man is not clearly defined. Not the way John Wang had been in my apartment, when he had sat before me. No, this shape was staticy and not solid—and not entirely complete either. Sometimes I can see through him and sometimes parts of his body fade completely. His right shoulder is now wavering in and out of existence. Prior to that, it had been his hands.

It could have been a hologram. It could have been a special effect. It could have been fake. But it was none of those.

It was, I was certain, the ghost of my deceased partner.

I feel my heart picking up, my breath quickening. Betsie looks up at me for a moment, then back at the ghost in front of us.

My ex-partner—a partner I had rendered into this condition because of my recklessness—doesn't appear to notice me. Hell, he doesn't appear to even move. He just sat there, holding his imaginary cup of coffee. Or maybe the cup was real to him. Maybe a ghost cup is steaming away in his hands.

He continues to flicker in and out of existence. No, I am seeing straight through him to the table beyond, where a young man is sitting with a laptop, although the laptop is much thinner than anything I'd seen before.

Mitch continues staring down into his hands. And it is Mitch, I'm sure of it. Maybe I should feel frightened. Maybe I should be questioning my sanity. I feel neither of those, other than mild shock. Truth is, I am just as surprised that I can see the man sitting behind Mitch—and sometimes even through Mitch. That I can see at all is just as wondrous and bizarre and alarming. That a ghost is also in the frame is just an added bonus.

Now, Mitch takes on more detail. Whether he can do this at will or not, I don't know. I can see what looks like a lot of damage to the left side of his face. The glow of blue-green splatters over his face and neck and shoulder is, I think, a ghost hint of blood.

I sense great sorrow from him. In fact, I can see it coming off him in slow waves of low energy, energy that eddies around him, as if the vibrations around him are sick and weak. Then again, I don't know what the hell I'm talking about, either. Still, the entity sitting before me, staring down into his imaginary cup—who seems to be composed entirely of slow-moving, low-energy light particles, looks lost. And I don't know what the hell to do about it.

Before I did anything, I absorb this moment, take it in, revel in it, even. After all, my old friend is sitting with me again at Chango.

Like old times. Or not.

Indeed, we are at our same table, sitting across from each other again. That one of us is 'seeing' through spiritual eyes and the other is dead, suddenly seems irrelevant. We are here together again.

I take it in, soak it in, and wonder if I am smiling in the physical world, too. I shouldn't be smiling. My friend is lost and haunting our old coffee shop. All because of me.

Does he see me? Does he see anyone? Does he even know he's here? Or is this just a ghostly memory of my ex-partner? I don't know any of this, but I decide to find out.

I slowly reach out with my right hand. In this world of light and energy, I see my physical right hand just beginning to move forward when I am plunged into complete darkness. I understand that the physical act of moving takes me out of my deep meditative state, a state necessary to enter the Winter Wind.

I find myself focused in my body again, feeling the small wind, the cool shade, my panting dog, and sensing a presence sitting across from me again. Try as I might,

I am not able to slip back into a meditative state, and so I sit there quietly, unmoving, until I sense the presence across from me leave. I know this because my dog turns her head and watches him go. To where, I don't know. The air itself is less energized. The agitated hair on my arms settles down, too.

Goodbye, buddy, I sign.

38

Jacky, the little old Irish boxer, is here again.

This time he came alone. No John Wang. I'd been hoping to see John Wang again. I had questions. Lots and lots of questions. About seeing and the Winter Wind. About how to sustain it, about how to move around in it.

Jacky had been boning up on his sign language, I see. Or feel. Although slow and methodical, he has learned the individual letters of alphabet. Hell, he can be as slow and methodical as he wants. I am touched beyond words, even the signed variety.

His seemingly frail fingers spell into my palm: "Are you ready to knock some heads today, cowboy?"

I nod and we begin our lesson. He first guides me through some jabbing exercises, and I lash out with my left hand, jabbing, jabbing, all while holding my right hand up in the cocked position, ready to unleash like a cannon shot. A wild, blind cannon shot. He has me moving in circles, jabbing and ducking and weaving. I feel silly, of course. I do not know how my form looks. I do not even know if he is throwing practice punches at me. Occasionally, I do feel air whoosh past my face, but that could be anything. My own breath, maybe. Or just barely missing a bookcase. He steps around my punches and sometimes taps my shoulder to stop me. He'll correct my form, guiding my hands and arms and shoulders through the motion. I wonder if he's this hands-on with his other clients. Probably not.

We do this for another thirty minutes, by which time I am sweating and dizzy from the turning in slow circles. My head is spinning and I am sucking wind hard through the small opening in my throat and now Jacky is patting my shoulder and rubbing my arms the way all boxing trainers do. I am grateful for his undivided attention. He lets me catch my breath. I suspect I am wheezing through the tracheal tube. Jacky rubs my arms and shoulder and neck the entire time I'm hunched over and doing my best to suck in enough air to feel satisfied. I feel spittle and drool forming at my neck, no doubt bubbling out of the fluted opening, and Jacky wipes it away without missing a beat. He is going far beyond the call of duty. When I stand again, breathing a little more normal, he pats my face... and puts me through another round or two of workouts. I dodge and weave invisible punches, all while punching through the combinations he has been teaching me. We take a short water break, and he signs to me that he will next be wearing punching mitts. I nod and soon I find myself swinging wildly at his mitted hands, mostly missing, but soon I get the hang of where they are, and my jabs and combinations and straight punches and hooks start landing with more consistency. I can't hear the sound my hands are making, but I feel the firm jolt as some punches land more squarely than others.

Soon I am hunched over again, gasping, hurting, hungry for air, and now, I feel his arm around my shoulders, patting me, rubbing me, helping me through this, and whoever Jacky is, I think I might just love him.

39

Betsie and I take an Uber ride to the beach.

The process seems fairly smooth to me, but perhaps, in reality, it is a clumsy one. Perhaps the driver isn't too keen on transporting a blind man and his dog anywhere. Perhaps he doesn't want the responsibility. Perhaps he is glaring at me even now. Perhaps he is sweating. Perhaps he is texting. Perhaps this is just another lift. I hope it's just another lift. I'd like to think that my existence doesn't disrupt too many lives.

As we head steadily onward, his car moving through space and time so smoothly that I often think we are at a standstill—and confident this is an electric vehicle—I think again about my brother and realize the great mistake I had made.

I had leaned too heavily on him, and he had crumbled. I should have sensed it long ago. But he kept offering, kept volunteering. I think in the beginning he had enjoyed helping his older brother. The goof-off little brother wasn't such a goof-off now, was he? How long that sense of pride had lasted, I don't know. And that it had segued into resentment, I had no doubt. I'd sensed his change long ago...and had felt helpless to do anything about it, except to be as pleasant and easy-to-work-with as possible.

But now he was gone. To where, I don't know. When I would hear from him again, I don't know either. My brother was famous for cutting people from his life. His ex-wife, and even our own father, whom my brother hadn't talked to for the last twenty years. I had no reason to doubt he would do the same to me: cut me off.

I think about this as the car comes to a stop. By my own internal clock, we have certainly been driving long enough to reach the beach. Indeed, I feel the rush of fresh air as the driver opens his door and, a moment later, my door is opened, too. I don't need my door opened, but I appreciate the gesture. Per my written instructions, he has let me off on the east side of the Santa Monica Pier. I hope. If he has dropped me off anywhere else, I will be lost.

Once standing outside, he takes my hand in both of his, shakes it, seems reluctant to leave me on my own. I give him the thumbs-up sign and smile and, a moment later, finally releases my hand and pats my shoulder, and now, I am alone with my dog.

Well, not entirely. This is, after all, Santa Monica Pier.

I snap my walking stick open, take in some air via the tube in my throat, and we move forward carefully along an arcing bridge, and then onto the pier itself.

Once there, I feel my way along the railing to the steps I am looking for...steps that will lead down to the beach below. At one point, I feel a hand on my shoulder, firmly guiding me away from the stairs. I think someone thinks I am unaware of the stairs. I smile and mouth the words thank you, and point to the steps and make little walking movements with my fingers, letting them know that all is well. The hand releases me—again reluctantly—and then

Betsie and I are working our way carefully down the pier, to the beach below.

———

We are on the sand, maybe a dozen feet from the shore-line, and a few dozen feet from the pier itself. Not quite far enough away for me to get disoriented. I hope.

I remove my backpack and spread out a blanket. I click open the oversized umbrella and lean it into the sun. I guide Betsie into the shade, where I set a water bowl in front of her and fill it with water from my bottle. Half for her, half for me. Soon, I am sitting comfortably, legs crossed, mostly in the shadows. I had already applied sunblock.

I do not know if the beach is crowded, although I sus-pect it's probably not. It's a Tuesday morning, after all. But who knows. Maybe the world, in general, is more crowded than I remember. It's also my first time here since the explosion. The beach, admittedly, loses some of its appeal when you can't see the blue ocean or hear the crashing surf.

Still, I can feel the wind and, if I'm lucky, I can even smell a hint of salt on the air.

Good enough. For now.

Betsie is breathing fast. Already it's a warm morn-ing. She's hunkered down in the shade and that's all I can really do for her. That and the water. I ease away from the shade, sit full in the sun, and cross my legs, resting my forearms on my knees. The malleable sand takes pressure off my ankles and knees, and I settle into a comfortable position.

I lift my face to sun and wind and the sprinkle of sand. I sit quietly, breathing slowly, deeply. As I do so, I feel the faintest of vibrations beneath me. A small, but deep echo that seems to emanate from the center of the earth. There it is again: another seismic groan, another shiver of sand. Again and again, so faint that I sometimes think I am making it up.

No. It's the ocean waves crashing over the nearby shore.

Betsie's harness handle rests under my knee, always connected to me. She is still in the shade of the umbrella, no doubt sound asleep: a good place to be.

I breathe calmly, easily. My clothing is loose and comfortable—workout sweats and a comfy t-shirt. I brought with me a wide-brimmed, straw hat that took some time to find…but I finally did find it on a top shelf in my closet. The hat is still in my backpack. As of now, I am enjoying the sun on my face and forehead and arms. That might change, though. If it does, I have the hat and more sunscreen, too.

As I sit and rest my hands on my knees and feel the earth groan beneath me, I am determined, once and for all, to get a handle on this Winter Wind business.

I begin with the breathing exercises that John Wang had walked me through. Slowly in, faster out; slowly in, faster out. I do this over and over, feeling spittle forming and dripping down my neck, spittle I cannot control. I let it drip. It's not hurting anything. I'm not trying to impress anyone here. Hell, I haven't tried to impress anyone since, well, since Rachel recently.

I let that thought slip away, as I continue to breathe. I try to let all thoughts slip away, breathing as easily and comfortably as I can, although I never truly get enough air through the single opening in my throat. But I am used to the amount now, although a part of me remembers when I could take big, beautiful, blissful breaths.

I let that thought slip away, too.

Letting thoughts slip away is not as easy as it sounds. Many thoughts return, over and over. Many thoughts lead to other thoughts, and I have to mentally step back and start over again. I keep starting over, keep trying to clear my thoughts. Sometimes I focus on my breathing longer than other times, and now, I have decided to focus on the wind and the sprinkling sand and the occasional whiff of salt and surf, and this seems to be doing the trick. It occurs to me at some point that, even with my eyes closed and shades on, that I should be seeing some brightness in the sky above me, a brightness that can pierce through even closed lids, until I remember, with a jolt, that I have no eyes. I do an admirable job of releasing that thought, too, and I soon find myself swaying in the wind, pushed this way and that, my hair whipping and clothing flapping. I feel the heat on my face and the sprinkle of sand and the vibrations under the earth.

It happens quickly. One moment, I am in complete darkness, and the next, blue light appears in my thoughts, filling rapidly.

I watch it fill before me, spreading, taking on shape and depth. I watch as a world of light fills my thoughts, a world of light and vibration and energy.

Once again, my perspective seems higher, as if I am standing just behind myself. I wonder if this is my soul's perspective, but let that thought go, too. There's Betsie, crashed under the umbrella, tongue lolled out, her water bowl nearby. I did a good job of setting up camp. I look down. I did a good job dressing myself, too. Looks like I mostly covered myself in sunblock, but I see I missed a swatch on the inside of my forearm.

I shift my perspective further out, and see others on the beach. A couple in front of me are hugging. The woman occasionally looks back at me. She is in a bikini and he is in shorts. Both wear shades. Neither have guide dogs. The woman crinkles her forehead as she looks at me. Now the guy turns and looks, too. They exchange words, and he shrugs and turns back around. Her gaze lingers on me, then she turns around, too. She is unaware that I am watching her in return.

So very, very weird.

The beach is indeed quiet, but not empty. No, not even on a Tuesday morning. Umbrellas and blankets are staked here and there. Kids play near the shore. Mothers watch. Others appear fast asleep, half-naked and baking in the sun.

I shift my focus further, and realize I am reaching the limits to how far I can see. *Good to know.* In this bluish light, in this world of flowing energy and vibration and ideas, the ocean looks almost as it should. The color seems right, even. I watch a smaller wave roll in—and watch a little boy run away from it, a plastic shovel in his hand, probably squealing. The wave foams and churns and then disappears seemingly into the sand.

I am overwhelmed by this and want to bury my face in my hands, but I know that if I do, I will lose my connection to the Winter Wind. Any movement, so far, breaks my connection.

I power through the gasps and the rolling tears and watch the seagulls circle overhead. I find myself fixated on the foaming, retreating surf, perhaps even mildly hypnotized. Everything I am seeing, sensing or feeling, I had thought was lost to me forever. And so, I find myself soaking it up, making up for lost time, with no guarantee I will ever see any of this again, or if this Winter Wind business will dry up and disappear…

Or until I finally wake up.

I spend many long moments in this position, my physical body unmoving, but my spiritual eyes seeing everything they can, soaking in everything they can, memorizing everything they can. I can only see so far, maybe twenty or thirty feet in every direction. I cannot see the far horizon, or even the end of the pier. But I can see enough and I am happy.

So very, very happy.

———

When I have had my fill—but already hungry for more—I turn my attention to the other reason why I am here.

I look down and see my physical body sitting on a corner of the blanket. My legs are crossed, my hands are resting on my knees. I am composed of tens of thousands of particles of light, all moving, all forming and reforming over myself. It is, I know now, the ever-flowing light of God, the light of creation, the light of love, the light of everything.

I take in some air and see my chest rise a little. I expel it and raise my right hand slowly, doing my best to maintain my connection to the Winter Wind, to remain in a deep meditative state. With mounting excitement, I watch my hand rise one, two inches—and then the world goes black, and I am plunged back into my broken body.

I gasp, and curse under my breath. Way, way under my breath.

Although I had been prepared to lose my tenuous hold on the Winter Wind, I am still jolted by the sudden darkness. I take a few minutes to collect myself. Then I go through the meditative steps again, breathing evenly, clearing my thoughts, and this time, the blue-green light returns a little quicker than before, and I find myself looking out toward the ocean.

I can do this. I want to do this. I want to be able to *move* and *see.* Is that too much to ask for?

Actually, yes it is. In fact, I have no right to ask for such a thing, or hope for such a thing. Ever.

But I am asking for it, dammit.

So, I continue breathing. Continue focusing. Continue staying calm...and lift my right hand again. This time, I watch it raise maybe three inches—definitely higher than before—before my world once again plunges into a blackness deeper than black. A Stygian darkness without hope of ever seeing light.

But I do have hope—and I now have the skills to access the creative force of the universe.

Whatever that is.

Again, I slip into a deep meditation. Again, I enter the Winter Wind. Again, I move my hand, this time not quite as high as before. And again, I find myself reeling in darkness. I do this again, and again throughout the day. I pause and add more sunscreen and drink from my bottle and continue working on meditating and connecting to the Winter Wind...and moving my arm. Higher, dammit. Higher and higher.

And higher.

40

Detective Hammer and Rachel make a surprise visit. It is later that same day, and I am officially burned from my prolonged stay in the sun. I had just popped in the last of my frozen dinners—again, my brother could have had the decency to shop with me one last time—when my phone buzzes at my hip. My phone that's hooked up to my doorbell.

Now we are sitting around my living room like old times. I offer coffee, only to discover they have brought me one from McDonald's, which Rachel sets in front of me and guides my hand to. She sits next to me, her thigh brushing mine. I can't remember a time when the brush of a thigh has been so exciting.

I think Rachel is sensing my excitement, because she takes my open hand, squeezes it and spells out: "Detective Hammer is here about your brother."

I set my coffee down, and sign: "Did you say my brother?"

She pats my arm, her indicator for yes. She next spells out: "He's been missing for three days."

"I know this already," I sign, although I'm feeling alarmed. "He told me he was leaving. He needed a break."

Rachel signs: "Detective Hammer wants to verify you've spoken with him."

I nod. Feeling sick, I sign: "He came by a few days ago. He said he needed a break. A break from me. He made it seem like he was moving."

After a pause, I feel Rachel nod as she listens to the detective before translating into my hand: "His work reported him missing. So did his girlfriend. Your brother left behind his car and his money, his computer and phone. Everything. There's no indication of foul play or that he booked a flight, bus, train or boat anywhere."

I turn away, take off my sunglasses, and wipe away the sweat that is gathering along the bridge of my nose. I sense Rachel nodding some more, listening to Hammer speak. A moment later, she takes my free hand and signs: "Hammer says that other than talking to you, his disappearance matches the others."

I find myself nodding, getting sicker by the second—and thinking back to my conversation with my brother. I had been numb and confused and if he had indicated in some way that he was planning on literally disappearing, I had missed it.

"Lee," signs Rachel, "Hammer wants you to know they have him on the Greek's video."

"When?"

"Three nights ago, near midnight."

The night he left me. I drop my hands in my lap.

After a moment, Rachel carefully picks up my right hand. "I'm sorry, Lee," she signs.

Hammer and I go over my final conversation with my brother. I do the best that I can. My brother hadn't said much, only that he needed to get away, from me, and that he was taking his girlfriend with him.

"That didn't happen," says Hammer, through Rachel. "Anything else?"

I shake my head. I was angry at my brother, hurt by my brother, confused by my brother, still reeling from his departure, still wondering if he might come to his senses and return. It had never occurred to me that I had been the only person with whom he had discussed leaving. That he had, in fact, disappeared entirely.

I look up suddenly. "He mentioned moving to Florida once he passes a few tests. At the time, I had thought he was talking about his driver's license or something. Hell, I wasn't sure. I was still in shock that he was leaving."

"Could be anything," signs Rachel for Hammer.

I nod, and sign back: "But it's something."

We all sit quietly for a moment or two. Shortly, I feel the small shift in the floorboards that seems to indicate someone is standing. Hammer drops a big hand on my shoulder. He squeezes. Now I sense him talking to Rachel, and then, I feel the floorboard moving again. A small burst of displaced air later, and the detective has left and I am alone with Rachel.

41

We sit quietly, until Rachel leans over and kisses me softly on the lips, and the sensation is jolting—and so perfect that I never want it to end. I do not remember lips being so soft and supple, but hers are. I do not remember lips being so perfect, but hers are. When she pulls away, I feel momentarily incomplete.

Until I remember that Hammer was just here to tell me that my brother is now officially part of the Big Case. Hell, they even had him on video entering the park.

Like the others...

"Once I pass the test," he had signed. And I'm pretty sure those were his words, or close to them. I don't have an eidetic memory, but I have a solid one. The blast took much from me, but not my memory. If anything, my memory is only stronger these days.

"I have more information on the first of the missing," Rachel signs a moment later.

"The zoo employee?" I sign.

"Not just an employee, but a veterinarian."

I sit back with the coffee in one hand and hold my other out for her. That I enjoy her touch so much isn't very surprising. In a way, I feel lucky that our communication is so intimate. Other people listen and wait for opportunities to touch. We touch continuously, and it's heady stuff indeed. At least, heady for me.

I sense her flipping through some notes. "Dr. Nathan Diamond had been, in fact, the lead veterinarian for the L.A. Zoo."

I nod, impressed.

"As you can imagine," she continues, pressing her small fingers into my hand, "it's quite a coveted and well-respected job. Although not as big as the San Diego Zoo, the L.A. Zoo consistently ranks as one of the top zoos in the United States."

I cradle my coffee cup in my lap and sign: "Are you reading this from Wikipedia?" I spell out Wikipedia letter-for-letter. If there's a new sign gesture for Wikipedia, I don't know it yet. And if not, someone should invent one, stat.

"How do you know about Wikipedia?" she asks.

"Hey, my accident wasn't that long ago."

She pats my hand, and continues: "Two years ago, he was under investigation for animal cruelty."

I perk up when I learn of this.

Rachel continues: "According to an article in the *Times*, he had been doing experimental research on some of the zoo's animals. Experimental and unauthorized, apparently. He was let go, pending a criminal investigation. Apparently, some of the animals had to be put down. And, according to zoo officials, some of the tests were somewhat disturbing."

I lean forward and set my coffee down on the coffee table, which, I think, just might be what it's there for. "We need to speak to someone at the zoo."

She pats my hand. "One step ahead, Detective. We have an appointment with the head of security in one hour."

42

I find myself in a musty office, sitting in a plastic chair in what I presume is a small office.

Betsie is at my feet, panting. I hold her harness in one hand. Betsie and me forever. Rachel, who had guided me into this place, continues holding my elbow loosely, occasionally rubbing me or lightly running her fingernails over my skin, both of which send nearly uncontrollable shivers through me. Yeah, my sense of touch might just be a little heightened.

After a few short moments, I feel the whoosh of a door opening and I presume we are not alone. Next, Rachel stops rubbing and lightly scratching. I feel the small movements of her as she communicates with whoever just entered the room.

Rachel opens my palm, signs: "Her name is Anne Gottlieb and she's head of daytime security. She has only a few minutes."

These days, I tend to get to the point, especially when my poor translator has to spell out each word for me. I sign: "We are here about Nathan Diamond."

"She understands," signs Rachel.

"Are you at liberty to discuss his dismissal?"

"She's not."

I remove my wallet from my back pocket and show her that I am retired homicide with a service-related disability.

I let her know that I am here at the request of the LAPD, working off the clock, so to speak. If need be, I can have homicide here in a few minutes, and she can answer their questions if she prefers.

"She understands. She prefers to talk to you."

Victim? I ask myself. There is no hard evidence yet that the missing are victims of anything. Yes, one did show up dead a year later, but for reasons unknown. For all I know, my brother is in the Cayman Islands, free of responsibility and life, and waxing surfboards for a living.

But a part of me suspects the worst—and that's the homicide investigator part of me. Why would Jesse DeFranco end up dead in the harbor, with a bullet in his head? Why had he been eating vermin in the forest? And how had he contracted tuberculosis?

Strange questions indeed...perhaps some of the stranger questions I've asked myself on any case, ever.

So, I begin with: "What was Dr. Nathan's title here at the zoo?"

"He was the chief veterinarian," came the response through Rachel.

"And how long did Dr. Nathan Diamond work for the zoo?" I sign, and our conversation for the next few minutes is punctuated by many seconds of drag time, as messages are interpreted and signed and relayed.

"Nearly fifty years. In fact, he used to work at the old L.A. Zoo, one of the few remaining employees who had made the transition from one zoo to the next. He was the chief vet at the Los Angeles Zoo for the last ten or eleven years."

"And why was he fired?"

"Dr. Diamond, along with many a top veterinarian, was also an accomplished researcher, noted for his contribution to finding a vaccine for leprosy, among other things. Unfortunately, it was discovered that some of his more recent experiments were inhumane and unacceptable. He was terminated immediately."

"When was this?"

"Just over a year ago."

"Are you aware that Dr. Nathan Diamond has disappeared?"

"Yes, we were interviewed maybe a year ago. Just after his firing."

"Did Dr. Nathan Diamond appear distraught over his firing?"

"You could say that. He was quite angry."

"Did he threaten anyone?"

"Not quite, but he let it be known that he would be back."

"Back, in what way?"

"I can't answer that."

"Did he come back?"

"Not that I'm aware of."

"Did the doctor appear suicidal?"

"I wouldn't know."

"What were his experiments?"

"I'm not a doctor or a scientist, and I can only tell you what I know. If you need more information, I can have another vet here explain in more detail. But from what I understand, he was searching for a cure for tuberculosis."

As Rachel finishes signing the final word, she squeezes my hand tightly and I sit up and would have gasped if I could. Instead, I suck air through the tube in my throat and hope like hell it's clean of spittle. I absently swipe at my neck…so far, so good.

I collect my thoughts, even as Rachel continues squeezing my hand. Finally, I work it free from hers and sign: "Where did the doctor do his experiments?"

"He had free reign of the zoo's facilities. As you may or may not know, the zoo is massive, over one hundred acres, with many outlier buildings and facilities. These particular experiments were done in some of the older buildings, deeper in the park. Far away from his main veterinarian facility."

"How, exactly, did he go about researching and experimenting with tuberculosis?"

"Again, I'm no expert, but from what I understand, he was using possums—rare possums, too. Apparently, they are known for having a robust immune system, which makes their study appealing."

"You did say possums?" I sign, wanting clarification.

"From our investigation, we learned that possums are immune to just about anything—from snake bites to ricin. Mind you, from what we gathered, it's not illegal to perform studies and experiments with possums. Apparently, there are many researchers around the country doing the very same. But that wasn't what Dr. Diamond's job was here. Not to mention, the conditions for the animals were atrocious."

"You saw the conditions?" I ask.

"I did. It was a nightmare scene. The man is an animal, with little regard for living things."

"What happened to the research facilities after the doctor was released?"

"Gutted and locked up."

"How long had he been using the facility?"

"As far as we can tell, a few years."

"And how had his research gone unnoticed for so long?"

203

"The building in question was buried mostly in the hillside, and had been used for storage. He'd gotten special permission to transform it into a secondary office of sorts, which he tended to use after hours. It was in the back half of the building—the half far away from prying eyes—that he'd turned into his personal research laboratory. His lab of horrors. And to answer your question: he was trusted, respected, and a valued member of the staff. He was mostly left alone."

I think about this, then ask: "Is it possible for Dr. Nathan Diamond to enter the zoo premises even now?"

"We do not have security checkpoints. This is a family park. But more than likely he would be recognized." There is a short pause, and I feel Rachel pressing more letters in my palm. "Detective Jordan, are you suggesting that Dr. Diamond, who has been missing for nearly a year, is secretly using zoo facilities to continue his tuberculosis research?"

I smile, sign: "Only a crazy person would suggest that. But since you brought it up: what's the likelihood of Dr. Diamond secretly using zoo facilities to continue his tuberculosis research?"

"Highly unlikely."

"Or that someone is giving him access to zoo facilities?"

"Again, very unlikely."

Except she had said *highly* the first time. I would grade *highly* slightly above *very*. "What do you know of the Old Zoo?" I ask.

I'd heard the Old L.A. Zoo, although I'd yet to visit it myself, and doubted I ever would. Apparently, Griffith Park was home to the original Los Angeles Zoo, built over a hundred years ago, and lying abandoned a few miles from the new zoo.

"The Old Zoo is not part of our patrol."

"I understand, but would Dr. Nathan Diamond have access to it?"

"Anyone does. It's open to the public."

"Can you describe the Old Zoo?"

"It houses a number of abandoned buildings and structures and cages. It's a popular hiking destination here in Griffith Park."

"Why hasn't it been torn down?"

"It's a relic from the past. And it's not hurting anyone."

"What are the chances any of the Old Zoo being used for research?"

"Zero. The buildings are empty, gutted. Tourist attractions only. Home to vandals and drunks and late night parties. Not crazy scientists." Another pause, and she adds: "If you want to know more about the research Dr. Diamond was conducting, there's a vet here who can explain it further. I've made arrangements for you to speak with her."

I tell her that will be fine, and I sense her leaving the room. Rachel squeezes my hand and I squeeze hers back, thinking, thinking…

43

A few minutes later, I feel Rachel sit up a little, then reach out and shake someone's hand.

A moment later, Rachel signs into my hand: "Her name is Dr. Linds, and she's been a veterinarian at the zoo for seven years."

"And she's familiar with the research Dr. Diamond was conducting?"

A pause as the information is exchanged from me to Rachel to the doctor. Then from the doctor to Rachel and finally into my palm: "She is very aware of it. He had spoken to her about it often, although she had been unaware of the conditions of his secret lab."

"Secret?"

"His official research lab here at the zoo was a front, so to speak. His real research was going on in an abandoned facility deeper in the park."

"This keeps getting crazier," I sign into Rachel's hand. "But don't tell her that." Rachel pats my hand: she understands. For the doctor, I sign: "Can you tell me more what he hoped to accomplish? I may not know much, but I thought tuberculosis was on the decline or under control."

"In the United States and Europe and most advanced countries, yes. But tuberculosis, or TB, takes months, sometimes up to a year, to eradicate. Although curable, three people die of TB every minute. Many poorer countries do not possess the expensive medication to fight TB. Dr. Diamond's goal had been entirely altruistic. His expressed aim had been to develop a cheap drug that all countries could use. A cheap drug that worked fast."

"And how was that going?"

"Hard to know. He worked secretly, although he spoke of making headway. I admired him for his tireless work, his dedication to eradicate a global public health problem."

"Was he funded?"

"Oh, yes. Dr. Diamond was funded by WHO—World Health Organization and the Stop TB Partnership. He was a leading researcher, in fact. Not to mention, the Los Angeles Zoo took great pride in his work and helped provide him the facilities and additional funds."

"How long did his research last?"

"Officially, a number of years. Unofficially, in his back room of horrors, who knows?"

"I understand he was working with possums?"

"Oh, yes. Possums are of great interest to researchers fighting infectious diseases. Their immune system is legendary. Of particular interest to Dr. Diamond—and ultimately, his downfall—was his use of the bushtail possum of Southeast Asia, a critically endangered species. But a species that is known to be resistant to many strains of TB."

"His downfall being he used endangered species for his research?"

"He had them shipped here illegally. It was quite the scandal once it was discovered the animals were not, in fact, being displayed, but were being used for research purposes. Worse yet, were the deplorable research conditions he subjected the animals to. It was quite a stain on the zoo's image. They had no choice but to fire him immediately."

"Did you speak to Dr. Diamond again?"

"Never again."

"Can you think of any reason why the doctor might fake his own death?"

There's a pause, and Rachel finally signs into my hand: "Dr. Nathan Diamond is all about the greater good. The needs of the many outweigh the needs of the few, and all of that. I always suspected he would continue his research, one way or another. He had been, after all, making great strides. As to why he would fake his death, I haven't a clue."

44

We are in Rachel's car when I ask her to make a call to the detective and to relay to him, as best as she can, everything she just heard.

I wait quietly while I assume she is on the phone. The windows are up and the air conditioner is on and the car is running; I feel the small vibrations and thumping of an engine that might need to be tuned. The cool air feels very nice.

All of my senses are crackling, and I am flying high. Everything I know tells me we are onto something big, and that there is something very, very strange brewing here at the Los Angeles Zoo...or near the zoo. Or, at one time at the zoo.

Dr. Nathan Diamond...what the devil was going on?

I think back to my brother.

"Once I passed the tests..."

I should have pushed for more information, for him to explain himself. Jesus, I had dropped the ball.

That is, until I remember my brother had blindsided me, sucker-punched me, and had left me reeling gasping and grasping. Still, I should have seen it and pressed him for something, anything.

Too late now.

No, definitely not too late.

My brother is out there, not very far away, perhaps. Somewhere nearby, in fact, if I have to guess. And guessing is all I have.

I think about the old veterinarian...if the old man is behind the disappearances, what on God's earth is he promising? A new lifestyle, a new beginning, if one just... what? Partakes in a few harmless tests. Was that the old vet's angle? Had his inhumane animal testing now graduated to human testing?

If so, I doubt he worded it in such a way. I am certain he painted a much prettier picture. We are doing some innocent safety tests, and all I ask is a few hours of your participation. Once you are done, we will provide all the legal documents you will need to start a new life. Oh, and we will throw in twenty thousand United States dollars for your efforts, so no need to bring any money. Oh, and here is a checklist of how to permanently disappear. Which would explain why all the disappearances—except his own—have been nearly identical.

I consider how desperate one needs to be to agree to such terms. I am certain there are many who would take the good doctor up on his offer. The money would be enough. The lure of starting a new life would be almost irresistible for those who need or want or have to do so.

And my next thought sickens me to my core: those who want to disappear are exactly the kind of patients—or test subjects—the doctor wants. Yes, I suspect they are very much disappearing. I also suspect they are not leaving his lab, ever, wherever it might be.

I am feeling sick to my stomach, certain I must be wrong, certain that there is a flaw in my line of thinking, but the depths of my nausea, the sickening in my stomach, suggest otherwise.

And just as I am about to open the door to get some fresh air, Rachel touches my wrist…and opens my palm. "Are you okay?"

"No. I am scared."

She pats me and squeezes my hand in both of hers, then opens my palm again and signs: "Hammer is putting together a search warrant."

I nod and sign weakly: "The zoo's facilities?"

"Right. Everything is going to be okay, Lee."

I take in some air and nod, and suggest we head back to my place. The warrant will take a few hours to get from a judge, and Hammer and his team certainly don't need us here getting in the way.

We had done our job.

I hoped.

45

We are back at my apartment, on my couch, drinking hot tea and honey.

Rachel had made the hot tea with honey while I had cleaned my tracheal tube in the bathroom. Not exactly a girl's dream date, but what else can I do?

Now, we sitting together, drinking, and she uses my free hand to spell out: "When will we know something?"

"Tomorrow," I sign with my right hand, which is easy enough to do with one hand, rotating my thumb up from my chin, up and over, rolling my wrist in the process. A fast gesture that's unmistakable.

"What do you think they will find?"

I set my tea down. "My guess?" I begin, and these days I never wait for a response for a rhetorical question. "Nothing. I doubt he's there. Crazy, remember?"

"But it makes sense, doesn't it?"

"It does," I sign, "…to a crazy person."

"Which Dr. Nathan Diamond just might be."

I shrug and reach for my tea and sip. My throat is often raw and sore and dry…and, well, just beat up. The tea and honey helps and I revel in it, until Rachel taps my shoulder and I hold out my right hand.

"It does make a sick sense that he would want to experiment on those who want to disappear. After all, if some of

212

the missing accidentally die in the testing phase, there's no repercussions for him. They've already disappeared."

I nod, feeling sick all over again. Jesus, Robert, what have you gotten yourself into?

She continues: "But how does he find them?"

"My guess: the Internet. A cleverly placed ad. Even back in the day, I'd heard of the darker corners of the Internet, the Dark Net as we called it. From what I'm told, one can find anything there. Anything crazy and illegal. I am sure it has evolved now, into what, I wouldn't know."

"Maybe how he found them isn't as important as finding them now," she signs.

I nod and rub my head and use one hand to sign: "Exactly."

A moment later, she takes my hand. "Maybe they will find something, Lee."

"Stranger things have happened."

"But you don't think it likely."

"I think this guy is a sick son of a bitch and he won't be easy to find. The zoo might be big, but not that big. They would have seen or heard something suspicious."

"Perhaps they don't look into every building. Perhaps some buildings have gone forgotten."

I nod. "That's what I'm banking on."

"But you think it unlikely?"

"I do," I sign. "But it's a start. We'll have some answers tomorrow."

"What about the Old Zoo?"

"You heard her," I sign. "Abandoned, filled with graffiti and not many buildings."

"Sounds creepy."

I nod and think about it, and as I think about it, her small hand travels up from my own, up my arm and over my shoulder and to my face, which she cradles, and then leans in and gives me a soft kiss.

46

We are in bed together.

It is *just after*. Just after we have been together intimately. Or, more accurately, just after I have thrashed and flailed about, and no doubt, made a fool of myself. Luckily, she is still by my side, naked and a little sweaty. I'm naked and dripping and nearly out of breath. My heart is hammering hard enough that I am concerned. I suck wind steadily through the tube in my throat and, of all things, wonder what Betsie thinks of what just happened. I hope I haven't traumatized her. Or, for that matter, traumatized Rachel.

And we lay there—catching our breaths and cooling off and wondering what just happened—I am certain I am going to hell. My brother, for all I knew, is in a very, very bad place...and I'm sleeping with the first girl who gives me the time of day?

All while my brother might be in a very, very bad situation. My brother who had told me he was leaving me, perhaps forever. My brother who had abandoned me.

I don't fault him, but I damn well wasn't going to give up living, and if someone out there was hurting him, or had hurt him, then that someone had hell to pay, one way or another.

For now, though...for now, I was gasping and trying not to pass out and reliving every single, beautiful moment of the last seventeen minutes.

When my panting and heart rate return to something resembling normal, I discover that we are holding hands, fingers interlaced, which rules out small talk. I do not know if the lights are on or not, but I suspect we are in the dark. At least, I hoped we were in the dark. Other than my daily walks and my recent boxing sessions, I had long ago given up on exercise. My body, I knew, was scarred. I had serious damage to my throat, shoulder, chest, and some of my face. Mercifully, the wounds on my face had mostly healed, or so I had been told.

So, yeah, I hoped to God the lights were out. As far as I could remember, I hadn't had a light bulb in my bedroom for five years. Or had I? In any event, they *felt* out, and that's something only one blind person can say to another...and understand exactly what they mean.

She turns over on her side, and presses her own naked body against mine. I am still on my back, my sunglasses off, my eyes closed. Always closed. Permanently closed.

Rachel's warm breasts are pressed against my arm, and I feel myself reacting to them. She trails her fingers along my mostly smooth chest. Some chest hair, nothing to write home about...just enough, apparently, for Rachel to play with. I lay there and revel in her touch, her attention, the waves of love that seem to pour from her, although that might be my imagination. Then again, what else did I have if not for my imagination?

And as her hand glides over my chest, as she soothes and caresses me, it happens.

The blue-green light appears, even as Rachel's intoxicating touch seems to recede. Even her scent and warmth seem to take a backseat to the shining, beautiful, living light. My perspective is from my bed, but from about where my headboard would be if I had a headboard. I don't. My perspective seems higher than my prostrate form. Higher, but just the same too. So weird, but somehow perfect.

I *should* be a little higher, I decide. I *should* have a broader perspective—especially if I'm looking outside of myself, or standing outside of myself, or whatever the hell is happening here.

My soul's perspective.

The light flows through the room silently, from a source that seems everywhere at once. It flows in rolling waves, and each wave is composed of many thousands—tens of thousands—of separate light particles that come together to form images. In this case, the various objects in my room. My dresser, my bed, the two forms lying together on the bed beneath me.

Not light. Vibration.

Indeed, according to John Wang, I am seeing vibration, which only appears to me as light. I am also seeing source energy flowing. Source energy may or may not be God. But it's something, and it's powerful, and it's everywhere. *Everywhere.*

It is in all things, surrounding all things, filling all things.

No. It is all things—and all things are it.

I am contemplating this as I watch Rachel's fingers leave behind glowing trails along my chest. Trail after trail, pulsing, burning furrows that disperse a few seconds later. More intriguing is the bare arm that leads to a long, bare body. All of which glows brightly—and I can't help but feel a little guilty soaking her in. After all, Rachel doesn't know about the Winter Wind…or that I can see her now.

I am feeling at peace. I shouldn't feel at peace. My brother could be in a bad way. My brother doesn't deserve to be in a bad way. Yes, he was a shithead for leaving me, but he doesn't deserve to be where I think he might be. And so I am at peace, but also know my brother may not be at peace. He might be hurting and scared...or worse.

I am at peace, but not at peace. I am content, but distracted. I want to soak in this beautiful moment, but my brother's plight gnaws at me.

I am about to sit, maybe pace the room a little, about to break my connection with the Winter Wind, when I see it. There, the right side of her face, the side that is mostly turned away from me. Turned away, I am certain, on purpose.

I shift my focus fully to the side of her face, even though I do not move from my prone position on the bed. If I move, I break my connection. As my perspective swings around, I feel a discombobulating jolt...and feel more out of my body than ever. I should not be able to see from this perspective. After all, my physical body is on one side of her face... and yet the camera of my focus is now swinging out to the opposite, further and further away from me. Remarkably, the movement feels natural. Once I get used to the initial jolt, I focus on what I am seeing...What I am seeing doesn't make sense at all. What I am seeing looks a lot like my own wounds. So much so that I gasp sharply, sucking hard at the hole in my throat, and then coughing violently because my tracheal tube needs to be cleaned in a bad way, all of which jolts me right out of the Winter Wind and back into reality.

Rachel pats my back as I sit up, cough up the mucus, and clear my lungs. I slip out of bed and head over to the bathroom, which is out through the bedroom door and at the end of a short hallway, a path I have taken thousands of times before. I splash cold water on my face and wipe my throat clean—all while reliving what I had just seen.

Shortly, I am back in bed. Rachel is sitting up, propped up on her elbow. I feel her eyes on me, studying me, worried about me. The room is dark, I know, but there would be enough ambient light for her to make me out. Or try to make me out.

"Are you okay?" she signs into my hand.

I nod, but I'm not okay. Not after what I had just seen. An irrational, sickening dread is coming over me. Irrational, because this cannot be true. What I saw cannot be true. Sick…because it was all my fault.

I am not very surprised that the hand I am reaching up with is now shaking. Or that the rest of me is shivering, too.

Please let this not be true. Please.

My fingertips graze her left cheek, and she flinches. The flinching is common. In fact, she often flinches whenever I touch her face.

But I have never touched the *right side of her face.* Even my initial exploration of her face a few nights ago had been only the left side. Even earlier, as we were making love, she had kept my hands away from her face, redirecting them elsewhere on her body.

No. Please…

I cup her left cheek gently, even as I feel her pulling away. She's taking short breaths. Gasps, if I had to guess. The proximity of my hand is making her nervous, I think. She reaches up and gently guides it away—or tries to—but I am persistent and won't be denied. I slip my fingers out of hers and keep them right there on her face.

Her breathing is coming sharper and faster. She is tense and I sense her wanting to get up, to get away from me. But I hold her cheek, I hold her here with me. My hand is moving away from her left cheek, and over to her right. Her rapidly rising-and-falling chest stops altogether. Her warm breath against my neck stops altogether. She's holding her breath, tense.

There...a row of fleshy bumps along her right temple, bumps that are surprisingly hard, too. I shouldn't have been surprised; after all, I had them myself, along my neck and eyes. My own scars had healed better than I could have hoped. Rachel's scars? Not so much. Everyone heals differently. Everyone reacts to trauma different. And Rachel had been through some serious trauma.

My fingertips move from the bumps along her temple to the outside corner of her right eye where the damage is worst. The scar tissue is thick and tangled, seemingly criss-crossed. Whatever had happened had torn up her face... and no doubt, her eye as well.

Now, I feel her tears, working through the corrugated scar tissue, and I feel her take a short, sharp inhalation. She lays there and weeps as my hand continues over her face, following a trail of scars from her eyes to her right ear, which, I note is mostly missing. I carefully, carefully run my fingers over the damaged flesh, the ragged, yet smooth contour of her mostly missing ear, and as I do so, her body convulses and heaves and now, my own tears are running free...and I know....

I know.

There were three victims in the bombing. My dead partner, myself, and...

I take a deep breath—or as deep as I can through the opening in my throat—and hold Rachel tight as I can as she weeps into my neck. I do not know what to say or think or feel or do, but my own tears flow...

And flow.

47

We are sitting up in bed, legs crossed, knees touching, facing each other.

She returns from the bathroom where, I assume she freshened up and, perhaps, considered fleeing. I am glad she did not flee. I am glad she is back and sitting with me and holding my hands.

Whether we are sitting in the dark or not, I do not know, but I suspect she has turned on a light or two somewhere in the apartment. I don't know. I don't care. We sit there for a long time, until I use my right hand to sign: "I'm sorry."

She squeezes my left hand, but I pull it away, and sign: "I'm so sorry you got hurt—"

Now, she takes my hands and holds them in hers, tightly, so tightly she is shaking, but not from tears. Just emotion. I do not know how long we sit like that, but it is significant. Maybe even thirty minutes, maybe longer. I weep some of the time, and sometimes, she brings my knuckles up to her lips and kisses them, and each time she does, I weep a little harder.

Now, I take in air, feel her heartbeat through her hands, and feel a draft of air moving over my back from my open bedroom window. Our knees are still touching. She has not stopped holding my hands, squeezing them. Only occasionally will she lessen her grip to rub my knuckles with her thumbs.

It is much later when she turns my right hand over and opens my palm and signs into it: "But I am not sorry, Lee."

I wait, with open palm, and know I need to clean my tracheal tube in a bad way, but I power through. I can feel mucus seeping out and sliding down my throat.

She continues: "I am not sorry because I would never have met you. I would never have gotten close to you. I would never have…"

I wait, and as I wait, more mucus seeps out, but I do not care. More tears flow, too, because I can hardly believe what I am about to hear…

"Because I would never have fallen in love with you." I pull her into me, hold her tight, and weep into her neck, shoulder, and mouth. Over and over again I mouth how sorry I am, but I know she cannot hear me and that's probably just as well. Finally, I pull back, and point to my heart and cross my arms over my chest and open my hand to her. It is, I am certain, the first time I have made the sign, ever.

"I love you, too."

———

She had been home cleaning that day.

Alone in her apartment, she had taken the day off from work to get caught up on chores. At the time, she had worked in insurance investigations, which might explain how she was able to readily get me the information I needed so far. After the accident, she decided to go a different direction with her life…and became a sign language translator. In fact, she is the LAPD's official translator.

She'd always gotten the heebie-jeebies from her neighbor. There was a darkness around him. He wouldn't look her in the eye. Late at night, she would often hear him working in his apartment, especially in those last few months before the shooting spree. Now, she understood what he was doing. Booby-trapping the place with nearly 75 different explosives, some of which went off when I had kicked in the door, especially those near the front window, where Mitch had been standing, and a handful of bigger ones that ended up blowing a hole in the wall that separated her apartment from the killer's. A wall that led to her own adjoining kitchen, where Rachel had been doing dishes when the blast occurred.

She had awakened in the hospital later...to discover she was blind in one eye and deaf in one ear, and that a policeman had died and another was in critical condition. She would also soon learn the extent of her neighbor's depravity and barbarism, and regretted not mentioning her concerns to someone. She was so angry with herself, even years later, and it occurs to me now that the woman I had just told I loved, the woman I had nearly killed, the woman I had blinded and deafened, blamed herself for everything. Herself.

"All I had to do was make one call..." she signs into my hand, then stops. Her hand is heavy in mine.

"And tell them what?" I sign. "That you have a weird neighbor who's up at all hours of the night?"

"Eleven people, Lee, including your partner. All dead, because I didn't act."

"All dead because one man was intent on killing."

"All I had to do was make one call—don't you understand?"

"And all I had to do was wait for backup," I sign into the air. "Or listen to my partner. Anything, but do what I did."

What I had done was kick the door in. I hadn't conferred with my partner. I hadn't told him my plans. I saw only the dead and blood—and I saw only red.

"I knew he was dangerous, Lee. I felt it. A dozen times, I nearly called the police. A dozen times I chickened out. It's my fault. All of this."

She spends the next few minutes crying hard into her hands, so hard that I thought I might have heard it. I held her close and couldn't believe the turn of events. I had gone from blaming myself to consoling her. And her blame was real. It is something she lives with, daily.

Jesus.

She is deaf in one ear, blind in one eye. Her wounds are significant...perhaps even more obvious than my own. In fact, definitely more obvious than my own. As far as superficial wounds, I had escaped fairly unscathed. I had puffy scars around my eyes where shrapnel had entered my face. I had significant damage to my throat, but that is mostly hidden by collars. I don't do scarfs or turtlenecks. First, I still need an opening to breathe; second, this is Southern California—not exactly turtleneck or scarf weather.

We are silent, motionless, lost and found. I feel myself wanting to slip into the Winter Wind, but I resist for some reason. I want Rachel to have these quiet moments alone and unseen. Later, I will tell her about what I can do. Now does not seem the time. Or maybe it is. When is the correct time to tell someone that, yes, you've acquired the ability to see vibrations when in a deep trance. I'm not sure when the right time will be, but I'm pretty sure it is not now.

And so we sit like that, knees touching, holding hands, as intimate and close as two people can get, I think. Always touching, always connected, and not just through sex. I liked that about us. I liked feeling the deep connection with another human being, especially this one...

Finally, she leans forward and presses her forehead against my chest, and I run my hand over the wounds along her exposed cheek, reading the tragedy of her pain, her loss, her guilt.

Each puffy bump, each jagged slash, each furrow and divot that make up the wounds, brings me closer to her, connects me deeper to her, and makes me love her more.

As we lie back on the bed, I think about our divine matchmaker, whoever or whatever it might be. I think: God, there has to be an easier way to bring two people together.

48

Next day, late afternoon.

Rachel is with Detective Hammer. She'd left early in the morning to work a gig or two, and now she is back for gig #3. As luck would have it, I'm gig #3.

We are sitting around the coffee table. This morning, with Rachel gone, I had slipped deeply into meditation and into the Winter Wind, practicing my movements. I was almost—almost—able to raise my arm all the way up while in deep meditation—and to maintain the Winter Wind, too. As in, I could see myself move. My goal, if possible, is to someday move around with sight, and to slip in and out of the Wind on cue.

Don't break the wind, I kept thinking this morning, and cracked myself up enough to, indeed, slip out of the Wind, and back into the darkness of my reality.

Now, in the living room, all is dark and quiet. I might as well have been in the vacuum of deep space. A vacuum with the slightest of ringing.

Ignore the ringing, I tell myself again. And again.

My hand is open and resting lightly on Rachel's thigh, waiting for her communication. It is all I can do to not pull her into me and kiss her deeply. After all, it is easy to imagine we are sitting here alone. That we are, in fact, the last two people alive.

In the past, I often convinced myself that I was dead, and this is the afterlife. Eternal blackness. Eternal silence. Sometimes, I long for real death—just on the off chance that I might hear birds sing again. Or, listen to some Nirvana again. Or Jimmy Buffet. Or, once and for all, listen to my first Lady Gaga and see what all the fuss is about.

Usually, I don't think I am dead. Usually, I am aware enough to know that I am alive—but when one sits for days and weeks and years in darkness and in silence, it is easy to forget one is among the living. It is easy to forget that there is a world of beauty and of sounds and interaction and living. It is easy to think that I am dead, actually. Or, worse, that I am nothing at all. Just a memory. Just an echo. Just pure thought.

Or even worse, that I never existed. That hell is, in fact, believing I had once been alive and lived and loved and laughed.

Shitty thoughts for sure. Luckily, when I am in these dark moments, when the darkness feels like a living thing, heavy and suffocating and all-consuming—when I beg for some semblance of light, a spark, a flash, anything—I will feel a wet tongue on my hand or arm or cheek, or wherever Betsie can reach me. Perhaps she senses my hopelessness, and she's always there to bring me back. Always.

I squeeze Rachel's hand. She squeezes back. I am alive. This is real. She is real. Love is real.

I sense her nodding and speaking and I wonder what Detective Hammer thinks of the two disfigured freaks sitting in front of him, now that I know Rachel is a fellow freak. That is, until I realize that I don't care what Hammer thinks—or what anyone thinks. Rachel might care. She had done a helluva job hiding her injuries from me, guiding my hands subtly as we explored each other. I wonder when she was planning on telling me. Probably soon. It was only a matter of time before my hand slid to the right side of her face. She had probably spent the past five years with men looking at her funny, with children openly staring at her. Five years feeling less than the woman I knew she was. All because of me.

No matter what the hell she says.

When Hammer is done speaking, Rachel begins signing into my hand, her touch as soft as ever, if not a little more urgent.

"He and his team served the zoo a search warrant early this morning, before it was open. They searched the buildings in question and found nothing. They searched similar abandoned buildings around the zoo. They searched janitor buildings and storage buildings and anything they could think of. They even headed out to the Old Zoo and took a look around there, too. They found nothing, but he appreciates the tip. So far, it's the only lead they have… at least, the only lead that was worth getting a search warrant for. Too bad it didn't pan out. Hammer thinks the doctor sounds like a nut job, and just crazy enough to pull something like this. They'll keep investigating that lead."

She says all this over many minutes, with many pauses, and when she stops, I unconsciously rub her fingers, which are, no doubt, tired from all the signing. At least, mine would be.

I feel their eyes on me after she is done signing. Rachel isn't nodding her head, isn't moving. Both are looking, no doubt, at me. Waiting for me. I was a senior investigator at the LAPD. I had many, many years under my belt, many closed files, and many still-open files, too. I was used to people waiting for me, waiting for me to lead.

Hammer may not be used to deferring. He was a good detective in his own right, but, undoubtedly, overworked, and this Big Case is a thorn in everyone's side. Not really my side, but I can imagine it is taking a lot of resources and time and manpower to get a handle on this one. The search warrant today has probably been a nightmare of logistics and timing, too.

The problem is...

Well, the problem is, I know they are wrong. I know there is something there, even if they didn't find it.

Everything in me—call it instinct, intuition, sixth sense, whatever—knows there is something still going on behind the scenes at the L.A. Zoo, hidden from public consumption, and hidden from even a search warrant.

Or not. Maybe my instincts are shot to hell. Except, I could feel the electricity of it, the knowing of it, the power of it. This knowing is real in me, more so than ever. Except...

Except I will not be able to convince Hammer of this. Not after he and the other investigators turned the zoo inside and out.

Finally, I nod and sign: "We did our best. I'll let you know if I think of anything else."

He pats my hand once, and I feel him rise. I sense him patting Rachel, perhaps lightly on the shoulder. And then he is gone.

Rachel takes my hand to sign to me, "He did mention one more thing, Lee."

I nod and wait.

"The department's cyber guys scoured what Hammer called the Dark Net, and found no solid evidence of anyone advertising to help people disappear in the Los Angeles area."

"Solid evidence?" I sign. "But they found something?"

"Just a single post on a forgotten message board, buried deep in the hidden net and nearly impossible to find. Someone had posted something with the keywords, 'Los Angeles Zoo.'"

"What did they post?"

"Someone had asked: 'But is it safe?'"

"And?" I sign.

"There was no answer." She pats my hand, then signs into it: "You did your best, Lee."

I nod and wonder if I have, and sit back with her as she rests her head on my shoulder and I rub her neck, slowly, thinking.

Thinking...

49

It is late.

Rachel is gone, and I am thinking of my brother and the missing victims, and the disgraced veterinarian, and Jesse, who had been found dead and infected with tuberculosis. I think of my brother's cryptic words in parting, words about getting past the testing.

I don't drink much, but I'm drinking now, on my balcony. Drinking hard, actually. Being buzzed, I note, hinders my ability to enter the Winter Wind. Still, as I sit there quietly, the blue-green Wind flashes through my thoughts, but the images are staticy, unclear. I see amorphous trees before me. Amorphous cars parked on the street. All crackling with energy, coming in and out of focus, and then sometimes disappearing altogether.

I wonder if it will always be like this—the Winter Wind coming and going, seemingly at random—or if I will truly gain mastery over it. I don't know about mastery, but I do think someday I will gain more control of it. Already I have been able to slip into it with more and more regularity. It's just the drinking that's causing the frenetic energy.

And so I let it, and watch the world before me appear and disappear—electric, bright, sometimes dull, sometimes clear, but mostly amorphous, fuzzy. Certainly as fuzzy as my own brain.

Betsie is lying over my feet, breathing fast and steady. Sound asleep, no doubt. I wonder if she can see the Winter Wind, too.

I consider all that I have learned of the Big Case. The improbability of ten—now eleven—people going missing in exactly the same way. No, that's not true. There were some variations. Jesse, who showed up dead later. And my brother, who indicated to me that he would be leaving, once he passed the test. I considered the improbability of one of the missing—the first, in fact—living and working in the same general area of the missing. A rogue veterinarian who experimented in his lab on critically endangered possums...and who had been found to mistreat his animal subjects, and subsequently fired.

You can fire the researcher, but can you stop his research?

I doubted it. And the crazy bastard might even fake his own disappearance—to hide in plain sight—all while continuing his research on the unsuspecting. But this time he ditches the possums, and instead goes after...

I swallow.

Crazy. All of it is just nuts.

If this guy had been advertising his services on the Dark Net, his site is down now. Or, perhaps, the police didn't know where to look. My brother was a computer geek. He could have figured out the Dark Net, if motivated enough. He would have found his answer...and I suspected the doctor's pitch might have been too good for my brother to resist. Apparently, my brother wanted out—out of my life, that is—very badly.

Of course, I'm certain the good doc mentioned nothing about the tuberculosis research, and had no intention of ever allowing his test subjects to leave his experiments.

But one had left. Or had he escaped?

232

Crazy. I continue to sip on my now warm beer. My fourth, I think. Enough for one night. Especially when I have work to do.

I stand, and Betsie stands, too. I fetch my light jacket, my phone and Betsie's harness.

After all, Hammer and the boys might not have found anything at the new zoo...but there's still the Old Zoo. I wonder how thoroughly they had searched it, and decide probably not very thoroughly at all.

That is about to change.

50

The Uber driver is particularly attentive.

He helps me into the car, spreads a blanket for Betsie, and soon, we are off into the night. There is a slight chance I have a buzz. Okay, more than a slight one, but it's only a buzz and it will wear off soon.

I'd written on my notepad where we are going, and the driver had patted my shoulder. He understands. And where we are going is not very far at all. So, I sit back and enjoy the ride and try to imagine all the landmarks we are passing: the apartment and condo buildings, the street corners, the bridges, the streetlights...

We turn a corner, and another, and now, I am thinking we have entered the long curving road that will take us, eventually, to the Los Angeles Zoo. After all, I had just been here, and I remembered the route...the gentle curve around the base of the small mountain range that spines the center of the park, the range that, on the south side, sports the Hollywood Sign, Griffith Observatory, and the Greek Theatre; and on the north, the L.A. Zoo. The closer we get, the harder my heart pounds.

A good sign.

A sign for what, exactly, I do not entirely know, but it tells me I am on the right path for answers. Or maybe not. Maybe I'm not on any path at all, other than getting lost in Griffith Park, to wander aimlessly until I dehydrate or starve or break an ankle. At least Betsie will eat well.

Dark thoughts, for sure.

I have no intention of getting lost in the woods. After all, there is always the Winter Wind, and, if used correctly, I should be able to find my way around the park. With luck, I might even find some answers, too.

As we continue around the bend, as I feel the small force of the turn press against me, I note that my buzz is mostly worn off. Betsie is pressed up against me. She has been staring at me, I think, the entire time. If the hint of doggie breath was any indication.

She is wondering where we are going. She has noted that the midnight drive is out of character for us. Way, way, way out of character. She is concerned. Maybe I should be, too.

Then again, she is just a dog.

No, I think, recalling Jack's words. *An angel.*

I'm not used to being concerned. I'm used to finding answers. I'm used to following leads all the way to the end, all the way to the bad guy. Some cases don't have ends. Some stay open forever. But I cannot sleep well at night until I know that I have exhausted every lead.

The Old Zoo lead has not been exhausted, and my brother is still missing. And just because the initial search at the new zoo turned up nothing, I'll be damned if I was going to sit back and do nothing.

Of course, I don't have to go alone in the middle of the night. Except the middle of the night feels right. The middle of the night is when the Old Zoo might give up its secrets, or when others have let down their guard. Did I have to go alone? Probably not. Had I not enjoyed the benefits of the Winter Wind, I would have waited for Rachel, or tried to convince Hammer to join me.

But I don't want to put Rachel in harm's way, or to try to convince a busy homicide detective that I'm not crazy. Now, thanks to my newfound gifts, I could indeed venture out alone, into the night. Looking for answers.

Soon, I feel the car roll to a stop. Kind of hard to tell these days with these newfangled electric cars, cars that hardly even vibrate, let alone spew telltale carbon monoxide. Virtually invisible, so to speak, to someone like me. Anyway, Betsie is sitting up and alert and panting, drool dripping onto my arm, all good indicators that something exciting is about to happen. At least, exciting to a dog.

A whoosh of air and now Betsie is standing—mostly on my crotch—and I feel a light hand on my shoulder. The Uber driver is doing his awkward best to let me know we have arrived. I nod and ease my legs out, snap my walking stick open. Betsie jumps out behind me.

We are on the back side of the massive Griffith Park, surrounded, I know, by trees of all shapes and sizes. As I plant my walking stick steadily on the ground and take firm hold of Betsie's leash, I do my best to get my bearings. I had asked him, in my handwritten note, to be dropped off at the closest entry point to the Old Zoo. According to Rachel, the Old Zoo was about a half mile from the new... and up a trail.

The wind is scented with freshly mowed grass and sweet evergreen needles and something that might very well be trash. I love when my sense of smell is firing on all cylinders, or through both barrels. I take everything I can get. Every bit of stimulus I can. There are days when I can't smell at all. I don't like those days. Give me something, anything.

And I've been given a lot recently, haven't I?

I had. More than I could have ever hoped or expected or asked.

But I had asked. I had prayed. With a little girl.

It's 12:33 a.m. No time for a blind, deaf, mute to be wandering in Griffith Park alone, especially after having recently read a trilogy of zombie books, set in this very park. Now, with zombies on the brain, I wave off the driver's concerned grip on my elbow and nod and give him the thumbs-up. Finally, he releases his tenuous hold on me and, a few minutes later, I suspect he drives off, although with those electrical cars, one never knows. Maybe he's still here, watching me.

Either way, I tug on the harness and head forward, sweeping the land with the walking stick, and soon find myself heading up an asphalt road.

51

When my walking stick hits grass, I decide it's time. I steady myself and begin the steps necessary to slip into the Winter Wind. It doesn't happen immediately or easily. But I do relax enough to get a second or two of staticy, bluish snapshots of my surrounding area.

And from what I can see, I am alone, and pretty damn close to where I wanted to be dropped off. I am about five hundred feet along a side road that leads from the parking lot.

According to Rachel, who had researched the Old Zoo for me, it is a popular hiking destination for park goers, who explore the abandoned cages, stairways, and walkways.

Getting to the zoo requires a short hike, probably one that is easy and fun for the sighted. Me, not so much.

I pause and take one more mental snapshot of the surrounding area—a snapshot infused with blues and green and wavy, staticy energy, then I suck in some air, grip Betsie's harness, and step onto the grass...and up toward the Old Zoo.

52

According to Rachel, there are a number of old roads and trails that lead to the Old Zoo, which is buried off the main roads into the park, nestled far enough away to not be an eyesore, and just far enough away to be a fun day hike.

Or a not-so-fun night hike.

I feel Betsie jerking and pausing a little more than usual. She would never pull me...and she would certainly never run. My guess: she is seeing squirrels and other critters.

A dog and squirrels, it's a beautiful thing.

Ten minutes later, I pause, focus my thoughts, and slip into the Winter Wind. Within seconds, the blue-green landscape comes into startling sharp focus.

I'm getting better at this.

Most important, I see the glowing, winding trail that, I hope, will take me up to the old L.A. Zoo.

With the details of the landscape imprinted on my memory, I set off for the winding trail.

———

The grass gives way to a dirt path, which I follow up.

Whenever my walking stick hits something—a rock, tree root, or bush where there shouldn't be one—I pause

239

and reassess and sometimes even slip back into the Winter Wind to get a better feel for where I am.

Of course, with the Winter Wind, I get more than just a feel—I get an honest-to-God snapshot. A dream come true.

Higher I go, moving quickly now, swiping the walking stick like a metronome, back and forth, back and forth. Twice, a tree branch nicks my face. Hard to protect your face and feel your way with a walking stick and hold tight to your guide dog all at the same time.

I need one more arm.

Instead, I keep my face ducked down, and soon take the brunt of a few more branches along the top of my skull, but no serious damage. Gone are the days where I worry about poking an eye out.

Later, I hit something solid. Not a rock, not a tree root. I hit it again, and feel the hollow vibration ring up through my stick and along my hands. A trash can, if I had to guess. Set to one side of the trail.

I move on, in darkness...but not quite blind.

Not anymore.

———

I stumble over a small rocky protrusion and use my walking stick to right myself.

I've been cocky, careless. Moving faster than I should have. The trail up to this point had been relatively smooth and clear of hiccups. The rock was a hiccup. Not quite big enough to register on my sweeping walking stick, but protruding just enough to catch the toe of my running shoe.

I pause and steady myself. I'm not helping anyone with a twisted ankle or a broken leg. Betsie is good, but not so good that she can warn me of small, rocky protrusions.

I set off again, and slow my pace.

I pause to catch my breath.

Losing one's breath with a tracheal tube is hell. I think of it as akin to breathing through one nostril…and one nostril only. But I have long since learned to relax and breathe steadily and calmly.

When I am ready, I move on again.

Another snapshot.

A hill before me, choked with trees. Small, super-bright spots dart in the undergrowth. Sometimes they jump. Rats, I think. Or mice. Off to my right is a bigger bright spot. Something is lumbering with its tail raised. A skunk.

The trail leads into the thick copse of trees, and I head forward again, breaking my connection to the Winter Wind, and sweeping my walking stick before me.

My next snapshot.

Before me, the path opens up into a clearing, with a grassy field on one side and the stacked, rocky forma-tions of a long-neglected zoo exhibit on the other. The ruins look a lot like something you might see buried deep in the Honduran forest. Indeed, I could have been an explorer in a South American jungle, stumbling upon a lost Mayan city for the first time, a city that hasn't quite been overgrown, a city that, apparently, was built with cages and pits and enclosures.

Or a mostly blind man stumbling through the Griffith Park on a wild goose chase.

The image of the manmade stone grottoes wavers as I lose my focus. I don't want to lose my focus. Not now. I take a deep breath and re-focus, and sink deeper into my meditation.

There are many walkways, paths, stairs, and graffiti is everywhere. Most interesting are the abandoned cages, which line the many corridors. And broken bottles everywhere. I imagine the abandoned zoo is a favorite for teenagers looking to get high and drunk. And a favorite for the homeless, too. A beacon for derelicts and the wayward. Next to me is a small shack that I can only imagine has housed its share of the homeless.

So much decay. Yet, so much beauty, too. I see where nature is reclaiming some of the corridors and cages and abandoned buildings. In fifty years, the whole damn place will be forgotten.

And it's all open. All abandoned. Anyone could be here. Anyone.

Even a blind man looking for the impossible.

I enter the Old Zoo.

53

I pause often, taking more Winter Wind snapshots, picking my way along corridors and between cages, not sure what I am looking for, and not even sure I'll know it when I see it, either.

While I scan, I remind myself that nothing is so lost that it can't be found, my brother included—and all of the missing for that matter. I put myself in what I call a receiving mode—a mode that is open to any possibility, no matter how unlikely. Such a mode had helped me connect the dots on some of my toughest cases.

I continue scanning the abandoned zoo. I only need one shred of evidence that something is going on here. One tiny shred and nothing more.

And so I search….

———

As the minutes pile up, and as the cool wind turns cooler, I am beginning to think that coming out here is a very bad idea. I am thinking of turning around, of trekking back through the woods, until I remember how far I have come tonight, the hassle I went through just to get here, to be here now.

Stay positive. Stay in that receiving mode. Just a little longer.

Throughout this whole inner dialogue, I never slip out of the Winter Wind, which impresses me. Except the more I am impressed, the more it wavers and flickers.

Focus.

I stand there, motionless, in the night, in the misty coolness, and watch the light show in my mind. The energy show, perhaps. I watch it roll in through my thoughts in waves. Sometimes it scatters, like frightened fish. Sometimes it collects its globs, forming shapes that seem vaguely human, and then those scatter, too. Mostly, the ripples of energy move over physical objects, giving them shape, giving them life, bringing them into stark contrast. At least for me.

From where the energy originates, I don't know. Where it goes, I don't know that either. But here it is, flowing over the land and through my thoughts, touching on everything, alighting everything, giving it substance and depth, even for the blind. Even for those without eyes to see.

I do not know what I am looking for, or even if anything is here worth seeing—

(*No,* I think. *It's all worth seeing.* All of it, every last broken shard of glass and trailing curlicue of graffiti.)

—but I tell myself, over and over again, and with more and more certainty, that if there is something here to be seen, I would find it. Here. Now.

Somehow, some way.

What I think I'm looking for is an entrance below ground, an entrance to a subterranean chamber. That feels right to me. The Old Zoo was built on a forested hill, with many levels, and many rooms built into the hill itself, like bunkers. These were basements to maintenance buildings, administrative buildings and perhaps even veterinary facilities.

Or, maybe, research facilities.

The rooms would have been cooler, especially when there wasn't air conditioning a hundred years ago. I suspected those rooms were here, too, locked up and sealed away…empty rooms, abandoned rooms.

Forgotten rooms.

I focus my attention on the steps leading down into the lower levels.

There are a number of stairways in the Old Zoo. Many are narrow and covered in enough graffiti to make you almost appreciate the art form. And I appreciated it now. I appreciated the crap out of it. I wish I could see the scrawls clearly enough to read. For now, I see only hints and outlines and shapes. One such shape, and it appears to be a predominant one, is the penis. And there are lots of them, of all shapes and sizes.

My perspective is from above. How that works, I don't know, but I seem to be viewing the park about three or four feet above my physical body. The view spreads out many dozens of feet in every direction, seemingly at once, penetrating the dark shadows and, apparently, even passing through walls, as I can see into hallways, grottoes, and even nearby maintenance buildings.

This gives me an idea.

I break my connection to the Winter Wind and move closer to an abandoned maintenance building. I pause and slip and hold my walking stick with one hand, bow my head, and slip into the Winter Wind. I shift my focus into the building—through the flimsy sheet metal and find myself in what I can only imagine is a very dark space.

Except, for me, it's alive with light. Stagnant light, which moves in slow eddies, pooling within the room. Brighter lights huddle in the far corner, and a long, winding light slithers across the floor.

Great...snakes.

The room is littered with leaning beams of wood and broken machinery. Old pumps, I think. Hard to tell. There are no doors or stairs or anything that seems to indicate there might be a basement. I try something, almost as a lark, and project my focus beneath the building. I am surprised when a small crawlspace comes into focus. No, nothing beneath this building except the land itself.

Feeling like I'm onto something, I scan the nearby cages and walkways and buildings. In particular, I look for hidden rooms behind doors or walls. Hidden staircases. Anything that looks like it might have been used recently, perhaps.

But I find nothing of worth. Sure, there's a walkway hidden from view behind a nearby building that seems to be popular with smokers and drinkers, but certainly not what I am looking for.

I move off another direction, pause, slip into the Winter Wind, and scan the surrounding structures... and find nothing of worth, certainly nothing that would indicate anyone was using this park for anything other than what it was intended for: drinking and getting high, apparently.

Finally, after many minutes of doing this, I pull back my awareness, lift my head, and break the connection to the world of blue-green vibration.

The Old Zoo is large, but there isn't an endless procession of abandoned buildings. I am certain I have searched all that I've come across. I am about to give up hope, about to look for the path out of the zoo, back through the park, and back to the parking lot where I can, hopefully, conjure up an Uber ride, when I recall the old shack on the way into the park.

The only structure I had yet to scan.

Feeling little hope, I strike off toward the shack…and toward the exit.

54

I pause where I think the shack is.

The night has grown colder, with a small wind seguing sometimes into a bigger wind. My sense of smell has abandoned me completely, but the air feels fresh, crisp, and far removed from the nearby big city. Big, big city.

My brother feels both nearby and so far gone that I am at a loss. That this is the last building in the Old Zoo gives me little hope. Maybe I had missed one here or there. I could always come back in the light of day with Rachel. Maybe she would humor me.

I pause and grip my walking stick, steady myself, and slip into the Winter Wind, perhaps faster than I'd ever done before. It is almost instant, and I am impressed, excited, and a little nervous, too.

The surrounding vegetation comes quickly into view, sharper and clear. The trail is leading before me, down into the parking lot far below. A forest to my left, and the shack just to my right, almost within touching distance.

I shift my focus to the shack. Shifting my focus is a new and interesting concept for me. Although I can see around me, 360 degrees, I can also focus my attention where I want. After all, I am not using eyes to see. I am using a sort of expanded awareness that I am only barely grasping.

With this being the last building, I give it special care and attention. After all, what had I to lose?

The outside is rectangular, dilapidated, although it rests on a cement foundation. Cement steps also lead up to a front entrance. It is similar to other storage buildings I have come across, although this one might be bigger, and it's surrounded by a chain-link fence.

Like something out of a video game, or a Hollywood movie special effect, I push through the corrugated metal siding and find myself inside the structure.

The energy here is staticy, yes, but also a little more lively than the other buildings.

Someone's been in here, I think. Perhaps even recently.

Then again, what did I know about energy?

The room is bigger than I had expected, no doubt making either an excellent security office or administrative building, or a large storage room. Hard to know, as it's been gutted, although many beams crisscross the room, lying on top of bigger slabs of metal sheets and wood panels.

There is much graffiti in here, more so than the other buildings. Maybe because this is the first building in the park. I make out the words: "Don't Trust the Man" and "Bow Down Before Me." I see a pentagram or two, but mostly, it's all just random inanity. Stick figures running up and down stairs. Gang tags. Words that start off looking legible, then trail off into incoherence. With nothing really to say, they tag for the sake of tagging, deface for the sake of defacing, rebel for the sake of rebelling. I say if you're going to spend the money on the paint—and the time hiking up here—then have something proactive to say. Better yet, get a blog.

I move my focus away from the graffiti and look down at the dusty, cement floor, mostly covered in wood and metal. Most of it seems to have come from the open ceiling above. All of it litters the floor and forms a haven for the many brightly lit rodents that I now see burrowed under the debris.

I focused again on the floor, and in particular, the particularly big slab of wood that seems to be centered perfectly in the room. Too perfectly?

I shift my focus again, this time to beneath the wood, and gasp.

So loudly, that I am jerked out of the Winter Wind.

And now I am moving.

55

Had I not known that the building was empty of human life, I might have been nervous. Then again, what's darkness to me? Of course, darkness is an emotional response...and knowing I was entering an abandoned building in the middle of the night, struck an emotional response, an old fear. An old fear I quickly squashed.

I push forward, feeling my way up the exterior cement stairs, and step through the doorless doorway. Here, just inside the entrance, I pause again and slip into the Winter Wind.

The path before me is littered with debris. I fear there might be an upturned nail that could hurt Betsie. Although I can see within the Winter Wind, I am not so sure how much my dog is seeing in the pure darkness of the room. Perhaps a little, perhaps a lot.

In my mind's eye, I study the floor before me as best as I can, noting the debris, but I do not see any upturned nails, or anything else that would cause alarm.

With the path clear in my memory, I move forward again, over the uneven floor, littered with wood paneling and metal siding and two-by-fours. And one big slab of wood.

Betsie stops. She's trained to stop when she senses changes in elevation, such as curbs, and when confronted with obstacles. The piled, loose planks of wood might qualify as both. But I was also sensing something else from her. Some hesitancy. Nervousness. Trust me, I know my dog.

I would have made cooing noises for her, gently coaxing her forward, if I could. Instead, I pause and kneel down and pat her head reassuringly. She turns and looks up at me, and I can almost see the questioning look in her eye—especially now that I know exactly what her furry mug looks like. I smile and nod and motion with my head to continue. We continue forward, but I suspect Betsie is doing so under protest.

When I feel that I'm in the right spot, I kneel down and release Betsie's harness. I remove a latex glove from a pocket and slip it over my right hand. Like at a crime scene. Next, I feel carefully over the floor—and I'm not liking what I'm touching. Rat turds, I'm sure. Lots of them. A mask would have been nice, now that I think about it. I power through, covering my tracheal tube with my shirt, although I doubt that does much.

Better than nothing, I think.

Now gripping the edge of the wooden slab, I give it a push. It moves, begrudgingly. After all, a lot of wood is piled on top of it.

But I keep pushing and pushing, and push it all the way to the far side of the room, no doubt collecting more wood and rat turds in the process and likely making a helluva racket, too.

Most important, I expose what is underneath.

Now standing again, I slip into the Winter Wind to see exactly what I have here.

The floor is shimmering.

In fact, everything is shimmering. It's the dust, I realize, floating and drifting in the air, alive and sparking with its own vibration of life, disturbed and displaced, much like the rats that have, I suspected, long fled the room in the presence of a canine.

Just me and the ghosts.

Almost immediately, through the sparkling, swirling, living dust—looking like so many fireflies—I see the glowing rectangle in the floor. Two glowing rectangles, side by side. Glowing, because they're metal doors, in fact.

I spy the handles in the center, and the seam in the middle, looking for all the world like twin cellar doors.

My heart is racing. Maybe it's my fear kicking in about possible hantavirus in here. I don't think so. No, it's racing because I had just found, for all intents and purposes, a hidden basement door beneath the Los Angeles Old Zoo.

56

wait for my heart to calm down, for my breathing to normalize. This could mean nothing. This could mean everything.

When I have regained some control over myself, I reach forward—and almost immediately, the Winter Wind disappears. I still haven't mastered movement within the Wind, but I am getting better at it. Darkness, yes, but I still have the memory of where I am and the floor layout before me.

Next, on hands and knees, no doubt confusing the hell out of my poor dog, I feel my way to the handles. Once there, I take hold of one and stand back and pull on the door. How silently it opens, I don't know. Does it creak like hell, waking the dead? I don't know, but I suspect it makes some sound, certainly.

Either way, I feel the rush of cool air immediately, up from wherever this opening leads. Perhaps to hell itself. Or perhaps just a small storage room. Perhaps, even now, a man is rushing at me, wielding a knife, but I don't think so. In fact, I know so. Betsie is only mildly agitated. Anyone rushing me would, of course, be met halfway by Betsie.

I carefully walk over to the far side, using my walking stick as a guide, and pull open the second wing of the double cellar door.

More cool wind, and now something else.

Yes, something indeed.

Apparently, my sniffer is working after all. I smell something. Something foul. Not necessarily dead, but close to it.

57

Another snapshot.

A long cement corridor, packed with old shelving and tools and tables and metal grates. The corridor heads in only one direction, away from the building and toward the zoo itself.

I pull back and think about my next step. I think hard and long, and wonder what's going on here. Mostly, I wonder who uses this tunnel and why, and how someone could conceal it again, once they were inside. I had seen the stairs leading down. Someone who is motivated enough could stand on the stairs and slide the massive wooden slab back over the floor again, lift it above their heads, keep it up with, say, one hand, while closing a metal flap. It would take some balance. The flap and slab, with some practice and luck, would fall together, concealing the opening again.

Unless a second person conceals the metal doors again. Yes, a partner, I think. After all, someone had hunted down Jesse DeFranco, and I am beginning to think it wasn't the good doctor.

I don't know, and, at the moment, I don't much care.

All I know is that there is a very good chance that my brother might be at the end of this tunnel. Crazy as it seems, and crazy as all of this is, my instincts tell me there's something here, and there's something going on now. Right now. Real people are disappearing. Real people are showing up on surveillance video at this park. Real people are showing up dead. At least one of them.

He used to work here, I think. *The bastard worked here and knows the layout and knows what's here and has been planning this for a long, long time.*

I consider my options. I can call the police. Or, in my case, text the police. I could text Detective Hammer directly. Or text Rachel. Not a bad idea. Whether or not they would believe me, I don't know. Would they come out here and help, I had no doubt they would. Except, of course, there was no way in hell I was going to get Rachel out here alone.

And tell them what? I had found a hole in an abandoned building?

No, but I can at least tell them where I am, should I never come up for air again. Grim thoughts, but safe thoughts, and so, I extract my phone.

I go to contacts and type in Hammer's name. I know how to work this phone. I use it blindly all the time. I don't need to see. Once I bring up his info, I press the raised message button. I next type in where I am, and what I am doing, and hit send.

He will, of course, think I'm crazy. And if he is sleeping, he won't get this until morning. And if I have no reception here, he may never get the message. Still, if he's awake and binge drinking—an old joke—then I might see him in 20 or 30 minutes. Maybe.

Either way, I'm flying blind for the foreseeable future. Either way, I'm looking for my brother, come hell or high water. Or down the world's creepiest underground tunnel.

I'm really doing this.

Next, I consider my dog. I don't want to tie her up. I want her to have a fighting chance if, say, someone comes around. I decide to leave her here, untethered, in the building. More than likely she will stay here, waiting desperately for my return.

I reach over and rub her furry face. Funny, how I always know where she is. Except she pulls away. She's not in the mood for rubs. She wants out. I smile at her and ease down into the hole, my foot finding the first rung of the metal ladder, then the second and third.

When I am at ground level, Betsie lowers her head to the floor, paws in front of her. I press my forehead to hers, then reach over and feel around until I find the interior handle to one of the metal doors. I lift the heavy door up, then pull it shut, sealing off one side. Next, I grope until I find the handle of the next metal flap. I push her big head out of the way, my message clear that she must move.

Her saliva drips on me as she obeys and moves back from the flap. She does not want to be separated from me.

When I know she is clear of the flap, I pull it down on top of me, sealing myself in what I imagine is complete darkness.

What else is new?

58

I pause often for snapshots.

As I do, I wonder if Betsie is whining above me. If so, I wonder if she can be heard. I imagine her waiting for me, by the opening, come hell or high water.

So far, I see nothing but an empty tunnel. A cold tunnel, too. A wispy wind often slaps at my clothing, and I wonder where the hell it might be coming from. I suspect I will know soon enough.

As I pause, I scan forward and backward. After all, other than a weak sense of smell, I have no other way of knowing if something is coming up from behind me or not. That is, until it's right on top of me.

I can see about twenty feet in either direction. And not just either direction, but through the walls, too, which reveal only dirt and rocks and slow moving energy. Very, very slow moving energy. And even here, in this place far removed from prying eyes, buried deep in the earth, in darkness, in suspended animation, alone and forgotten, are bright spots of energy. Insects, worms most likely.

The stench seems to be growing stronger, even pushing through my damaged olfactory system. A stench that suggests death…and something else. I was either going to come across a dead deer, a mountain lion's den, or I was going to find…what?

I don't know.

In fact, I don't have a fucking clue what I will find.

No, I think, as I move forward in the darkness, feeling naked and exposed without Betsie by my side. *I do know what I might find. Something out of a nightmare.*

Not the kind of thoughts you want while inching along a seemingly forgotten tunnel beneath the Old Los Angeles Zoo. I almost don't know what to do with my right hand—the hand that holds Betsie. And so, I held it up before my face. I don't think there is anything too low in the corridor, but I've hit my head in the past—on everything from low doorways, to low signs to tree branches—and I've learned to take precautions in unknown places. Granted, in the past, I didn't have the benefit of taking snapshots of the route before me. Still, while I traveled in darkness, the snapshots were only just that—snapshots in time. I moved now through space and time—and I might have missed something. Something low. Something sharp. Something dark. Something waiting to reach out and snag me.

Again, not the kind of thoughts you want, not here, not ever. I pause again, take a deep breath, calm myself, and slip into the Winter Wind. I survey the path ahead, verify there is nothing low-hanging or blocking my path, and continue forward, sweeping my walking stick to keep me straight and true, reaching my free hand up to protect my head—and walk another twenty feet—or what I think is twenty feet.

Again I pause, slip into the world of blue-green vibration, survey the path before me—and behind me—continue forward again.

The temperature is dropping. I am wearing only a light jacket and wish I had something heavier. I had not expected to be so cold. I should have been prepared.

Off my game.

A very big part of me tells me to turn around, especially now that the smell is growing stronger. Sweet, pungent, and rotten...all rolled into one.

Had I not known better, I would have thought I was coming upon a hallway full of decaying mushrooms. Except, of course, I know better. I know exactly what I am smelling...and the closer I get, the surer I am.

There is something dead down here. Something dead within a few weeks, perhaps. Dead and rotting.

Most troubling, perhaps, is that my brother has been gone for about a week.

Not him. It can't be him.

And I keep thinking this, as I shuffle deeper into the darkness.

59

The wall and door emerge out of blue-green light, both shimmering, both blocking my path.

I am maybe fifteen feet from them. I am still far enough away that the wall and door are hazy at best. The door looks old, and so does the door handle. And the longer I stand there and study the door, the more the surrounding shadows come into focus.

Stacked to either side of the door are metal cages.

The Winter Wind shows me that many of the cages contain living creatures within. Possums, I think. And maybe raccoons. Fat rats, too. Some are alive, pacing their cages. But many are dead, too. And not just dead, but partially consumed. Grotesquely consumed. I can see maggots crawling. I can see bones and entrails and dried-out skin. Yes, the picture is becoming clearer. The dead are in varying stages of decay, and many are in the same cages of the living.

Most are pacing, overly stressed, malnourished, dehydrated, dying. Some are staring at me. There is a long hose nearby, dripping water. The cages have filthy bowls but not much else. A small possum is watching me from the corner of its cage. He's chewing on something…his own tail, in fact.

Sweet Jesus.

Someone, I'm certain, has been coming in and out, perhaps even recently. Perhaps even tonight, judging by the dripping water.

The stench comes to me now, stronger than ever, and I turn my head and fight a gag reflex. Even back in the day, even after coming across horrific murder scenes and viewing autopsies and death photos, I had to fight a gag reflex. My partners didn't know it. I hid it well. But it was always there, and I was glad it was there. It made me feel human. It made me feel less robotic, like some of my partners and others on the force.

I took in some air through the tracheal tube in my throat—air that I knew was rancid and putrid and fecal, and calmed myself. Or tried to.

Once I was calm, I took one last, deep breath, and lifted my head—and all went black.

I was out of the Winter Wind and moving forward again.

60

I am close to the door.

My walking stick has lightly struck a cage, and I pause again. I detect vibration all around me, movement—scratching, perhaps. In my mind's eye, I imagine the critters pacing their cages, clawing the cages, smashing up against their cages. Either to get out or get my attention. Or eat off my face.

I need to slip into the Winter Wind, but my mind is racing. The smells, the animals, the pain and horror of what I've already seen. How the hell can I calm down enough, to focus enough, to relax enough?

I don't know...but I needed to see what was beyond this door.

Instead, I push forward, carefully working the walking stick between the cages until I hit something solid.

The door.

I'm shaking hard enough that I am having a hard time controlling my free hand enough to look for the door handle. Finally, I find it and try it. Locked, of course.

Calm down, Lee. Deep breaths. You've been in some crazy situations before.

But none this crazy, and none where I was at such a disadvantage.

With my hand on the cold handle—a handle that seems to vibrate as well, although that could have been my imagination—I try to regulate my breathing, to control my thoughts, until I realize that neither are happening.

I'm still sucking in air—and all too aware of the horror that's immediately around me, even if I can't see it or hear it.

I can smell it. Sense it. Feel it.

Worse, I am almost certain someone is coming up behind me. I'm not sure when the goosebumps came, but they're here now, studding my skin and raising the hair on my arms and the back of my neck.

No one's behind you, I tell myself, over and over...but to no avail. Maybe there's a side door I missed. Maybe the ruckus the animals are making—that I'm sure they're making—have alerted someone. Maybe even now this someone could be coming up behind me, gun raised—or lead pipe raised, or knife raised...or, hell, fist raised.

Calm, Lee. Deep breaths.

Except I *can't* control my breathing. I am having what must be close to a panic attack, although I've never had one before. Then again, I'd never been in a tunnel of horror before, either.

Breathe, breathe, relax.

It's one reason why I have my hand on the doorknob. In the least, I will know if this door is opening.

Breathe, relax, good.

A dim blue-green flickering teases at my thoughts. I ignore the smells, the small vibrations around me, vibrations that seem to indicate the many confined animals, scratching and clawing.

Breathe slowly, breathe deeply, good, good...

Flickering, flashing, and I am in the Winter Wind.

I shift my focus *behind* me. So fast that I disorient myself. Twenty feet of empty tunnel. I see only cages, crates, boxes. All glowing and amorphous in the blue-green, staticy energy.

I pause, calming further. The anticipation of someone coming up behind had left me a nervous wreck. I continue holding the doorknob while scanning behind me. At the very least, there is no one twenty feet back.

Good enough.

I shift my focus again, this time to the door. In particular, what lies *behind* the door. Magically, the energy swirling and spitting around me pushes through the closed door, through the surrounding wall, and into something I am not fully expecting.

No one could have expected this. Hell, even if I had been expecting this…there is just no way to be fully prepared for what I see.

61

A room with cages.

Big cages, too. Obviously remnants of the Old Zoo. I picture them being unloaded from an old traveling circus. The kind of cages that would have been filled with lions and tigers and monkeys, and whatever else traveling circuses brought with them.

Of course, these weren't filled with lions or tigers or monkeys—or animals of any sort.

I almost pull back. I almost turn and get the hell out of there, as fast as I can go. I know the way out. I can cover ground pretty quickly, especially ground I've already been over.

But there's no way in hell I'm running.

I scan the cages, I scan the men and women within, huddled and asleep, or drugged. They are mostly naked. Many are covered in sores. Many appear quite ill, and most are curled in the fetal position. I can't hear them, but I suspect the few that are awake are moaning or calling out for help or weeping loudly. Also, two are dead. Just left there in the cages. I know they are dead because their forms do not radiate bright white light. Their bodies, much like the dead in the animals' cages around me, just lie there, motionless, absorbing the vibration around them…not radiating.

There are ten or eleven cages in view, with more, I suspect, just beyond my seeing radius. My brother isn't in any of them. In the center of the room, between the rows of cages, there is what appears to be an operating table. I can make out feet. Male feet, I think. Strapped down. Tight.

The room comes into sharper focus. The dead have been dead for a long, long time—way past rigor mortis or bloating—and well into decay. They are at the far edge of my seeing, but I can see the dried skin, and their skeletons just beneath. The more I look, the more detail I can see. And the deeper my vision seems to stretch.

But I can't quite see who's on the table.

Maybe if I stand here a little longer. Try a little harder. But the horror of what I'm seeing is challenging my ability to stay calm enough to remain in the Winter Wind. I feel myself wanting to gasp, but I don't. I feel myself fighting to turn and get help, but I don't, not yet. Mostly, I want to kick the door in and take out my badge and gun, and take care of business.

But I had done that before, hadn't I?

I had. I had acted recklessly and now I am who I am, and my partner is dead, and the woman I have come to love is maimed for life.

No kicking in doors. And no rushing around like a crazy man. Be calm, think, observe...

There, on the table, I can now see a torso. A naked torso. I can see a stomach rising and falling rapidly. Someone is scared. And probably cold. I can't imagine there are any comforts in this room of horror.

Now a woman is rattling her cage, screaming, I think. She is responding to the person on the table, I think. They are both, I suspect, crying out. But their cries are falling on deaf ears, literally. And I suspect they are deep enough down and sealed away so that no one can hear them.

I continue holding the doorknob, continue stretching myself to the limits of my seeing, the limits of my new abilities.

But I can't quite see far enough. Can't quite see...

Almost. Almost.

And now, animals around me are chattering, shaking their cages wildly. From my peripheral, I see them going apeshit...crazier than they had even when I was approaching. The ground is veritably shaking. The figure on the table fights his restraints, fighting so damn hard I can see the blood around the straps cutting into him.

He's kicking and jerking and struggling—rocking the operating table...

He fights just enough, rocks just enough, shifts the table just enough for his face to appear in frame, just enough for me to recognize my brother. It is the first time I have *seen* him in five years. He looks so different. Emaciated, terrified, hurt.

Holy sweet Jesus...

And that's when the animals in my peripheral vision go ballistic, and I am just shifting my attention to them when I see something drop from the ceiling above, directly behind me.

Another trap door, much like the one I had dropped into further down the tunnel.

I turn—but not fast enough. Something heavy and blunt slams into my lower back.

62

The force of the blow does not hurl me into the door; instead, it drives me to my knees.

White, searing light—anything but the Winter Wind—explodes in my head and it's all I can do to find my breath and cover my head at the same time.

The weapon—a metal baseball bat, no doubt—comes down again, this time squarely across the middle of my back and I can feel my bones crunch under it. Several ribs, in fact.

I am driven straight to the ground, straight to my stomach—and I curl in time to cover my head when the bat comes down again, this time across my upper arm and left hand. But the force is strong and true, and several bones in my hand shatter, I'm sure of it. But I keep it there, protecting my head.

There is a good chance my arm is broken, too. I won't know it until I try to move something, and right now, all I am doing is preparing for the next blow—and trying to breathe and trying like hell to figure a way to protect myself.

But the blow from the bat doesn't come. Instead, a kick is leveled to my midsection, but it doesn't land true, and this seems to piss off the kicker, because he hits me twice more, rapidly, with the bat. Blows that hit my damaged ribs again, but also my upper back, knocking out what little air I had been able to recover.

Another kick, this time leveled at my face. It hits me square and knocks my sunglasses off. A plastic shard, I think, has lodged deep into my empty right eye socket. And then, the bat comes down again, harder than before, and connects with my left shoulder, neck, and ear. I see more white light and feel the blood flow from my head, certain the blows have broken my humerus and clavicle.

Mostly, I am certain the attack has rendered me nearly useless, not that I would have been any match against anyone in a fight, let alone someone with a weapon.

I wait for the next blow, certain I am fading in and out of consciousness. And as I drift in and out, sputtering blue-green light appears and disappears. Briefly, haltingly, and even more amorphous and blurry. But it's there, and as I lie in a growing pool of my own blood, I see the man, flickering in and out of my thoughts, approach.

I see him reach a hand down…

Now, I feel my head lifting, being hauled up roughly by my hair. Painful, yes, but the pain is barely a blip on my radar.

More blue-green flashes…

I see him lean down; he appears to be studying me closely. He is young, that much is sure. Maybe mid-twenties. Lean and roped with muscle.

Darkness again, and now I can smell his breath and I can smell the disinfectant on him. He smells like an operating room, or a hospital, or a laboratory. His breath, blasting my face over and over, reeks of tobacco and halitosis. Bad breath is the least of my problems.

Another flash of blue-green light as I slip a little more out of consciousness. My perspective is a little above and behind me. I seem to be looking down at myself. So strange...

He's holding up a flashlight, shining it straight into my eyes.

More darkness, as I feel the rubber coupling of the flashlight probe around my eyes. He uses it to roughly lift a lid, which digs the embedded piece of sunglasses plastic from my sunglasses deeper into my empty socket.

His hand shakes and air bursts into my face and, if I had to guess, he has snorted. Probably with some sort of derision or relief. It is a blind man wandering the hallway, after all. Surely nothing he should fear, right?

There is a slight pause and now he releases his hold on my hair and my head slams down to the concrete floor. More bright lights erupt in my skull...and I black out...

———

I awaken in darkness, alone and cold and certain I have been out for only a few seconds. But that's the thing with blackouts: it's hard to judge time, especially when one lives in perpetual darkness anyway.

No, I think, not perpetual, *and not any more. And certainly not if I keep taking his punches and blows.*

The next one, I'm certain, will kill me, especially with me lying here like a sitting duck.

One chance. And one chance only.

Where he is, I don't know. Where I am, I don't know either, but it feels like the same cold spot on the floor, the same metal wall against my back. I think one of my fingers is caught in a nearby metal cage. A miracle it hasn't been gnawed off. At least, I don't think it has.

As I come to, the blue-green light erupts around me. I try to sit up, and when I do, searing pain shoots through me and plunges me back into darkness. Shoulder is definitely broken. Maybe my upper arm, too. And there is something seriously wrong with my hip. Something is broken there, I'm certain of it.

I breathe and the Winter Wind returns. I find myself hovering above, looking down at myself. I see the blood now, sparkling like an effervescent fairy pool in the middle of a forest. Except this is a pool of my own blood, and it looks like it's coming out of an ear and an open gash at the base of my skull.

Dizziness sweeps over me as I find a way to my left hip—my good hip—and put my weight there. I can feel knives digging into my hip; shards of bone, I suspect. Sooner or later, one will puncture an internal organ. Then again, dying a slow death is probably not an option, not here in this forgotten tunnel.

Unless, of course, I end up in a cage on the other side of this wall, or on a gurney like my brother.

The crackling, snapping vibrations that are the Winter Wind reveal I am alone in the hallway. The animal cages are still around me. The animals are mostly going apeshit. The living ones, that is. I reach into my empty eye socket and pull free the broken plastic shard. As I do so, the Winter Wind escapes me again, and I am in darkness. I feel blood splash free from the wound. If I hadn't already been blind, that would have done the trick.

Breathe, breathe, and I am back in the Winter Wind. A glow from further down the hallway, back in the direction from where I came. The man with the bat is down there, beyond the limits of where I can see. He's making sure I am alone, I realize. He'll soon come back and finish the job, or drag me into a cage where they will do...what? I hadn't a clue. Experiments, no doubt. Torture, maybe. But more than likely...

More than likely, one clean shot to the head...and then feed me to whatever's alive in the cages.

The light in the hallway is getting brighter.

The son-of-a-bitch is coming back.

63

I move to sit up; the blue-green light winks out, and I am plunged into total darkness. I'm also left gasping for air and fighting through more pain than I think I can handle. I want to vomit and pass out all at the same time. But I fight through it, air blasting out through my tracheal tube, along, with, I think, blood. Lots and lots of blood.

Punctured lung, for sure.

My right hip feels ruined, shattered, useless, and so I do my best to shift my weight to my right leg, and I am mostly able to stand when I feel a disturbance in the air, the vibration of the excited animals.

He's back.

And I know he's coming at me, with the bat. One good swing will crack my head open...

———

I stand there, breathing and bleeding and leaning to one side, and tell myself I have, at least, a small handful of seconds. He's not here yet. But he's crossing the small antechamber, and no doubt, raising the bat at the same time...

I do my damn best to control my breathing, knowing that at any moment, the son-of-bitch could be on me, knowing that at any moment, the mother of all explosions is about to erupt in my head, knowing that at any moment, I will be dead. I stand there and breathe and the light returns, flickering around the edges of my consciousness, bright, blue, green, flickering, flickering...

I see the glowing mass approaching me from the darkness, coming at me rapidly, something is on his shoulder, the bat...

Flickering blue-green light, appearing and disappearing in my thoughts, bright one moment and total darkness the next.

Too excited, too terrified, too much pain...

The light returns and I see he has stopped before me. He cocks his head to one side, and then disappears again, and when he reappears in my thoughts—I see the bat jumping off his shoulders, coming around hard and fast, and directly at my head...

And that's when the Winter Wind winks out of existence.

———

I don't need the blue-green light to know to duck, and I do so now.

Air whooshes over the back of my head. I stagger, gritting through the abysmal pain in my hip, certain I might fall at any moment, but praying like hell that I don't.

Breathe, calm, relax...

The Winter Wind returns, this time clearer and sharper than before, and I see the young man regain his balance. He'd apparently put a lot of weight behind what he surely thought would be a killing blow. He regains his balance. A young guy, muscular. I imagine him hauling bodies in and out of here, transferring grown men—no doubt drugged—from cages to gurneys. Yeah, he could do it, especially with the help of a crazy old doctor.

Mostly, though, he looks confused as hell. He hadn't expected me to duck.

Now, he is nodding and circling me, and I realize I have somehow staggered away from the wall and am standing more in the open.

As he circles me, I follow him, shifting and turning my body, and this confuses him as well. Maybe he thinks I can still hear.

Now he stops, realizing he is giving away his position to me somehow, and I am impressed that I have been able to follow him without slipping out of the Wind, without losing my meditative focus.

You've done this before, I tell myself, remembering my time at the beach, my time practicing moving my arm and staying in the blue-green world of vibration.

I can do this...

He takes a step toward me, carefully, and I don't move. He smiles and thinks he has me. He thinks I can't see him—or hear him. He raises the bat and this time aims for a bigger target, somewhere around my mid-section.

He swings, faster than I am expecting, but I am able to contort my torso enough that most of the bat misses. Enough grazes me to hurt, but nothing like before, and I show no reaction and regain my balance, even though the searing white pain knifes through my hip. My seriously damaged right hip.

He stumbles again, and pulls up; I am relieved beyond anything that I have managed to maintain my hold on the blue-green light, this world of pure energy.

Breathe, calm, relax.

He is pissed now. He doesn't understand what is happening. I can see that on his face. In his eyes.

So clear. Everything, so clear.

He comes at me, bat raised, swinging wildly, thinking he is going to damage me with brute force. No more sidestepping for him. No more near misses.

He comes at me.

I see it clearly, so clearly.

I lash out, just as Jacky had taught me. I snap my fist out from my shoulder and put all the weight I can into it. The blow hits him straight in the face, over his right eye. It is a hell of a punch. Maybe the hardest punch I have ever thrown, and I watch calmly, quietly, serenely, as he goes down in a heap at my feet.

——

I look up in time to see another man standing in the doorway nearby. An old man who is holding a gun.

Something flashes to my right, something big and bright and faster than anything I've seen so far. It's a blur of teeth and claws and fur. A big creature, and it slams into the old man.

A super white explosion briefly fills my thoughts as the gun goes off, and now, the man is rolling with the animal, fighting it, but not winning. Definitely not winning.

Something skitters across the floor, something small and radiating heat. I calmly pick it up, maintaining the Winter Wind...

I hold out the gun before me, as my guardian angel pins the old man to the floor, teeth bared, and looking as frightening as hell.

64

It is later, much later, and I am in a hospital, recovering from surgery.

I have been slipping in and out of consciousness, in and out of the Winter Wind. In the room, I sometimes see nurses and once even a doctor. But always, always I see Rachel. Sometimes she is pacing. Sometimes she is sitting and texting. And sometimes she is reading on her Kindle. Often, she is just sitting there, holding my hand, watching me.

Although I am only half-conscious, the clarity of the living vibrations around me is startling, and I can sometimes see clearly her many wounds. Wounds caused by me.

In and out of consciousness.

I am in no more pain; I can see the IV, and where my shoulder has been set and cast. I note I am leaning to one side, and I suspect some surgery had been done to my hip. Bandages and wrappings secure my torso and chest, and I know there is only so much you can do for broken ribs. They are often the hardest to heal, take the longest, and are the most painful.

Oxygen is directed straight into my neck. My vitals appear strong, steady, and the nurses do not seem anxious or worried, and so I slip out of consciousness again, and again, throughout the next few days.

And always, I awaken to find Rachel in the room or by my side.

Always.

I am barely able to lift my hand to sign: "Betsie?"

She signs back: "I have her at my place. She's fine."

———

I come to and see Rachel's forehead pressed into the mattress, her hand holding mine. She is asleep, I think.

I can see a bald spot now on the right side of her scalp, where most of the damage was done by the explosion. The bald spot has mostly been hidden with creative hairstyles and hats. The exposed scalp is badly damaged, her skin mottled and scarred and discolored.

I reach out and cover the patch with my hand and hold her as I drift back into sleep...

More time, more dreams, more visitors, more blue-green light, more attention from Rachel. Attention I don't deserve, not after what I had done to her. But she doesn't see it that way. She sees my injuries—and the death of my partner and the murder of the innocents at the convention center—as her fault, due to her inaction.

We both need therapy—or each other. I drift back to sleep.

———

It is, I think, two days later, when I feel a pressure on me, and I awaken from a deep, dreamless sleep—and emerge into the Winter Wind. I see the face I have been most hoping to see: my brother.

His hand is on my chest as he speaks to a nurse and occasionally shoots glances at Rachel, who looks at him with suspicion, concern and pity. She knows he left me. She knows he hurt me. She knows my brother is a troubled man.

Aren't we all?

I do not know if they have introduced themselves, but when the nurse leaves, my brother turns to Rachel and says something. Interestingly, I see the vibration of his words leave his mouth. I watch them imprint a pattern in the air, a sort of sound wavelength, and I wonder, at the back of my mind, if I can someday read these patterns and understand what people are saying to me.

I wonder...and I hope.

My brother, apparently, has requested to be alone with me, because Rachel finally nods, acquiesces—but doesn't seem too happy about it. God bless her loyal heart.

Finally, she gets up from her spot in the chair next to me, looks at my brother, looks at me, then turns and leaves the room.

I am alone with my brother.

———

My brother appears relatively unscathed. There are wounds along his wrists and forehead, where I can almost picture him slamming his head against something, per-haps trying to push through something. The injuries to his wrists are obvious. I suspect there are similar injuries to his ankles, where he'd been restrained.

What happened to him, I don't know. That he had been experimented on, or had been about to be experi-mented on, was the only thing I can surmise. But none of that matters now.

All that matters is that my brother is standing before me, alive and healthy—and had my mother been around, she would have been weeping incessantly, holding both of us, and never allowing either of us out of her sight again. She had been a good mom.

As my brother moves around and sits where Rachel had been sitting, I wonder if he's still planning on leaving. If he does, I'm gonna be pissed...and hunt him down myself.

He's speaking to me, I see. Vibrations warble out of his mouth, forming a pattern in the air. I smile at this, and absently wonder what the vibration for "hi" might look like. Or for "I love you." I wonder if I can someday discern such vibrations. Maybe, I think. Maybe.

Now the vibrations issuing from his mouth turn staticy, abrupt, and halting. I look up from the sound waves to his eyes and see tears flowing. Tears that glow almost supernaturally, rivulets of diamonds.

He lets the tears flow, untouched, unconcerned who sees them, never guessing that his eyeless brother is watching them even now.

He takes hold of my right hand and holds it with both of his, and still, I do not move. I let his emotions play out...but mostly, I am enjoying seeing him, being with him, looking at his familiar sharp chin—hatchet jaw, as my dad used to call him. Reveling in his broad shoulders and his thick brow. I remember our time growing up. I remember the sports and the games and the fights and the forgiving and the long conversations, and I am so happy that he is here, now, holding my hand, and not in some faraway state, never to be seen again, or, worse, hidden deep underground in a madman's laboratory of horrors.

My brother is lucky to be alive, I know that and he knows that. I had seen at least two of the dead, and there might have been more. I wouldn't know the full extent of the doctor's experiments until later, if ever.

No. I need to know.

But now, I stop thinking of the horrors I'd witnessed, or the horrors I had experienced, and just lay there next to him, watching him from somewhere above me, reveling in his touch, remembering the good times, and wishing like crazy for many, many more good times to come.

When my brother is finished with his soliloquy—his words lost to me and known only to him—he puts a hand on my chest and pats me.

I choose now to lift my hands and weakly sign, "Don't leave me again, asshole."

I see him stare at my hands, then at me, then throw back his head and laugh, shaking the whole bed as he does so. He eases up out of the chair and sits next to me, managing to wrap his arms around my damaged shoulder and bury his face into my neck, holding me in a way that somehow doesn't hurt too much.

He holds me like this for a long, long time.

65

It is a few days later and I am at home with Rachel and Detective Hammer. And Betsie, of course.

I am leaning on my right side, taking pressure off my right hip and, concurrently, trying to ease the discomfort in my chest. Neither seems to be working, which is why I am glad I am still on lots of pain meds. Vicodin, in fact. The doctors and nurses have all lectured me about dependence, and to stop once the pain is mostly gone.

When the pain goes away, I'll cross that bridge when I get there—just as long as the crossing of the bridge is pain-free.

For now, addiction is the last thing on my mind. Getting through a full minute without wincing is my first big goal.

Meanwhile, Detective Hammer is talking while Rachel signs rapidly into my palm: "Your brother was one of the lucky ones. We found nine dead, most rotting in cages or stuffed into sacks or barrels. Filthy horrible business. Many more were in various stages of dehydration and malnourishment, and still others had been infected with, of all things, tuberculosis, which is what the mad son of a bitch had been hoping to cure.

"Before being fired from the zoo, he had been secretly experimenting with animals—possums, I think. Rare ones, too. Apparently, these little guys have a remarkable immune system that science is still trying to understand, but I think you know all that, right? Anyway, he goes about it in the wrong way, experiments on endangered possums, gets canned…and then, a year or so later, decides to kick his experiments up a notch with people.

"The guy—Dr. Diamond—says he did it to help mankind. That he was close to a breakthrough. He doesn't see it as killing people. He sees it as a sacrifice to the good of humanity. A real whack job, if you ask me."

"And his helper?" I sign.

"A hired thug, no more. We're sure he's the one who offed Jesse, and did a lot of the heavy lifting."

I sign: "How many total were found?"

"Nine living and eleven dead. Twenty total, that we know of. We're still digging through that mess."

"Where did the others come from?"

"From what we gather—and from what the good doctor has told us—they picked them up along Skid Row, with a promise of a hot meal and some clothing. The others, as you know, were lured his way via an online ad buried deep in the Dark Net."

"Where he prepped them how to disappear," I sign.

"Exactly." There is a pause, a long one, then Rachel signs into my hand: "One thing I need to know, Lee: how the hell did you manage to get all the way out there, find an underground tunnel, and fight off a guy with a bat and a man with a gun?"

Rachel, I sense, is as confused as the detective.

I reach down and pat Betsie's head. "I had a little help."

"Just you and your dog?"

I smile. "Just me and my dog."

"I'm calling bullshit."

"Call it what you want, Detective."

I sense the detective staring at me, probably with his mouth hanging open a little, confused as hell, and rightly so, anyone would be. Now, I feel a shift in the floorboards, and suspect the detective has stood.

"He says he'll be back in a few weeks to check on you and hopes you get better soon—and that you are a lucky son of a bitch."

"Tell him I love him, too."

"He says to piss off, but he's also laughing."

When he is gone, I take a few short breaths...and slip into the Winter Wind. Rachel is sitting next to me, holding my hand, looking concerned and relaxed and beautiful all at the same time. Betsie is at my feet, sleeping.

Rachel signs into my palm: "The detective raises a good point. What did happen back there, Lee?"

I smile, then sign: "I have something to tell you, baby."

She looks at me, frowning, then signs into my hand: "What?"

"Have you ever heard of the Winter Wind?"

———

It's later, and I have done my best to explain Jack, John Wang, and the blue-green light of creation and vibration. Rachel stares at me, tears in her eyes. Confusion on her face. But there is hope in her eyes, too. She is sitting straight, and I see she is shaking. I would be shaking, too. Finally, hesitantly, she points to her heart and slowly, slowly crosses her arms over her chest. She holds the position for a heartbeat or two, then releases it and points at me.

I smile, and wipe my tears, and sign back:
"I love you, too, baby."

The End

Also available:

SILENT ECHO
A Mystery Novel

by J.R. Rain

ABOUT THE AUTHOR

J.R. Rain is the international bestselling author of over fifty novels, including his popular Samantha Moon and Jim Knighthorse series. His books are published in five languages in twelve countries, and he has sold more than 3 million copies worldwide. Please visit him at www.jrrain. com.

22669237R00191

Made in the USA
Middletown, DE
05 August 2015